I S.P.I.

Supernatural Paranormal Investigations

Mischievous Magic

❧

Michelle Lee

BLUE FORGE PRESS

Port Orchard · Washington

For Ax, Wylene, Chad, and Jonielle
and in loving memory of
Risa, Dan, Gage, and Jameson.

Mischievous Magic

Michelle Lee

Book 1
Surf & Turf

Chapter One

I kicked my feet back onto my desk and the ancient office chair supporting my finely rounded buttocks gave a wail like rusty fornicating ducks that were swimming in boiling water. The back of my head bounced on the floor where I was deposited and the chair shot out from under me as if it were a greased sled on compacted snow.

The resulting sound of old metal meeting a crumbling office wall blended with the curse words that spewed from my mouth in a bout of verbal diarrhea. Perfect. Hopefully, no other tenants in the high-class building saw my fall from grace. The thought of this place being high-class made me snort but it's where my business, I S.P.I., was housed. Supernatural Paranormal Investigator.

Risa Daniels is my name. I'm a spy, or at least that's what I liked to say. A P.I., or S.P.I., a bounty hunter, a mother, along with a list of other titles bestowed on me by many who thought less favorably of me. Some not so savory. I couldn't begin to tell you what race I was; my gene pool is heavily chlorinated. My parents were the equivalent of magical hippies.

There were no racial lines in my history. I stem from a long line of free love, break the race chains, sleep with everyone, and be a little of everything; only the magical waters become muddy and powers become diluted.

Thanks, mom and dad, for that kick in the girl nards.

I know that I have some fairy blood in me but I didn't get any of their cool elemental magic. Let me rephrase that. I have some of it but it doesn't work when I want it to, only when it's the worst timing possible. I got the fairy longevity, though. There's a trace of pixie blood in the mix and I did get tiny wings, but I can't fly and much like the fairy magic, they appear at inopportune moments. There has to be siren D.N.A. somewhere down the line, but it only seems to work when I'm on the phone and people mistake me for being the type to deliver a telephonic happy ending. I am positive that there is a good percentage of leprechaun because I get lucky a lot, not just between the sheets. You probably get the picture by now; I'm a magical mutt.

I have three sons and it shouldn't come as any shock to you that there are, of course, three different baby daddies. I have no defense to that other than I was young. Remember the longevity thing? I'm about three hundred and seventy-two years old, as a rough estimate. What? I'm still a woman; I can't reveal my actual age.

My oldest son, Gavin, was an oops, surprise, you're going to be a teenage mother type of pregnancy. His father was a troll. Literal and figurative. Stupid teenage hormones and tequila. I have to say, screwing a troll as your first lover at eighteen, not the best choice. Size matters and that hurt. Anyway, Gavin tends to take after his father a bit with the attitude, which isn't all that pleasant. He's my son, and I still love him, even when I want to wrap my hands around his neck and squeeze.

My middle son, Gage, is about the sweetest boy ever to have lived. I'm not biased; everyone that knows him says that. He was named Gage because my meter of picking good men was broken like the gauge needed replacing. I'm awful, I know. Gage's father was a selkie. Someone captured him and skinned him when Gage was five. Glad he was useful to someone during his life.

Then there is my youngest, Jameson. If you are wondering about his name, that was what I had been drinking the night I met his father. I had to switch it up since the tequila didn't produce good results. Come to think of it; I shouldn't drink. I digress; Jameson is a joy. Equal parts devil and angel, which makes sense since his dad is a fallen angel. I should have figured that would mean he wouldn't be faithful. Oh well.

I live in Glimmering Rock, a magical city hidden within a large human bustling town called Branstone. Here is where it all gets complicated. Humans, supernatural beings, magical beings, paranormal beings, myths, and legends, all live in harmony. Of course, that is because humans have no idea we exist and live among them.

Glimmering Rock had a magical council where the heads of the prominent races made laws. By that, I mean the ones that have the most population within the city. Then there was the law enforcement for us magical types, separate from the council, and then human law enforcement, and finally, the black market in both worlds often intertwined amongst all of them. Then there was me.

All of the groups knew who I was. Some respected me; others thought of me as a joke. A scant few were terrified of me, those were the smart ones, and the rest only thought of me when they needed someone not affiliated with any of the authorities. I worked in a substantial gray area.

The cases I took on depended on the client that walked through my barely still hanging office door. Human or magical, I worked for both. Beggars can't be choosers and living isn't free. A girl's gotta do what a girl's gotta do to make the mortgage payment.

It was the moment that I was bent over; my ass

pointed right at the door to my office while wiping my hands on my shins and trying not to pee myself when I sneezed from the dust that kicked up that a would-be client walked in. My luck didn't work in this instance.

At the sound of a clearing throat, I righted myself as quickly as possible, squeezed my legs together as if that would hold in the pee, and pivoted on my heels. My blond hair fanned out around my face, the ends whipping me in the eyeball before it settled back down. With my green eyes watering like a mud puddle after being stomped in by a rambunctious three-year-old, I smiled.

"Hello," I managed to get out while the potential client picked up my chair and slid it back across the room to me.

"Ms. Daniels, I presume?" the man said with one of those deep, rumbly, gravel caught in his throat voices.

Thank goodness I wasn't drinking; I'd have tried to put moves on him. "Correct. Thank you for your assistance. My chair was tired of me and hit the eject button."

"No complaints," the man who would be my latest mistake smiled. He had dimples. "The view was pleasurable."

I was doomed. I caught myself before readjusting my boobs, which had managed to work their way free during my meeting with the floor. I didn't need to call attention to them; his eyes kept wandering that direction of their own volition.

"How can I help you?" I sat down, putting my elbows on my desk in front of me, trying to block the lumpy boobs from sight. I made it a point not to sleep with people who hired me. Was it wrong to hope he didn't hire me?

"Let me make my entrance again," the man smiled and stepped back into the hallway, closing the door behind him.

Not one to look a gift horse in the mouth, I quickly

set my boobs back where they belonged, smoothed my shirt down, and tried to strike a feminine pose and look classy. Total long shot but I had to try for my pride's sake.

The rickety door opened and the good-looking man stepped back inside with a brilliant smile, his eyes dropping to my chest. Biting back laughter was brutal and how I managed was beyond me. He took a seat across from me and held out his hand.

"Ms. Daniels, correct? My name is Ivan and I'm looking to hire an investigator," he introduced himself as I shook his hand. "May I ask what the initials in your business name mean?"

Rough skin, calloused palms, dirt under his nails, firm grip, and large knuckles, I cataloged quickly. Ivan was a man who was used to manual labor, outdoor work if I had to guess. Non-magical, as that familiar zap of energy failed to materialize when our skin touched.

"Call me Risa," I answered, releasing his hand after the quick thought of wondering what it would feel like undressing me passed. "Sexy private investigator. What can I do for you?"

"You have an interesting reputation, Risa," Ivan started with a giant grin. He leaned back into the plastic chair, and when it creaked, I desperately hoped it didn't break under him. Ivan crossed an ankle over his knee and grinned at me again. "I have an open case with the police department in Branstone. However, I'm not sure they can help me."

The barking laugh that came out of my mouth surprised us both. I coughed, not in the least embarrassed. "Why do you think that?"

The police of Branstone were an eclectic bunch. They had a few good cops in the department and those cops knew of both cities. There were also clueless cops that wouldn't know a unicorn from a rhinoceros.

"Because when I told them that my cows were disappearing, they asked me if they were in my freezer," Ivan replied with a straight face. "I'd probably know if I butchered one of my cows. The cop took my statement and opened a case, yet I am almost certain they won't investigate it."

Hmm, that response didn't tell me if Ivan knew of Glimmering Rock and its inhabitants or not. All it told me was he didn't have faith in the officers charged with protecting his life. Not a stretch to agree with him.

"Branstone does have a few inepts on the squad," I agreed. "Do you think someone is stealing your cows? Or is your suspicion something more insidious?"

I was happy to note my assessment was right on the dot about him working outdoors. If Ivan had cows, he was a rancher or farmer. A hand reveals a lot about a person; I was also very observant. Ivan was correct that I had a reputation.

I was a thorn in the sides of all the authorities, not because I walked a thin line between lawful and blatantly illegal, but because I got answers when they couldn't. I might be a bit unorthodox but I closed all my cases.

"I'm not entirely sure." Ivan sighed and ran a hand through his hair. I am sure he had no idea that it was sexy, and if he did, who cares? "I noticed the first one missing about a month ago. I marked it in my log and noted where her last position was. I chalked it up to a natural predator. I'm aware these things happen on full moons."

Ah, he did know of us then. I pulled out a pad of paper and started taking notes. "Okay, so it happened on the full moon?"

"That was the first one I noticed, yes." Ivan let out a frustrated breath. "I had a deal with the pack alpha to notify me if one of his pack got a little carried away. He promised to make restitution but when I questioned him he firmly told me I was wrong in my assumption that one of his killed a cow."

Talk with Mick, I noted. "Firmly told you? Did he get aggressive with you?"

"I wouldn't call it aggressive; Mick was irritated with me for not believing him," Ivan corrected. "He's never lied to me before so I accepted his explanation and went back home. I poured over the security feeds for hours and saw not one wolf on my land. That was when I started to pay closer attention. About a week after the full moon, another cow went missing."

I wrote down the date and another tally for the cow. "Only one?"

"Yes. It was two cows total at that point. Three days later, four cows went missing. This time, I saw a blip on the camera. It was almost as if the camera had skipped itself. It was that quick. I took the footage to a friend of mine who is a tech person and he could see nothing that would indicate equipment failure or someone messing with the feed. Six cows disappearing creates a lot of missing income in my line of work. My ranch has both dairy and beef cattle and it was exactly three of each," Ivan supplied, his tone growing agitated. "All females."

"I understand. What is your friend's name?" I asked, noting it all. If I were Ivan, I would have suspected the pack as well. "Also, did you take this to the Glimmering Rock police?"

"Danny Reese," Ivan filled in the blank. "No, he suggested I speak to you and bypass the police."

Startled a bit at the admission, I tried to keep my face blank. I was sure I looked constipated. "Okay," I drew out the word.

Ivan laughed. "He said you were unconventional, but there was no one better. He also warned me you don't sleep with clients."

"There are a lot of things I'd do for a paycheck, but sex isn't one of them," I blurted out automatically. Of all the people, Ivan's friend was a booty call of mine. "Nice of him to share that."

Ivan's warm laugh made me want to abandon that rule. I kept taking notes as Ivan shared his ordeal. We discussed my fees, had a frank conversation about sex that made me pick up the phone and call Danny as soon as Ivan left to arrange a hook-up. It was probably the bastard's plan from the start.

Chapter Two

I had to admit that I wasn't expecting a case of missing cows to land in my lap. Humans stealing cows wasn't unheard of and happened more than people thought. However, in a magical city hidden within the human one, it wasn't a common occurrence.

The police should take anything affecting someone's livelihood seriously and my first stop was going to be the underground market. If someone was selling off stolen cows, chances are someone there would know about it. The trick would be getting those people to open up.

Reliable magic would be handy in this situation. With my mixed bloodlines, that wouldn't be happening anytime soon. Disaster would strike first. Thankfully, my leprechaun genes work in my favor most of the time. Plus, my dad made sure I knew how to fight physically since my magic couldn't dependably defend me when things went south, as they often did in the market.

I might also run into Gavin down there. He occasionally sold some of his goods there and, like a good mother, I didn't ask where he obtained them so I could plead ignorance if he got caught. I didn't condone his actions, don't get me wrong, but I wasn't above using him as a source either since he was shady anyway.

I slammed my old 1967 CJ5 door and winced at the way the old Jeep shuddered. She needed some tender loving care. For that to happen, I needed a payday. I patted the faded red paint and cooed some unintelligible words at her before I walked away.

The underground market wasn't underground, at least not entirely. It was a hidden pocket inside the magically enhanced parking garage. If a non-magical human drove in here and parked, they wouldn't think anything of the structure. A magical person would see a mirror image of the spaces whichever way they looked.

It was powerful fairy magic with layered illusions over glamour spells. No matter how many times you come here, it always appears the same and it's disorienting. The parking garage itself was linked to a popular shopping mall in Branstone and typically overflowing with the non-magical variety of humans. Yet, the garage always looked practically empty due to some nefarious fairy's intricate spell that wanted the market to remain extremely difficult to find.

For those individuals who made frequent trips to the market, one drain in the garage floor was the starting point on how to find the doorway, and it never looked the same. Fairies were deceptive creatures without breaking the not able to lie trait. Man, do I ever wish that my fairy magic worked.

The concrete jungle I was in was always cooler than the temperature outside the structure; dim and oddly silent. To make it even harder, you were dodging cars that appeared out of nowhere as they exited the garage. Getting out was far more straightforward than you'd think with all this magic.

Locating the drain, I counted fifteen steps to the east, turned clockwise, and moved another twenty steps. Inhaling slowly, I closed my eyes. This last part was always some mental challenge. Today it looked like you were going to step off the edge of a floor to plummet to your death.

Reflexively, I put my hands out in front of me as I stepped into the abyss and entered the market. My luck held and I didn't smack into anyone and quickly moved to the side in case anyone was coming in behind me.

This little pocket dimension of the market looked like an outdoor bazaar. Booths and tents lined the floors with every type of vendor you could imagine. Looking for a spell to make your farts smell better? The market had it. Not that I ever went and sought that out. It was just an example, I swear.

There was never a set location for any given booth or tent. It changed daily and someone led me to believe that sites were on a first-come, first-serve basis. I tended to think that the vendors that greased the palms enough got to pick wherever they wanted. You'd think it would be in the same place so that it was easier to find them; only that was the reason it was never in the same location.

Conveniently, there was always a spell booth near the entrance that sold locator spells to help you find what you wanted if you were in a hurry. I was and I wasn't. My motherly instincts told me Gavin was here and I simply followed them.

I went down a level and caught the scent of brimstone and vanilla cupcakes. Damn it, what was Jameson doing here? I quickened my step, rounded a corner, and almost walked right into Gavin's father. How could I have not smelled him?

"Risa," Braxton growled. "What brings you here?"

"I'd ask you the same thing, but I don't give a shit. Where's Gavin?" I tried to push my way around the troll. He was immovable.

"He's busy. What do you want?" Braxton stepped closer to me. "I don't need you harassing my son."

"Your son?" I screeched, drawing attention. "Why is it now that he's doing shit in the market that he's your son? Yet when I was raising him alone, you demanded a test to prove he was yours and still didn't support him!"

"Shut up, woman!" Braxton snarled the words at me and boxed me in against a wall. "You don't need to spread lies at the top of your lungs. You were fast enough to fuck me senseless and stupid enough not to take precautions."

All these years later and the dumbass troll still made me see red. "Ass-clown. Move!" I demanded with a swift knee to his nuts. Who's the stupid one that left them unprotected?

"Idiot! Mom, are you okay?" Gavin asked, yanking me away from getting head-butted as Braxton doubled over.

"Fine. We need to talk," I told Gavin. I executed a lovely donkey kick behind me into Braxton's ass, shoving him right over to the head-down ass-up position he liked to demand females get in.

Gavin led me to a small booth with some questionable potions displayed on a decorative silk scarf. Nice to see he was trying to make his wares look pretty. I refrained from rolling my eyes and followed him behind a curtain, where I found Jameson sitting and reading a potion book.

"Explain," I demanded of the two.

"You said you wanted to talk?" Gavin tried to steer the conversation away from the reason my youngest son (though, can two hundred and two be considered young?) was reading a book on potion-making.

"Asking for an explanation is talking," I pointed out heatedly. "Jameson?"

"It's only research, Mom," Jameson answered without looking up.

"Yeah, research," Gavin echoed, a guilty look crossing his face. "What's up?"

I'd pry the answers out of Jameson later. "What do you know about cows?"

"They make delicious cheeseburgers and milk," Gavin responded with a grin. "Odd question to come find me at the market to ask."

I fought the impulse to laugh and strangle him at the same time. "Not what I meant, smart ass. Has there been talk down here about cows? Cows are going missing in town."

Something flickered across Gavin's face and was gone the next instant. "Not that I've heard. Are they being killed?"

I searched his face for a clue that would tell me he was lying. "I can't say for sure. They are just gone without a trace."

"It's not like you can stuff one in your pocket and get away," Jameson looked up from his book. "There has to be some sign as to what is happening. You sure get interesting cases, Mom."

Gavin frowned at his brother. "I'll keep an ear out for any talk or information. That's an odd enough thing I can't ask around about without raising suspicion," he told me as he looked back at me.

"I'd appreciate it. What's your sperm donor want?" I changed the subject.

There was that look on Gavin's face again. Whatever Braxton wanted wasn't good and he was dragging Gavin into it with him. I should have kicked him twice for good measure. Even at eighteen, when I decided to test out my sexual prowess with him, he was a waste of oxygen.

"Dad asked me to procure some special items for him," Gavin answered cagily. "Client confidentiality and all that. You know how it goes."

"Right." I scowled at my son. "Client confidentiality," I echoed sarcastically. "Don't wind up in jail for the man who wouldn't even acknowledge that he was your father until he was forced to by the court."

"Oh, that reminds me," Jameson stood up. "Dad asked if you were dating anyone."

I winced and started to back away. "Please tell me you didn't say I was single."

"No, I don't think dating him again would do either of you any good," Jameson said with a smile. "He's just looking to get laid anyway."

It was time for me to escape. Danny was waiting for me and he'd take care of my getting laid issue without any entanglements or child production. The most uncomplicated ex to deal with was the one that got skinned and that was because he was dead. May he rest in mostly peace.

"Okay, I'm going to leave now." I pointed to the book Jameson still held and caught his eye. "We'll be talking."

"I love you, Mom." Jameson moved to hug me. "Be safe."

"Love you." Gavin gave me a half-hug. "I'll listen."

It was the best I could ask for under the circumstances. I left and took the circuitous route out, window shopping, or giving the appearance that I was. I didn't have extra money to spend on black market trinkets that may or may not work as advertised. The exercise's point was to surreptitiously listen to those tents where I knew the lips were loose.

I picked up on chatter about a new player that had moved into town. Apparently, he liked to throw money around and had a party boy vibe to him. I made a mental note to find out who he was and avoid him before he became another wrong choice.

I was almost to the exit when I felt that telltale prickle of magic inside me reacting to something. It typically happened when I was in imminent danger and wasn't aware of it. I immediately suspected my baby daddy with the bruised balls and slowed my step. Trolls weren't the brightest of creatures.

I grabbed hold of the building magic inside me and fervently hoped that it worked as I wanted it to perform. Stepping closer to the wall on my left, I turned in the direction I thought the danger was approaching from and prepared to let loose with whatever I could, only nothing was there.

When a hand touched my shoulder from the other side, I spun and released my hold on the magic. You'd think with as many years as I've dealt with faulty magic, I would know better to trust that it would be beneficial to me.

Elemental magic burst from my body in the form of ice. The ground around me turned to a sheet of it and my feet lost their purchase on the floor. Fortunately, I also wiped out whoever had touched me and caused the magical misfire.

In a tangle of limbs and one soon to be bruised ass, I went down hard. Unfortunately, the perpetrator landed directly across my midsection, whooshing the air from my body and winding up with a face in my crotch as the mystery man tried righting himself.

He took his sweet time getting up after that, too. With warm palms planted on my thighs, the man righted himself carefully, trying not to slip on the icy ground. I could feel the stares of the market's patrons at the spectacle I'd made and I wanted up, now.

I shoved the man and used the force to push myself out of his way and took note of the convoluted magic smell. It gave me my first look at him. Damn, he was hot enough to make my underwear melt. If my stomach didn't feel like a unicorn had gored me, I would have appreciated the face in my crotch moment more.

"I'm so sorry," the man said in the most unexpected voice I could have imagined. It was high-pitched, fingernails being peeled back by a toothpick with acid on it type sound. "I shouldn't have startled you."

"You think?" I guffawed, thankful that some retort didn't pop out about his voice.

"The ice magic would have been more effective if you had aimed it about twelve inches in front of you," the man said in a helpful tone.

"I repeat, you think?" I snapped and clawed my way up the wall to standing. "Do you mind getting the hell out of my way now so I can leave?"

"Sure. I'm new to town and wanted to ask you where is the best place to get invisibility potions? My name is Wiley, by the way," the ridiculously handsome man held his hand out to me.

It was the guy the people had been talking about and he was looking for invisibility potions; an interesting fact I filed away for further examination. "You're in the right place. Excuse me."

"Uh, sure." Wiley frowned and moved.

I slipped past him and kept going without introducing myself. He was trouble. I found it curious that cows go missing and the new man in town was looking for invisibility potions. Way too coincidental, but still noteworthy for picking apart when I wasn't running away from an embarrassing situation that I caused.

Chapter Three

The sizzle of the magic brushed across my skin as I exited back into the parking garage while I rubbed my sore backside. I glanced at my watch before heading to my Jeep. I still had time to burn before I was supposed to meet up with Danny and I didn't want to be early. I'd look desperate.

I decided to stop off at the police station and check-in with the officer assigned to Ivan's case. It wasn't necessary on my part but I liked to extend the courtesy that they usually didn't if our cases crossed paths. The last time it happened, I got accused of interfering with an ongoing investigation.

I knew it wasn't likely that they were actively investigating the cow disappearances but they should be. Vanishing livestock didn't happen every day. Poor Ivan. I didn't know his bank account balance and all I had to base my judgment on was his lack of arguing with my fees. And the fact that he had an active and working ranch, I had to assume that he had funds, yet commiserated with the lack of evidence in the disappearing investment that made him those funds.

I stopped dead in my tracks as my Jeep came into sight. All four tires were flat; the Jeep was resting on the rims. Fury tore through me so fast I didn't have time to try and quell the magic and it appeared in the form of a mini-tornado that ripped through the parking garage.

I dropped and kissed the pavement before the violent wind could flatten me into the position I assumed. Feeling my clothes wanting to be forcefully removed by the product of my instant rage, I could do nothing but wait and hope that I remained clothed when it died out. My saving grace was no one else was in the vicinity that I had to worry about protecting.

Luckily, with my wonky magic, the tornado lost steam relatively quickly. "Could have at least refilled my tires with that air, you useless magic," I muttered as I wiped my hands on my pants.

Grateful that the clients I'd recently helped had all paid in full, so there was money in my account, I fished my phone from my pocket and called my insurance company to come to fix my tires. Whoever had done it hadn't slashed them at least. They'd only let all the air out.

I leaned against my Jeep while I waited and called Gage, hoping that he might know what his brothers were up to regarding potions. Jameson and Gage were relatively close-knit. Gavin was usually the one who kept his distance from the other two.

Gage's phone rang and went to voicemail. "Gage, it's Mom. Call me when you have a moment," I spoke after the annoying beep. "I need info."

Hanging up, I looked around the seemingly empty parking garage. I knew there were other cars here. I could hear the sounds of people closing doors, engines starting, tires squealing, but thanks to the magic, I couldn't see them. Disconcerting when I was stuck waiting for assistance in a magical parking garage that they might not be able to see me in.

Not sure why that thought hadn't clicked when I made the phone call, I slammed the palm of my hand against my forehead. Idiot. In all these years, this wasn't a situation I had dealt with before. Even still, it's not like I didn't know it was a place imbued with more spells than a witch's grimoire.

With a heavy sigh, I lifted myself to standing upright and wondered if I'd be able to push the Jeep outside the entrance to the garage. Thanks to my muddy bloodlines, I was stronger than a typical person. It wouldn't hurt to try, I guess.

I walked around to the driver's side and opened the door. Climbing in, I shifted it into neutral, got out slowly, positioned my body so the door didn't slam into my back too hard, and began to push. It's an old Jeep, I've had to move it this way before but that was with air in the tires.

I managed to move the Jeep about a foot with some serious effort. Another couple of feet and I was drenched with sweat and thankful that I didn't drive a large, heavy vehicle. I wasn't sure how long the attempt had taken me but I was about ready to kiss the driver of the roadside assistance truck when he appeared from nowhere.

"Miss Sanders?" the man who was my new hero asked.

"Yes! Thank you!" I cried. I stopped myself from throwing my arms around his neck and managed only to smile. "I don't think there are any holes, but it looks like someone let all the air out of my tires. I was trying to push the Jeep out to the street where it would be easier for you to find me."

"I'll take a look," he smiled back, and I saw the name on his shirt said Tim.

I made another mental note to call the insurance company and sing the man's praises. I stepped to the side as he got busy and, after a few minutes, he determined the same thing I did. Someone had only let out the air; no one punctured anything. He pulled out an air compressor and got to work refilling the tires with air.

"You'll probably need to replace the tires soon. The tread is getting low," Tim told me helpfully.

"It's on my list of things to do," I replied, already knowing that bit of information.

"Gotta love these old Jeeps. They run forever and are almost indestructible," Tim kept up the friendly banter with me. "Collector items, as well, if I'm not mistaken."

I wanted to laugh. It was brand new when I bought it. Tim wasn't wrong, though; these old Jeeps were fantastic. "She's my old girl and I'll love her forever."

He finished up with the tires, shook my hand, gave me a flirty smile, and took off. I rechecked the time and realized I needed to head to Danny's house. There wasn't time for me to check in at the police station now. I would have to either do it tomorrow or later this afternoon.

I jumped into the Jeep with fatigued muscles and made my way to my current booty call's residence. Danny, being a tech guy and all, made good money. Me, not making good money and being a stubborn female, refused his help along with his offer of a more committed relationship. I'd more than proved I wasn't good at relationships at this point in my life and saw no need to torture him by tying him to me.

Poor guy didn't deserve that outcome. Besides, I liked the arrangement we had. Some days I needed my alone time and solitude after a day of playing with the scourge of humanity. That seemed to be what most of the cases were dealing with when the client walked through my door.

What Danny and I had was fun, mutually satisfactory in the sex department, and it might be wrong, but I was happy that I could walk away if I needed to. Not that I wanted to do that, it was just a peace of mind that it gave me knowing I could. My three baby daddies were mistakes but they each gave me something I treasured.

By the time I pulled into Danny's driveway, I was horny beyond belief and dismayed to find three other vehicles present. With a sigh, I dropped to my feet, rubbed my tailbone, and trudged up the porch and let myself in. I followed the sound of voices back to Danny's office.

The sight that greeted me was one of three locals talking to Danny about hacking someone's computer or equally ridiculous shit that I didn't want to hear. I wasn't precisely law enforcement, and I skirted the law several times throughout the day. However, I didn't blatantly break it.

One of the men, Petey, looked over towards me as I leaned in the doorway. "Lookin' for a good time, sugar?"

"You wouldn't know how to give a woman a good time, Petey," I replied with a smirk. "Not even if she drew you a detailed cartoon map using the easy words and bright arrows pointing to the right areas."

"Danny is a computer nerd; you think he knows?" Petey fired back.

"He didn't need a map, which is a good indication. Also, I keep coming back for more. What does that tell you?" I cocked my hip out and bit back a laugh as Petey looked me over.

The second man, whose name evades me, barked out a harsh laugh. "Poor Petey got shut down by a woman for the millionth time today."

"If you gentlemen are done, I think this conversation is over," Danny said as he stood. "I can't help you this time."

"You can; you just won't," Petey turned from me and glared at Danny. "You just want to get laid now that your flavor of the month is here."

"I think you are done with your tongue wagging, Petey," I interjected. "Time for you to go so Danny can get to wagging his tongue and tasting the flavor of the month, which happens to be a favorite of his."

I pushed off the doorframe, entered the office, pulled off my coat, kicked my shoes off, and sauntered over to Danny. I ran my hands over his chest and dropped them down to the belt buckled over his designer jeans. Working the buckle open, I started to unbutton his jeans when the other three men rapidly stood, protesting that they didn't want to see Danny's junk and beat feet out of there.

Danny chuckled and wrapped his arms around me. "Still got a way of clearing the room."

"You know I do," I agreed and stood on tiptoe to kiss him. "Talk dirty to me about cows."

"A sentence I never thought I would hear coming out of your mouth. How was your meeting with Ivan?" Danny asked with a smirk that made me give a love tap to his balls. He jerked back but not in time to avoid the gentle blow.

"Are you testing my fidelity? Because, damn, that one came close. He's hot and I wonder what he'd look like naked," I answered honestly and settled my ass on his desk.

Danny lifted me and had my jeans off in no time flat and set me back down on the edge, spreading my legs. "Tongue wagging?" he asked with a husky tone.

"Cows," I reminded him, feeling the dampness start to spread. Hopefully, I wasn't sitting on any critical papers; they'd be wet now.

"You are not a cow," Danny answered, leaning forward to kiss inside my thigh. "The surveillance footage wasn't tampered with; I can say that with certainty." He turned his head and nipped at the other thigh, higher this time.

I gnawed on my lip for a few seconds to keep myself from jamming his head right between both my thighs and holding it there until I screamed out my delight with his tongue wagging. "Any way you can check the dark web for cattle chatter?"

"You know I have skills," Danny replied with a flick of his tongue.

My thoughts scattered when the second lick happened and I forgot about cows for the two minutes and thirty-eight seconds it took him to turn me into a screaming mass of putty. I was lying over his desk with my chest heaving when I heard his pants hit the floor. I didn't get a chance to refocus my thoughts until fifteen minutes later when we were in the shower cleaning up.

"You want me to plant a bug that will show you chatter about cows?" Danny asked as he soaped up my boobs.

"If it doesn't cross any lines, yeah, that would be helpful. I need to go talk to Mick, too," I answered distractedly and decided to return the favor by washing his balls.

Danny didn't answer for a few seconds other than a long and drawn-out moan. "Damn, woman. No lines crossed for me. I'll do this on barter for you, at no charge. My fee is a weekend away uninterrupted."

That slowed my hands, and I pulled back to step under the spray. We hadn't done the weekend away thing before. The most we had done was an overnight at Danny's place with me dashing off before the sun rose. "Why?"

"Because we work well together and we can have a whole lot more of that shuddering body thing that makes those noises come out of you," Danny growled, pulling me back into him.

It couldn't hurt, right? "Okay. Do it," I told him.

As an answer, he did me again. Against the shower wall this time, though no less gratifying than the time spent on top of his desk. Danny had skills, that was for sure.

While we had never agreed to be exclusive, I knew that he was, and he knew that should the opportunity arise, I probably wouldn't be. It was another reason I hadn't moved him from booty call to relationship.

"Headed to Mick's office?" Danny asked me as we dressed.

"Yeah, so thanks for getting my pheromones all worked up and sending me off to a sexy alpha shifter," I replied with a laugh.

"It was my plan all along. It will distract Mick and he'll be more likely to answer those pesky questions you like to bother him with," Danny told me with a swat on the ass. "Now, give me your word that the weekend after you finish this case, you will go away with me."

Shit, he wasn't going to let this go. "Fine, you have my word."

"Say it, Risa. I get an uninterrupted weekend with you when you finish this case," Danny pushed.

"Don't press your luck. I just said I gave you my word." I made my tone match my glare.

"I know you, babe. Say the words," Danny's voice lowered again as he crowded into my personal space. His mannerisms were possessive without crossing that line into being demanding in a way that would push me over the edge.

I ground my teeth together and gave him a tight smile. "You aren't playing fair with that attitude; you know I like that." I huffed out an irritated breath. "Fine, when this case is over, I give you my word that we will have an uninterrupted weekend together at a place of your choosing."

Danny crowed out his victory and gave me a searing hot kiss that left me wanting a little more. Reluctant to let myself want more with this man, I pulled away. "Work to do," I replied breathlessly.

I was positive it looked like I was running as I made my way quickly back out to my Jeep. I gunned the engine and kicked up some of the gravel unintentionally and cringed. I yelled sorry out the window and kept going.

Chapter Four

Mick's office was in a pool hall called Blue Balls that bordered Glimmering Rock and Branstone. It served as the pack's clubhouse and an official business frequented by magical and non-magical alike. Mick built the club that way on purpose; Mick's office was on the club's side that rested in Glimmering Rock.

Mick designed it so that the non-magical people wouldn't truly see his office door since it was in the magical territory. It appeared to those people as a storage closet and they tended to look right past it. Ingenious on his part.

I parked in the lot and slid out of the Jeep, waving hello to a medium that lived near me. "Hey, Crowley," I called to him. "How's life treating you?"

"Girl, you got a danger cloud following you," Crowley shot back, his voice slurring a bit.

"Not unusual in my line of work," I told him with a shiver. I hadn't considered that this job would be dangerous. I am not too fond of coincidences, and my magic going wonky wasn't atypical but coupled with the flat tires, it could have been a sign. "Picking up anything specific?"

"Not that I can see," Crowley admitted. "I got a zap when you pulled into the lot that told me danger was nearby. Spirits are quiet. No one is shouting at me today, which I appreciate. I didn't sleep all that well last night. I kept dreaming of cows."

That made me pause mid-step. "Cows? What about them?"

"It's strange because I usually remember, only this time I woke up confused each time." Crowley shook his head, his silvery hair that was sticking out in tufts from under his hat, fluffing up and expanding. "I'd see the cows in what looked like a doctor's office. Who takes cows to a doctor's office? That's why I thought maybe it was some weird nightmare and not one of the precog dreams. The moos they were making were pathetic sounding and they echoed in my ears when I woke up."

A chill washed over me again, like someone dancing a happy jog on my freshly dug grave. "I'll agree, that's strange. Are you going to be here a while, or are you leaving? I might have some questions for you about those dreams but I need to talk to Mick."

"He's in a pissy mood," Crowley warned me.

"Sounds about right," I muttered and bent over to pat the old man's hand. "Will you still be here?"

"Most likely. I'm on a winning streak. I only came out for some fresh air and one of the spirits that linger here told me to sit outside for a bit. Possibly because I needed to tell you about the danger that's following you or maybe to tell someone about the dreams," Crowley shrugged.

"Okay, we'll talk soon." I straightened up and headed inside the club. A low growl greeted me from the left and I looked to see the pack's enforcer, Chuck, sitting on a stool watching the door. I gave him one of my patented fuck-off looks and kept walking.

Chuck and I had a history. He hit on me one night several years ago and I took him for a spin. I only ever intended a one-time thing and he got possessive in a bad way. Not like the sexy way that Danny used against me but the stalker way. It ended in a fiasco, the usual Risa way things like that ended. Mick got involved and had to pull rank. Now *that* had been sexy.

I put a little sway into my hips as I passed some of the pool tables and drew a few looks from some bad-boy types, causing one to miss the cue ball. I laughed evilly and kept walking, right down the hall to Mick's office.

I didn't knock. I just opened the door and waltzed in like I had a right to be there. Unfortunately, I caught Mick mid-orgasm. Instead of turning my back to let him finish, I watched him with my cheeks flaming. Not once did the alpha break my stare as he grunted out his release.

However, the woman he was using was about as embarrassed as could be and practically ran from the office, clutching clothes she'd snatched up from the floor to her chest. The door slammed behind her as she fled. I waited for Mick to button his pants up but all he did was tuck himself back in his jeans, leaving them open. Yeah, I looked.

"Risa," Mick drawled. "Want a picture?"

"Not particularly impressed, so that is a no," I retorted, flopping myself into a chair. The bold lie hung in the air between us. "Uh, I wanted to talk to you about Ivan and his cows."

Mick snapped to attention and his temper flared. "I told him it wasn't the pack," Mick snarled at me.

"I wasn't accusing you," I pointed out. "I merely said I wanted to talk to you. Ivan told me that he had spoken to you about it and has an agreement with you. I am more looking for suggestions on what to search for because it seems to be the timing of the disappearing cows is someone trying to set the pack up to take the fall for it."

Mick relaxed marginally, though I could still feel the snapping anger of his temper close to the surface. I fervently hoped that my magic didn't flare up and cause some mishap to get him right and genuinely pissed off at me. "Ask."

"So, that means you didn't understand that my words were a question without the upturn in my voice to signify that it was a question?" I purposely goaded him.

A slow, cold smile spread across his face. "You think I'm stupid?"

"Did the word stupid come out of my mouth once?" I backed off a little. "What could have gotten into the field undetected and moved quickly enough to not show on the camera?"

"With a potion, a lot of things," Mick growled. "You already know that. Spit out whatever it is you want to ask."

"Who have you pissed off recently that would want to set you up?" I fired the question at him.

"Probably half the town," Mick admitted with a grin. "To the point of setting me up for a crime, that's a different thing. I'm not sure that I've done anything to warrant that or that anyone in my pack did."

"Grudges?" I pressed him.

"Possibly. That will require a bit of time for me to think about; I think best during sex. Want a ride?" Mick stood and stretched, exposing the opened jeans and happy trail that tapered down his ripped abs to the hardening pole I glimpsed earlier.

"No. You can't handle me," I spouted off. "I was taken care of earlier, anyway."

"You only think you were satisfied. I can show you a different world," Mick stepped closer to me. "The smell is driving me nuts; you could have at least showered."

"I did. But I had another round in the shower," I offered up lamely. The unbuttoned jeans were as distracting to me as the smell of sex was to him. "Maybe you smell yourself."

"Nice try but no. Want to stick your face down here

and smell?" Mick held his hand open in an inviting gesture.

Verbal sparring with him was fun, yet I found myself at a loss for words for once. "There is no one you can think of right off the bat?" I hoped the change of subject worked.

Mick chuckled. "Point to me. I'm sure if I thought about it, I could come up with names. Do you honestly believe that someone is targeting me at the same time they are stealing cows? It's not like those are easy to hide. They have to be going somewhere."

I already knew that. "How about you come up with some names for me. Leave the rest of the investigating to me."

"Lucky for you that you are nice to look at, Risa. Not many people get away with talking to me like that, much less walking in on me and cutting my fun short. I've had some of my people watching the new guy in town; he smells off to me. Wiley, I think his name is. The day he moved here, he made it a point to come by and sought me out, told me that he wanted to be friendly with all the leaders in the city," Mick freely offered up. "Yet, I didn't see him seeking anyone else out or any of the other leaders visit him."

"You've been watching since the day he moved here?" I asked dumbfounded. I usually had a better pulse on things.

"Oh yeah. Rich guy moving into town and seeking me out? That raises suspicion with me." Mick nodded. "He has shifter blood, a race I'm not familiar with."

"He's a shifter?" I echoed, sounding dumb.

"Best as I can tell," Mick nodded again.

It didn't sit right with me; I'd have picked up on Wiley being a shifter. His scent was different; I *had* noticed that. It was eerily similar to mine in the mixed way it came across. To me, that meant he wasn't a shifter, or at least, not a full-blooded shifter. Strange that Mick would miss that.

"Anything else standing out about him?" I shifted my stance slightly and crossed my arms, drawing Mick's eyes to my boobs.

"I don't trust him," Mick replied distractedly with a smirk on his face. "I think he's dangerous. Most would take that as a warning that they shouldn't trust him either. Yet, I know you'll do whatever you want."

Mick moved and started stalking towards me, pushing me to the door. "You done with me now?" I couldn't help the snark.

"Don't get killed until I get a chance to sample the goods, darlin'," Mick bent over and hotly whispered in my ear.

Reflexively, my hand shot out and cupped his junk, squeezing it. "Keep dreaming." I turned on my heel and strode out of the office, leaving the stunned alpha werewolf standing there with his mouth open.

I'm sure my face was flaming and I didn't care. Something was alluring about the pack alpha. It was more than the size of his junk emblazoned on the palm of my hand. Alluring or not, he was also a cocky asshole. His warning about Wiley being dangerous hung in the back of my mind.

Chapter Five

I didn't have any more information on Ivan's case than I had before I came here. I had another mystery I wanted to solve. My instincts told me that there might be a connection between the two, but I couldn't see it yet. It wouldn't behoove me to haul off and accuse the new resident of a crime I had no evidence to support.

So what exactly did I have? I knew six female cows had disappeared without a trace. Video surveillance of the grounds showed no trespassers and a slight blip on one of the feeds. A new guy moved into town asking about invisibility potions. A son that worked in the black market and involved another son in whatever new scheme was afoot involving an ex. Invisible fingers were pointing towards the wolf pack. Tech guy looked at videos and they haven't been tampered with at all.

I wrote each of those things down in a bulleted list and stared at it while sitting in the driver's seat of my Jeep. Under the last bullet point, I noted that I spoke with Mick and spotted no signs that he was lying to me. Under the new guy bullet, I wrote that his scent was muddled and Mick felt he was dangerous. I didn't believe my sons were involved but I had to look into that angle as well, in all fairness.

As for Danny's part, I knew there was no deception

there. To not appear on a camera, someone would have had to have used a potion for invisibility, or maybe hyper-speed, and that's what the blip was. The other thing my brain huffed up the side of implication mountain to trip on was what if there was a portal on the property that no one ever stumbled over?

The thought prompted me to turn the page in my notebook and make another bullet list. Who can create portals? Where do they go? Is this a new portal or was it something that existed previously and was re-found by someone? Who would have access to the portal? Why take cows? That last thought led to, what if the cows just walked through by accident?

I tapped my pen on my teeth, staring at the side of the building, lost in thought about the possibilities that this might all be some weird fluke that the cows themselves tripped through. It wasn't a stretch but how did that tie in with the moon phases? That's what turned the whole debacle on its side.

A portal was highly plausible, as well as cows finding it by accident. The disappearances on moon phases were not, which told me that there was a person behind this, and they were trying to deflect attention away from themselves by throwing it on the wolf pack.

Mick, the well-endowed prick, wasn't altogether liked but everyone respected him. He kept his pack in line, behaving, and treated them fairly. He didn't use his position to bully his way into getting things, nor was he the most powerful leader. Mick regarded the law, upheld it, and meted out punishments when deserved.

The bear clan was more likely to step outside the boundaries of the law than the wolves were. For that matter, so were the wyverns. The unicorns had a few run-ins with the wolves a few years back. I was willing to stake my reputation on this having zero to do with the wolves.

For all I knew, it could be one of the humans that resided here and was in tune with the supernatural.

I sighed then immediately almost wet my pants when someone tapped on the window. So much for situational awareness, I hadn't even heard the crunching of footsteps on the gravel. Plus, I hadn't locked the Jeep door behind me when I got in. Not smart.

My head whipped around to see my middle son's smiling face pressed against the window. "Hi, Mom! I was driving by on my way to work and saw your Jeep parked here and thought I'd stop to say hello. Sorry I missed your call but I was with someone. I met someone!" Gage crowed and stepped back from the window so I could open the door and climb out.

I hugged him and then moved to lean against the Jeep. "You met someone?" I asked with raised eyebrows. Gage was always meeting someone. It was that selkie blood of his. Selkie's had incredible seductive powers yet didn't maintain long-term relationships well. As evidenced by Gage's father and now Gage.

"Yes, I did! He's amazing! My first satyr." Gage threw his arms around me again. "I met him at work. He came into the restaurant to have dinner and asked to meet the chef. It was love at first sight." Gage looked around the parking lot, "What are you doing here?"

Interesting and not surprising. Gage was a good-looking man and that's not my mother's bias talking. It also didn't hurt that Gage was a very well-known chef with unparalleled skills when it came to creating mouthwatering dishes.

"I'm working on a case. And congratulations, I hope the relationship works out for you." I patted his arm. "Do you know what your brothers are up to lately? Have you heard any rumors about cows? Black market meat or anything like that?"

Gage frowned. "That's disturbing and the answer is a resounding no. I haven't talked to Gavin recently but I did talk to Jameson a couple of days ago and he said he was helping Gavin with a project and left it at that. Do you still want me to probe?"

"No, Gavin will know I put you up to it and I don't want to create tension. Jameson will spill if I can get him cornered. What's on tonight's menu?" I asked him. Not that I could afford to eat at his restaurant.

"I'm going to marinate some portobellos in a wine sauce, sauté them, then stuff them with a seared veal and some fresh herbs," Gage told me with a crooked smile.

"Sounds rich," I quipped, playing with words.

"Want me to save you one?" Gage laughed, knowing I was referring to the flavor as well as the price tag.

"No. I'm sure it will be excellent but I'm not crazy about mushrooms or veal," I told him as I righted myself. "Get going. I don't want you to be late. If you hear anything else, let me know."

"Love you, Mom. We'll do dinner soon so you can meet Arion." Gage kissed my cheek and climbed back into his fancy Mercedes and zoomed off. He'd done well for himself and I was proud of him.

"Arion," I muttered as I got back in the Jeep. "A satyr." Maybe this time would be different, who knows. His last girlfriend only wanted him for meals and sex. At least Gage was an equal opportunity dater and didn't define his sexuality as the humans did; added bonus, he was luckier in love than I was, though that's not saying much.

Before I took off to my next location, I pulled my phone from my pocket and called Danny. "Hey," I greeted him when he picked up. "Do me a favor and look at those videos again and tell me if the cows are stationary when they disappear or are they moving around a bit."

"Got it," Danny agreed distractedly. "I'm working on your worm bug right now. I'll text you about the cows."

"Thanks, you're the best," I told him in my sweetest voice, which only made him laugh.

Hanging up, I decided that my next course of action was to check out Ivan's field. It carried some risk, yet I had to consider that Ivan hadn't disappeared and he had been in his fields. I shrugged to myself. Visiting another area via portal couldn't be all that bad, could it? I mean, if it happened, I'd probably find the cows, then case solved.

Chapter Six

Ivan, hi, it's Risa," I greeted the sexy farmer when he answered his cell phone. "I was wondering if it would be okay if I stopped by to look at the field?"

"Sure, I'm home," Ivan replied with a smile in his voice. "Should I cook us up some dinner?" he flirted with me.

I swallowed a groan at my stupid no dating client rules. I blame Mick for getting me all stirred up again after my sessions with Danny. I *was* hungry but I couldn't cross those lines I drew. "I appreciate the offer and if you are offering a raincheck, I'll take that."

Ivan's rich chuckle tickled my ears. "A woman with unbreakable morals, I like it. I'll see you when you get here. Do you need the address?"

I was pretty sure I knew where he lived, however, better safe than sorry. "Yes, please. I'm not in the office."

Ivan rattled off his address, I wrote it in my notebook, and we hung up. My conscience ate at me, and I sent a quick text to Danny, letting him know where I was going. I rationalized it in the back of my head, telling myself it was for safety reasons and not because I felt guilty for going to Ivan's. It was work, that's all. I rolled my eyes at myself and got the Jeep started. I wasn't in a relationship.

I considered driving by the city's new resident while

I was out to check out his place myself. I didn't want to do that alone; I talked myself out of it. If Mick didn't trust him, he was right, and I should exercise caution. Especially since I already had an encounter with him in the black market of all places.

I tried to shake off the frazzled feeling that was hanging over me. I wanted to blame it on the afternoon nookie, and I knew it wasn't that. It was the combination of Braxton, my sons, a weekend away with Danny, Ivan, and the possible chance meeting with Wiley earlier. I was used to a lot going on, only not in my personal life like that.

Thoroughly distracted while driving, shame on me, I didn't notice the fancy sports car practically crawling up my tailpipe until the engine revved and drew my attention. With a glance in my rearview mirror, I spotted the mysterious Wiley with a smirk on his face; he was that close.

I felt tempted to hit the brakes but my Jeep was as much my baby as my kids were. Instead, I smiled sweetly and flipped him off. I saw him throw his head back in laughter and then he sped around me, waving as he passed.

Now I hoped he was involved in this cow thing somehow, only to give me a reason to send the police after him. I didn't care if he had enough money to buy them off, which he probably did; it would still inconvenience him. I had a natural-born talent for pissing men off and Wiley just moved himself to the number one spot on my list. Cocky ass-clown.

Ten minutes of plotting against Wiley later, I pulled into Ivan's driveway for the ranch. He owned a large tract of well-maintained land. Cows freely roamed the fields with a scenic view complete with green rolling hills in the background. At the back of the property lie the dairy barns, a silo, and some other buildings I didn't want to know about lest I suddenly find myself not wanting ever to eat a burger again.

I parked next to a bright blue pickup truck and got out, looking around. It was a nice setup but the smell of cow shit would get to me if I lived here. I could tolerate it for the length of a quickie. The thought popped into my head before I could stop it and I laughed to myself, shaking my head. Honestly, I wasn't that quick or easy to drop my pants.

"What's so funny?" Ivan asked, walking up.

"Random thoughts of hook-ups that appear in my mind," I told him truthfully. "Want to direct me to where the livestock disappeared? Were they all in the same field?"

"I'm digging your Jeep; she's a beauty. And I can totally understand why Danny is lost on you," Ivan laughed. "I'll do you one better than directing you. I'll take you there myself. We can take the cart."

The cart turned out to be a Polaris RZR, my first time being in one of those. I could have fun with it, though it probably wasn't a great idea in the cow fields. Silently, I got in and kept my mouth shut while he drove us through the fields. It seemed like we were going for miles. I was glad he was driving and I wasn't walking through pastures of cow shit.

"Okay, all the disappearances happened in this backfield but not all in the same spot. Was there a theory that you were working on?" Ivan asked as he brought the cart to a stop.

"Possibly," I admitted slowly, drawing out the word. "How much do you know about the magical world?"

"My mom was a mage. I know a fair amount but I got none of the magical D.N.A., unfortunately. There are times I think it would be useful, though I am not bitter about it. My life is good, and I've done alright. Why do you ask?" Ivan turned in his seat, so his body faced mine.

"The thought that there might be a portal here struck me. I have Danny looking at the videos again and I wanted to scout out the area," I stuck with the truth. "There are different types of portals, and it's possible there was one here before you came here or that someone opened one and left it."

A stunned look crossed Ivan's face. "Can't say I considered that. How will you know?"

I laughed lightly. "Hopefully, by feeling the magic of it and not accidentally stepping through one to an unknown location."

Ivan's nervous laughter was tight and fear lined his eyes. "Okay then. I'll trail behind you given that answer. I guess, at least if you vanish into thin air, I'll know why. If that happens, how do I get you back?"

"Don't follow me in, that's for sure. Call Danny if that happens," I instructed him. "Which way?"

Ivan silently pointed and watched while I climbed out of the cart and gazed around. He followed my actions and kept his distance. I could see that the thought of a portal scared him. Honestly, it scared me too. Only because I didn't want to end up in some other realm with creatures ready to eat me, maybe I would mind less if my magic wasn't unpredictable.

My phone vibrated in my pocket, causing me to flinch; I pulled it out and saw the text from Danny. *Cows were in motion.*

Okay, that helped. That means the cows most likely walked or were led into a portal if there was one here. I slid the phone back into my pocket and watched my step. My shoes might not be designer shoes but that didn't mean I wanted them smelling like a cow pasture either.

I headed in the direction that Ivan had pointed and the tingle washed over me that told me magic was present. I held my hand up to halt Ivan and tried to feel it out.

"There's magic here or someone has recently used magic here. I can feel it on my skin," I whispered harshly.

My nerves felt like they were vibrating; it was so thick. I slowed my pace, so I didn't step through a portal, then stopped. I studied the ground around me without moving and found a stick. Bending over, I snatched it up and held it out in front of me like a sword. I glanced back and saw Ivan mimicking me and stifled a snort of laughter. We looked ridiculous.

I began moving again at a snail's pace, alternately watching my step and the stick. If part of that stick vanished, I would know the portal was in front of me. Hopefully, it wasn't one that would suck me in like a black hole. Portals weren't a topic I was overly educated in; I only knew the basics.

Creating a portal took an immense amount of magic, which helped me narrow down the list of suspects to those with a deep pool of power at their disposal. Most commonly made by fae, mages, or witches, though other races could produce the magic needed.

"If I get pulled onto a foreign planet, we might have to rediscuss your fee," Ivan called out feebly.

I snickered, "Relax. It will get me before it gets you. Have you moved your cows out of this area?"

"I did after I got home today," Ivan replied cautiously. "Figured it was a wise move and now I'm glad I did. If there is a portal here, can it be taken down?"

"Yeah. It might cost a pretty penny, though. It's not something I can do and I'll provide you a list of trusted people after we figure this out. Correction, after I figure it out. You don't have to follow me. You can stay back with the cart," I told him, turning to look behind me.

"Feels like the manly thing to do, you know, making sure you are okay and all," Ivan muttered warily. "Your balls might be bigger than mine."

Maintaining professionalism wasn't always a strong suit of mine and I'm not quite sure how I managed not to burst into laughter at his admission. I turned back around quickly before Ivan saw the amusement on my face and resumed my forward walk.

It didn't take long for the stick to find the portal. My skin felt like there were thousands of creepy crawly insects flowing over it. My curiosity was going to be the death of me someday. I badly wanted to stick my head through and see what was on the other side. I'd never been through a portal before.

"Don't come closer," I warned Ivan. "The portal is in front of me."

I threw the stick into the portal to see if the magic's feel changed when something entered it. I halfway expected the branch to be lobbed back at me. I jolted a bit when I felt Ivan at my back. He reached around me and jabbed his stick in the direction I had thrown mine and gasped as he saw the end vanish.

"You don't listen well, do you?" I giggled and took the stick from him. "Back up a few feet. I'm going to try and figure out how big this thing is."

"Fearless. Danny's words didn't do you justice. He underplayed you." Ivan shook his head and backed up.

I wasn't fearless. My heart was hammering out a bizarre rhythm in my chest. Granted, it might be that excited fear but it was still fear. I inched closer to the portal and swept the stick from side to side until I felt it hit the unseen edge of the invisible opening.

I bent over and made a mark in the ground to signify that it was the left end. To be sure, I moved the stick around on the other side of it and there was nothing there. I returned to the task and did the same thing until I found the right side and marked that.

To satisfy my curiosity, I moved the stick up until I

found the top. I didn't have a way to mark that, and it became evident to me that two cows side by side and stacked on each other could fit through this portal. It was good sized.

"I've been here for ten years. How is it that I've not lost any employees or myself in that thing?" Ivan asked with his eyes widened, looking like saucers.

"Maybe on some level, you can feel the magic of the portal and it repels you," I suggested, not entirely sure. "Maybe you are incredibly lucky. Got any wire fencing or stuff to circle around this to keep people out?"

Ivan blinked at me a few times, mouth hanging open. Finally, he shook himself out of the stupor and he pulled his phone from his pocket and called someone. "I'm in the far-field. Can you bring out the spare chicken wire fencing and some of the pink ribbon we use to mark the electric fences? You'll see the cart; stop there."

While he was relaying directions to whoever he was talking to, I marked the spot in front where the stick vanished. I moved around to the other side of the portal to see if this was a double-sided thing. To my utter shock, I couldn't see through it. Ivan was no longer in my sight.

"Don't move," I yelled out to Ivan. I waved the stick in front of me and sucked in my breath when it disappeared. "Good to know," I muttered and began making the same marks over here.

I made my way around it to where Ivan had frozen in place, making me laugh again. "Won't marking it like this make it obvious we know about this if there is a person behind this thing?" Ivan waved his hands around in front of him.

"Yeah, it will. I plan on spending the night out here to see if anyone comes through it at night. I guess if your offer of dinner is still on the table, you can bring it out here to me," I shrugged at the astonished look on his face.

Ivan pulled his phone back out of his pocket silently and called someone while he stared at me. "Hey, bring camping supplies with you. Tent, bag, pad, extra rope, several bottles of water, flashlight, and make sure the gate is closed behind you so the cattle can't get back into this field. Thanks."

Chapter Seven

Ivan hadn't argued with me, which I was thankful for, and I knew he wanted to. Solving his problem was what he hired me for and that's what I was going to do. I needed to observe the portal and if someone came through I had every intention of detaining them.

Now, Danny, he'd argued. He slightly wigged out that there was a portal on the property that no one knew existed. I suspect that someone knew and probably someone that worked for Ivan. No one might have ever run directly into the portal but since his cows started disappearing, I'm guessing that someone discovered it.

As much as I wanted it to be Wiley, Ivan told me he hadn't seen the man on his property. Wiley's search for invisibility potions said to me that if he had been using them, Ivan wouldn't have seen him. My gut told me this wasn't Wiley, though.

We'd set up the tent off to the side under a few trees to provide me with a little cover if someone or something did come through. I already knew Ivan's camera covered this area and my hope wasn't that he was gluing himself to the security screen to watch me. Not only would it make peeing outside more challenging but it would give away my plan to go through the portal.

It made me question my sanity, sure, but the thrill of

trying something new pulled at me and I rationalized it that it would help me solve this case and possibly get back Ivan's cows. Yep, total bullshit. I knew it. I was more than aware that I wanted to say I'd traveled somewhere via a portal. Who wouldn't? Come on, that's incredibly cool.

I also know that's why Danny argued with me so vehemently. He knew I was going to do it. I didn't even need to say anything, and if I knew Danny, he'd already hacked Ivan's cameras and was watching me as well. The thought made me roll my eyes again.

I checked my watch and kept my eyes on the portal for a few hours without moving my body. I wanted it to look like I was asleep. From my position, I could see both sides of the mystery portal, and the tingle of magic was a little less. However, I could still feel it.

So when the air changed and felt charged with volatile electricity, I noticed, and my eyes didn't shift away from the portal. Visibly you wouldn't know something was happening. Audibly I heard a faint crackle and pop sound, and then the air went back to normal.

I had no idea what it meant but I suspected that someone came through because I didn't feel alone. I feigned sleep with my eyes cracked open enough to see. Anyone who was watching wouldn't know that anything changed or that I was on high alert. There was nothing in this field for anyone to steal other than me and they wouldn't find me as docile as a cow. Hopefully.

My luck was holding out because my arm was down by my side and I was able to use my fingers to pat my hip and reassure myself that I had my knife tucked into my hidden pocket and with the way I was lying, the gun I had tucked into my waistband was pressing into my back.

I kept my breathing even and stayed as still as possible, which was a direct argument with my cells screaming at me to move and do something. Take up a defense, fight, seek, something other than lying here doing nothing.

"*Fuck!*" I heard someone whisper harshly and the chicken wire moving.

Confirmation I wasn't alone and someone at the very least was using an invisibility potion or they could make themselves invisible. Personally, I hoped the guy was using the potion, which would mean they aren't as powerful as they thought they were. Or so that was what my brain was reasoning out.

Inactivity wasn't something I excelled at, and I was itching to make a move. Only, where? Invisibility didn't mean silence and I was doing my best to listen to see if I could narrow down where the person was. The problem was the grass was dewy and not making its typical crunching sound. If I could turn on the flashlight, I could look for footsteps, though that would give me away in a split second.

I shouldn't have worried; I was noticed by the telltale hand on my ankle yanking me right out of the tent. Glad I'd had the foresight to wrap the exceptionally long rope around my hand and wrist and anchored it to the tree behind me, I held tight to it.

"Hey," I shouted. "Let me go!" I struggled and kicked weakly, no sense in giving my strength away. I wanted every upper hand I could get. I hoped someone, Danny or Ivan, was watching to see me getting dragged by nothing and that they heard me shout.

I received no response other than the hand around my ankle, tightening to an almost painful grip. I could gauge where the man was by my positioning and the hold on me, yet I didn't fight back too much. I needed to see who was behind this at the very least.

I didn't expect the violent kick to my midsection that left me without air for more than a few seconds. That had been uncalled for and quite painful. However, it worked as a distraction against the magic that began crawling over me the closer we got to the portal opening.

"Stop damaging the goods, asshole," I ground out when I could speak again. Not sure how whoever this was missed the rope trailing behind me, but I wasn't going to look a gift horse in the mouth. I was going to beat the shit out of this douche who thought they could get away with kicking me, though.

Too late, I realized we were at the portal entrance as the flash of pink ribbon crossed my vision. I hadn't even heard or seen the chicken wire move this time. What the hell? My magic started stirring and an aggressive bolt of something slammed through my organs. Whatever the mixed bag of genetics was inside me reacted with the portal.

It felt like an explosion tore through me. I heard a body landing somewhere away from me and I became disoriented. Shit. I better not be stuck wherever I was. That wouldn't end well for anyone stuck here with me.

I did a mental checklist; all my arms and legs were present, fingers and toes could wiggle. I could feel my gun and the rope. I shifted with a groan and felt for my knife; it was there. I forced my eyes open next. Wherever I was, it was dark, just like at Ivan's farm. I could breathe, which meant there was oxygen. Likewise, I was on the ground, so there was gravity.

Conclusion: I was somewhere on earth. Therefore, I wasn't stuck. I reached for my cell phone and saw that I had no service. It could be that whatever happened when I went through the portal ruined something inside of it. All I had to do was find a way to call Danny and he'd get me home.

Satisfied that I wasn't on a strange planet or realm, I sat up and rubbed my stomach where I'd gotten kicked.

Luck, stick with me, I thought and pushed myself to stand. I tugged on the rope and was disappointed to see that I couldn't tell if it was intact or not; it was too dark.

A loud screech sounded from in front of me and I involuntarily stepped back. That didn't sound human or like any animal that I'd ever heard. My magic rolled under the surface of my skin and a tiny fission of fear cracked my calm facade. Doubt about being on earth crept into my head.

Instinct had me throwing my hands out in front of me, and something slammed into me, shoving me backward. Wonky magic shot out of my hands in the form of a fireball and what it illuminated made me pause and my jaw unhinged itself as it dropped open.

Nope. Not on earth. It looked like I was in a Jules Verne world mixed with something Wes Craven would come up with for a horror movie. Those four seconds of light were long enough for my fear to grow. I didn't think there would be any calling Danny. That damn rope better be intact.

"You bitch!" a man screamed at me.

Well, there *was* a human here, the one who took me, I assumed. "You dragged me here unwillingly and *I'm* the bitch?" I retorted. "You need to rethink that."

I heard a moo in the distance; the cow didn't sound distressed, not that I would know the difference. I was guessing because I didn't appreciate the thought that a cow was suffering. The distant sound meant I'd have to cross who knows how far in the forest of trees that looked like they had teeth. Wait, could I be in the fae lands? They had scary shit.

Movement sounded from my right, and I pivoted, raising my arms again. This time a wall of shimmering purple light emanated from me and sat in front of me. The dude wasn't invisible here or had something I'd done make that happen? Whatever it was, he crashed into the wall with his face, which made me laugh. Priorities, laughter kept me sane.

"Ouch, that had to hurt," I called out snidely. "Where are we?"

"Fuck off, bitch. You ruined my paycheck and probably destroyed the portal!" the guy glared at me with blood dripping from his rapidly swelling nose.

"Okay, thanks for your assistance. I'll be paying you back for that kick, by the way. For now, I'll go retrieve the cows and make my way home," I casually replied. Luckily the heavy sarcasm in my voice masked the growing fear.

"They'll kill you," my kidnapper snapped with an evil grin.

"Many have tried; they all failed," I batted my eyes at him. "Including you."

Chapter Eight

All I could do was hope that the rope was long enough for me to find the cows. There was no chance I was letting it go; it was my lifeline at the moment. I picked my way gingerly through vegetation that felt like it was alive. Not in the way that plants are living on earth but alive like a sentient being. I had little doubt that everything here could be lethal.

I didn't know what magic had come from me with that purple wall but the ass-clown who brought me here was trapped by it. When he moved, the wall did too. It was impressive and I wished that I could produce that voluntarily.

Now I was inching my way towards what I assumed was a building. A chimney or something that passed for one was belching a foul-smelling smoke. It looked like a mud hut that primitive people of earth would have built for shelter. Only the mud appeared to be moving like a waterfall. Strange was an understatement.

Sometime in the past ten minutes, I had decided I wasn't in fae lands. I honestly had no clue where I was, and I felt trapped in a dream-like state. The one thing I was sure of was I wanted to go home. If I didn't manage to round up the cows now, it meant I'd have to come back. I didn't think my entrance would be as subtle as it was this time. If feeling like you exploded was subtle.

Bioluminescent plants were around the building, emitting an odd colored light that was almost red in appearance. If it weren't for those plants and the purple wall, I'd be utterly lost. Those were the two light sources. Otherwise, I'd be entirely dependent on the rope around my wrist.

I swallowed a girly scream that threatened to erupt from my throat when a Cujo looking Cerberus type dog appeared fifteen feet in front of me. "Nice doggy thingy," I crooned. "Please tell me you are a pet and friendly."

"No, I'm not a pet or friendly," the creature answered me.

Color me shocked senseless. "Uh, hi," I finally spit out. "Are you here to hurt me?"

"I haven't decided. How is it you understand me?" the speaking freak dog asked.

"You aren't speaking English?" I paused. "Where am I?"

"What *are* you?" the thing asked back.

"A magical humanoid being with mixed blood," I answered hotly, slightly offended. I reached behind me and gripped the gun. I didn't want to shoot the pup but I would if I needed to.

"You are like the one you trapped back there?" the talking dog sat back on its haunches and pointed with a paw.

I scoffed, "Hardly. That idiot is beneath me on the food chain. Tell me how to get the cows back. And your name and where I am and if I can go back?"

"You are a demanding creature," his tone changed to one more threatening than it already had been. A series of sounds came from him that sounded like a cross between beeping, choking on marshmallows, and sneezing.

"What the fuck?" I spouted off.

"I don't know that word. I told you my name and your location," the dog creature growled out.

"Uh, okay. I'll call you Cujo since that didn't translate and this place will be christened WTF world," I drawled, wondering if I was pushing my luck. "Where are the cows and can I get them out of here, back to where I came from?"

"Are those the smelly things that emit some disgusting form of gas?" Cujo stood on his hind legs and I found myself looking up into one of his three heads.

"Yeah, those. Will I be able to use the portal to get back?" I asked again, unnerved by this creature.

"It used only to work one way unless you had the charm to activate it from this world. Then you came through and now it's open." Cujo shrugged and waved his arm behind him. "Your creatures are over there. Scientists are doing something with them. The worthless one like you back there has been selling them."

"Cow trafficking. I've heard it all," I snorted. "Great. I'll be retrieving the smelly things and get out of your hair. I'll figure out how to disable the portal once I'm home. That way, your world won't be wrecked by people from mine." Crowley's dreams flitted across my mind.

Cujo gave a huff of disdain and I swear all three heads rolled their eyes at me. "Do what you will. I'm merely an underpaid and underappreciated guard for the scientists. I typically kill whoever comes through."

I shuddered, thankful my leprechaun luck was holding. "Much obliged for not killing me."

"For now. You are pleasing to look at." Cujo moved off to the side and motioned me forward. "I can't say what the scientists will do."

Great, I thought. I followed Cujo to the flowing mud building, trying to process everything that had happened up to this moment. It was pointless since I understood none of it. I was in an alien world, talking to a three-headed dog that guarded scientists who bought trafficked cows from Earth. *What?*

"Through there." Cujo opened the door.

I wanted to plug my nose. I walked past Cujo and into the dark building, managing not to touch anything. The world had to be toxic to create three-headed talking dogs. Danny might not put out if I sprouted another head.

I came upon another scene that froze my already paralyzed brain. Three millipede looking creatures were in the room wearing lab coats and swimming goggles, extracting milk and blood from the cows. No wonder Crowley hadn't remembered much about his dreams. There were no words to accurately describe the *what the fuck* thoughts flying through my head. Ivan's case shot to the top of my strangest list. And I'd seen some pretty weird shit.

"Hey!" I shouted, startling the hundreds of arms that were doing whatever constituted as science here and made them stop. Goggled bug-eyes stared at me in fascination, thoroughly creeping me out. "Those cows don't belong to you!"

The room filled with the sounds of nervous cows and that beeping, choking, sneezing sound as all three bug-people started making sounds. Why could I understand Cujo and not these things? Magic prickled against my skin and I didn't want to hurt the cows, so I drew my pistol and leveled it at the head of the closest bug.

"Don't kill them," Cujo said from behind me. "I'd have to defend them and hurt you."

What I could only assume was a conversation ensued and a sharp yank on the rope had me flying backward through the air, right into Cujo, who caught me by my boobs, of course. Add groped by an alien creature to my list of experiences.

"Hands off." I pushed away from him. I was glowing with magic. "Tell them those cows were stolen and didn't belong to the man who sold them. I'll be taking them with me."

I plugged my ears to block talking since it was giving me a headache and moved to the cows. Removing the very earthly looking modern medical equipment they were using, I tried to figure out how to get six cows to follow me. I had no herding experience. I couldn't even get my kids to follow me.

"They would like me to explain to you that they are extracting genetic material from the creatures to blend with another to create one animal that they can use as surf and turf. I am unsure what that means but those are their words, not mine," Cujo stated, sounding confused. "Something about duplicating a sustenance the other brought with him."

Dumbfounded once again, I failed to notice the rope attached to me was pulling tight again. Knocked off balance, I startled the cow next to me and almost got stepped on by a hoof. I unwound the rope and began to weave it over the cow's heads, hoping there was enough. The next yank made the first tethered cow move towards the door.

"Yes!" I crowed. My skin was still luminescent and wasn't helping the nervous cow situation. "Cujo, help me," I pleaded.

"I think I'd rather observe," Cujo replied drolly.

"Asshole," I muttered, working fast, trying to wind the rope around cow necks, hoping I didn't choke them out. With the last one finished, I followed, holding the remaining short end of the rope/harness next to the cow.

"What is surf and turf?" Cujo asked, trailing after me.

"Food," I told him. "Your scientists are trying to create an animal to harvest for food. Some weird hybrid cross between a sea creature and a land creature, if what you told me is correct."

"I don't lie," Cujo sounded cross.

I stopped responding to his questions and prodded the cows as best as I could. I wanted out of this place. It felt like it took forever for the cows to meander their way back to the portal and I wondered how long I had been here. Too long was the immediate answer that popped in my head.

Looking at my still trapped kidnapper, who was sleeping now, I wondered if I could bring him back with me and how I would get around the purple wall. First, my bigger problem was getting the lead cow to walk into the portal that obviously made them skittish. Not that I could blame them.

I tugged on the rope in a desperate attempt and hoped there was someone on the other end to pull back. It took a few minutes of me trying but it eventually worked and the first cow mooed its unhappiness with the situation. I got behind the old lady and shoved with all my might and she finally took the first step forward into nothingness.

One cow rescued, I sighed. I was grateful that the rest were inclined to follow the first, and the heifers, one by one, entered the portal. As the last one took a step forward, I turned to the sleeping thief.

Reaching my hand out, I tentatively touched the purple wall and watched amazed as it disintegrated at the contact. Interesting. The strange world had an odd effect on my magic. No longer hesitating, I grabbed the man by his neck and cracked the butt of my pistol against his skull, then threw him bodily into the portal.

Turning to look behind me once, I saw Cujo among the trees, watching me. I raised my hand in farewell and turned to the portal. Not wanting to wait around to be kept captive by a three-headed talking dog and his millipede goggle-wearing bosses, I entered the portal.

Once again, magic crackled painfully against my skin but it spat me out into broad daylight and a stunned Ivan and Danny. Not caring that they were looking at me, I dropped to my knees and kissed the grass.

"Damn, Risa! Are you okay?" Danny broke out of his stupor and raced over to me, hauling me to my feet.

"As far as I know. That asshole there kicked me in the gut. Fucker might have bruised some ribs." I looked over at Ivan, "Do you know him?"

"Sure do, he's one of my ranch hands," Ivan muttered darkly. "He's the one who took my cows?"

I broke down into hysterical laughter, no longer able to contain my happiness at being back. "Yeah. The asshole was trafficking the cows. Might want to have a vet check them out. The cows, not him."

"So, um, this new skin color you are sporting is different, kind of hot," Danny said into my ear. "Want to explain?"

"Later. I want a shower." I patted Danny's ass and looked back at Ivan, "What time is it? We can debrief later."

"Risa, you've been gone almost two weeks," Ivan sputtered out. "We can debrief in the morning."

Stunned, I looked back at where the portal was, sitting sight unseen. "Uh, well, I wasn't expecting that." I checked my phone; seeing a strong signal, I called the mages that I knew who specialized in portals and arranged for them to come and shut it down immediately. "I'll wait until they get here, then so long. We can meet at my office in the morning. Not before ten."

Ivan nodded numbly, then called his vet to check the cows. "Thank you."

Chapter Nine

All three of my sons came to dinner that night, each one worried in their way. Part of me wondered if the reason they came was to eat the dinner Gage was bringing. I'd do things I didn't want to do for one of his meals.

Jameson stuck close to my side the whole night and ended up spilling his involvement with potions, which didn't make Gavin too happy, but he felt shaken up that the guy he was working with forced me through a portal and assaulted me.

Mother's instinct was telling me there was more to it than that little involvement with the cow trafficker but I was too tired to push him on it. There was time; besides, Jameson would end up spilling the rest of it if Gavin didn't succumb to my angry mom stare.

I slept like a rock that night and texted Danny to let him know I was okay and was heading to meet Ivan. I splashed some water on my face and was finishing getting dressed when he responded.

I'll be there. Don't forget that we have a weekend date this weekend. Portal is closed; I made sure of it.

Damn, I *had* forgotten about the weekend away with him. As for him sitting in on the meeting, I didn't care. He'd been a part of it and as long as Ivan didn't mind, neither did I. It would also be amusing to see the look on his face when he found out the reason the ranch hand took the cows.

Grabbing one of the muffins that Gage had left for me, I headed to the office. The rundown building had never looked so good after the flowing mud smelly one I was inside. I huffed out an irritated breath at the mail piled up on the floor of past due bills and I marveled that I had been gone for two weeks. It felt like only a couple of hours.

Shaking my head, I gathered up the mail and stuffed it in my top drawer and lowered myself into my desk chair only to have it similarly eject me to what it had done when Ivan appeared in my life.

Growling, I stood to the sound of laughter. "Is this a pattern?" Ivan asked.

Rolling my eyes, I yanked the offending furniture back behind my desk and jammed my ass into it. "Seems to be. Danny said he was coming; you okay with that?"

"Yep. Danny freaked out when you disappeared. Can't wait to hear this." Ivan sat down and crossed his arms.

"You don't have to wait long. I'm here," Danny announced, entering the office and gently closing the door behind him. He set a thumb drive down on my desk. "The video of you disappearing is on there. Thought you might want it for any files you keep on cases."

Danny was the only thoughtful warlock that I knew. I tucked the drive into my desk drawer on top of the bills. "Thanks. You guys ready for some crazy shit?"

They nodded and I launched into a detailed account of what had happened. It amused me to no end, the disbelief written across the men's faces as they listened. By the time I finished, Danny appeared unhappy and Ivan looked like I had told him his dick talked to me and told me its secrets.

Ivan blinked a few times, then pulled out his checkbook and wrote me a check, padding it nicely. "Including hazard pay. I was hoping to get answers to where my cows went. Not only did you find them, and the thief, you went to a different world to bring them back."

I glanced at the check and smothered my surprise. Bills would get paid and I'd be able to get gas and groceries. Nice payday. As I was tucking the check into my pocket, my office door opened again. Ivan looked up in surprise and excused himself after another round of profuse thanks. Danny didn't move.

"What do you want?" I snapped.

"I believe I need your services," Wiley answered with a smirk.

"If you are hoping I can find your balls, don't bother. I don't take on cases with impossible endings. I can't find what doesn't exist," I ground out. Danny coughed into his fist. "As you can see, I'm in a meeting at the moment. Make an appointment," I said, standing and pushing him out the door.

"I've left several messages already," Wiley whined.

"They'll get answered in the order received," I quipped and shut and locked the door before he could come back in. I looked at Danny. "Feel like wagging your tongue with someone that's been out of this world for some surf and turf?"

Book 2
The Doxy Proxy

Chapter One

I let out a frustrated sigh only moments before the cylinder on my office chair gave up. It rapidly dropped, causing my heart to lodge in my throat, and then tipped me off like a dump truck dropping its heavy load of rocks. I landed on the floor with a thud.

Sadly, it was the most exciting thing to happen to me today. No clients had walked through my shabby chic door in a week. Okay, fine, it was just shabby. Cheap metal, hollow on the inside, probably made out of recycled soda cans, and paint peeling off gave it that rustic look.

I shook my head. Who was I trying to kid? Myself? Rustic and chic weren't words used for this building. It was more of the decrepit, crumbling, hole-in-the-wall, should be condemned variety of terms used to describe this place. The rent was right, though, because I managed to stay in the black.

I needed to up my advertising game. I'd briefly considered using my last synopsis as proof of a satisfied customer. Still, even in the magical town of Glimmering Rock, aliens experimenting on trafficked cows was a stretch to believe. I mean, it was true, but yet utterly unbelievable.

Picking myself up off the floor, I gave my chair a good kick, sending it flying across my one-room office and crashing into the secondhand filing cabinet I'd gotten for a steal at a garage sale in Branstone. Most of the people that resided in Branstone knew nothing of Glimmering Rock or its inhabitants.

There are exceptions to every rule. Some of the Branstone police knew about us, as did some of the residents. Everyone in Glimmering Rock knew of Branstone; how could they not? It was the city that hid us. We often frequented non-magical places. At least I did. It was nice to get away.

Speaking of getting away, I had been back five days from my promised weekend getaway with my booty call. It hadn't been as bad as I thought it would have been, but it still freaked me out, and I'd been avoiding Danny since. I knew he wanted more from me, and if I were to be completely honest, what we had was more than a booty call. I only refused to acknowledge it because my history with relationships was the definition of something going pear-shaped.

I glanced at my phone as its shrill ring broke through my chair rage. It was the youngest of the results of those relationships. I answered using my aggravated mom tone. "Jameson, son, what do you need?"

"Hey, Mom. I'm outside your office by your Jeep. Did you know there's a scary dude out here waving his arms around, looking at the sky, and arguing with it? I'm a little afraid to walk past him. I don't want to be mean, but he isn't right," Jameson answered softly.

The other businesses in this building weren't mental health offices, so by default, that meant if he was here to see someone, it was probably me. There was a chance he could be just walking by, but this wasn't a popular part of town. People didn't often take strolls through here.

"You came to see me?" I ignored the other part. "You have angel and demon blood running in your veins, don't let some kook scare you. Get in here."

I hung up, hoping he'd do what I said. Jameson was a good boy, despite his fallen angel's father's blood. My window looked out over the other side of the building so that I couldn't see my Jeep or the crazy man. I gave it a few minutes before I stormed out there to rescue my baby.

A minute passed before I heard Jameson's footfalls on the floor outside my door. "Phew! Not sure what is going on with that guy, but he's huge, and he smells awful," Jameson declared, shutting the door firmly behind him, then locking it for good measure.

"Magical?" I asked, looking out the window again, curious now.

"Yeah, I don't know what, though. Wow! Mom, you look gorgeous! That weekend away did you some good," Jameson crowed happily.

I blushed hotly, right down to the roots of my naturally blond hair. I was not about to talk about the weekend of wild debauchery Danny and I had performed. Jameson wasn't wrong, it had done me a lot of good, and my lady bits were still thanking me.

"What brings you by?" I asked without turning around until I felt my face cooling.

"Oh, I was dropping off some leftovers from the lunch I had with Gage. He was introducing me to his new love interest," Jameson said with a grin. "He's in love," he drawled. He set a container down on my desk and looked at the chair across the room.

"It broke again," I told my son defensively.

"That explains the dirt on your pants." Jameson dropped into one of the orange plastic chairs in front of my desk. Another of the bargain finds I'd picked up in a Branstone fire sale that a school had. They had to be fifty years old if a day, and I cringed when it creaked under Jameson's weight. "Want me to look at it?"

"You *are* looking at it. You can't fix some things, and I think that chair hates me anyway," I growled, sending a scowl to the offending furniture. I moved and kicked it back over to my desk. I was debating sitting in it and took the chance because I was interested in whatever was in that container Jameson brought.

"It's a chicken salad," Jameson answered my hungry look. "Has cashews, orange slices, some of those home-made croutons he does so well."

Sold, I'd take it. Gage, my middle son, was a well-known chef. Not only in Glimmering Rock, but in the surrounding cities as well. He split his time working at a restaurant in Branstone and one in Glimmering Rock. People from Branstone came here occasionally, and when they did, they ate at his restaurant.

"What did you think of the guy?" I asked with my mouth full of fresh, crunchy lettuce.

"He's nice; can't keep his hands off of Gage, which I didn't particularly want to see. He plays piano and sings at some club here," Jameson filled me in. "Gage is utterly smitten. I felt like a peeping tom."

"Well, he's a satyr. Combined with the lure of a selkie, I'm sure it was quite the scene, and I'm happy I wasn't there for that," I shook my head.

Jameson shifted, "Well, I wanted to drop that off. I need to head to the market for some ingredients I need to try my hand at potion-making."

"About that," I stilled him with a look. "Why? You have a great job with an architect firm. You don't need to get involved with whatever Gavin is up to."

"I like the challenge," Jameson admitted. "It's still construction, just with a different set of plans. I told Gavin I didn't want any part of anything illegal, and he promised me it isn't. Before you ask, no, I don't know who or what it's intended. I only know he has a client looking for a potion that doesn't currently exist, and I am going to try my hand at mixing some different recipes to see if I can create the outcome he wants."

"Which is what?" I demanded, shoving more salad into my mouth.

"Gavin asked me to keep it confidential," Jameson hedged, uncomfortable.

He was saved from further interrogation by the sound of someone approaching my door and knocking with a hesitant soft touch. Jameson swiftly stood, unlocked the door, and stepped back and out of the way.

My eyes widened, and I choked on a nut as it went down the wrong pipe. I coughed, trying to dislodge it, which caused my eyes to water, sending Jameson scurrying back to me. He thumped me hard on the back. I hadn't prepared for that, and my head struck the edge of the salad container before bouncing my forehead off my desk, salad flying everywhere. My chair chose that moment to dump me on the floor again.

"Oh, dear," the massive creature at the door muttered.

"Mom!" Jameson cried out, alarmed and amused at the same time. "Are you okay?" He helped me stand, and once he was sure I was uninjured, he chuckled and began to pick up the spilled salad from the floor.

"Laugh it up while you can, child. You have my genes in you too, remember that," I warned him, smoothing out my shirt and plucking leaves of lettuce off my boobs.

"I know, those are the ones I'm proud of," Jameson kissed my cheek before fleeing to safety, his laughter trailing behind him.

"Sorry about that," I gestured for the man to come inside. Not trusting my chair, I perched on the edge of my desk and salvaged what I could of the salad to eat after this guy left. "Come on in."

I winced and bit my tongue when he stepped forward and promptly smacked his head on the doorframe. I heard him mutter something, then he ducked under the eight-foot-tall doorjamb and walked into my office. Jameson hadn't been joking; this guy was huge.

At least nine-feet tall, his hair was bushier than a shrub getting fertilized with the best shit magic could produce. He was broad, and under his odd clothing choice, I couldn't tell if it was brawn or flab. The oversized bright yellow plastic football helmet on his head wasn't a usual fashion choice of adult males, nor was the rubber cape he had draped over his shoulders. Galoshes adorned his feet, and vinyl gloves covered his giant hands. The rest of his outfit paled in comparison, though brightly colored.

I coughed into my fist to stop the laughter that threatened me and realized he wouldn't fit into one of my chairs. He seemed to understand that predicament, and he leaned against the wall. "Greetings and blessings on your day, ma'am," he smiled at me, his words slurring as if he were drunk.

Coughing again, this time because his smell wafted across my nose, I smiled back. "Hello. What can I do for you?" How I managed not to gag, I didn't know. I impressed myself sometimes.

"I need help." He straightened up, "My name is Axoxias."

"Obnoxious?" I spluttered out; sure, I had misheard that.

Axoxias darted and grabbed a pen from the top of my desk. He wrote out his name and then pronounced it slowly. "Ax-oh-shus."

"How about I call you Ax?" I requested. I was positive that I would forget and mispronounce it and call him obnoxious again. Ridiculous, childish things like that stuck in my equally absurd mind.

"Sure, okay," Axoxias agreed. "I need help," he repeated. "The council is trying to run me out of town. Me, and my army, and Waffles." His arm movements became agitated. "I am the only of my kind here; I have a right to live here."

Army? "Maybe you should start at the beginning. I'm Risa. It's nice to meet you, Ax." I held out my hand for him to shake.

His grip was firm, and my arm felt like it was going to pop out of its socket when he shook it. Ax had some brute strength to him. It made me think that his bulk was muscle and not flab. I pulled my arm back when tears flooded his chocolatey eyes. He was a sensitive, brawny dude then.

When he dropped down to the floor to sit and crossed his legs, I did the only thing I could and joined him. It's not as if I wasn't down there already today. It also reminded me that I needed to clean. Or hire someone to do it for me if I could get a payday.

"Tell me why you think the council is after you," I prodded him, reaching up to grab my notebook off my desk.

"To be fair, I don't think it's the whole council, but I think it's one of them. I keep getting death threats," Ax wrung his hands. "The beginning," he trailed off, and his eyes got a distant look. "I'm the Doxy Proxy. I'm also the only sasquatch in the area."

I wasn't following. I got the sasquatch part; I could figure that much out with the process of elimination. "What is the Doxy Proxy?"

"The leader and spokesperson of the Dachshund Army I have created," Ax said proudly.

Chapter Two

Weiner dogs?" I queried, not sure I heard him correctly. It appeared that I had another case to add to my list of bizarre.

"Yes, dachshunds. The general speaks to me, and since I can understand her, I became their proxy. I can understand Waffles, too," Ax added as an afterthought.

"Waffles?" I echoed, afraid of the answers. If he talked to food, this wasn't a case; this was an escapee of some home for the mentally impaired or criminally insane. It could be either at this point.

"Waffles is my pet donkey," Ax added.

"You mean you are like the Doolittle version of a sasquatch?" I asked incredulously. "Amazing."

"You don't believe me?" Ax looked crestfallen. "That's the same tone the police used when I asked them for help. I believe these death threats are serious. My friends and I are in danger."

I sobered instantly. "I'm sorry, I am taking you seriously."

"Thank you. I live on the outskirts of town, not on the border, but close. There are great woods out there, and the legends get a few things right occasionally. Sasquatch's love the woods. Regardless, my neighborhood is quiet, just how I like it. One of the council members lives on my street, and I think it's her behind the threats. I had a pet chicken, Petunia, and she went missing. Two days later, the councilwoman stopped by introducing herself and brought with her a chicken casserole. Do you know those smiles that some people have that ooze evilness? That's how she smiled at me. It gave me chills," Ax shuddered violently at the memory.

"Which council member is this?" I wrote down a few notes and waited.

"Mercy Kane," Ax spit.

"Malevolent Mercy," I mumbled. I'd had a few run-ins with that bitch. I could see her doing something as cold as killing Ax's chicken and serving it to him.

"Apt name," Ax agreed. "There was no reason for her to stop by and introduce herself either. I've been living on that street for over thirty years, same as her."

I noted that on my archaic system of opening case files of writing them on my notepad. "Did Mercy say anything else?"

"It's wasn't long after that encounter that a petition floated around the neighborhood about banning animals that weren't born to fly from flying," Ax recited. "That was followed by anonymous complaints to the police about loud farm animals keeping people up at night. Waffles sleep's inside and doesn't make a racket."

Confusion marred my face. "Why the petition?"

"Oh," Ax frowned. "I probably forgot to mention that my dachshund army flies. A witch that I had a brief relationship with thought it would be funny to have flying dogs, so she put a spell on them. The affair ended after the general had an oops moment that landed on her head."

I snorted, then leaned my head to my chest until I was confident that the laughter wouldn't burst from me in a wild spurt. When the urge passed, I cleared my throat. "Is it possible that's what happened to Malevolent Mercy? I mean, Councilwoman Mercy? Could she have been hit with a bomb?" I giggled again. I would have paid to see that.

Mercy Kane was a harpy and a genuine bitch-of-all-trades; her attitude matched the legends of harpies depicted in old Greek mythology. I hated dealing with Mercy. The woman was one of the council members that had it out for me and went out of her way to make my life as difficult as possible. Petty and childish insults would spew from her twisted lips if she spotted me.

"I wondered that, but I don't think that's the case. When my army takes to the skies, we stick to areas that aren't populated, so those bombs don't accidentally happen. That's why I wear this helmet," Ax tapped his finger against the brightly colored plastic. "Also, I play *Flight of the Valkyries* as soon as their little feet lift from the ground. Kind of a way to help announce that they are taking flight and because it just sounds super cool."

I bit the inside of my cheek hard. "How do you play it?" I wasn't judging, but this was hilarious to me, and I was doing my damn best to not laugh at it since it was a serious thing to Ax.

"Oh, I carry a little boombox in my bag and pull it out when I know they'll be flying. The doxies also love that song," Ax smiled fondly.

All I could think about was John Cusack holding up the boombox playing *In Your Eyes*. I was awful sometimes. I found myself smothering another giggle and did my best to look serious. "Okay, so what do you want me to investigate? The death threats? Or are you looking to have me put an end to Mercy's torment of you?"

Ax looked sheepish, "Both. Is that possible? Mercy Kane scares me."

"She frightens most people," I admitted. Was it possible that his stench had fried my nose? I found it strange that I couldn't smell him anymore. "Do you have the death threats?"

"Yes!" Ax shouted, making me jump.

Nope, my sense of smell was still active. I don't know what Ax had eaten before coming here, and I was sure it hadn't smelled that way when he was eating it. Wow, sasquatches were an odiferous bunch. The things I learn in this profession are quite valuable.

Ax rooted around in the backpack I hadn't even noticed he carried. The sheer size of him made the bag look like a dainty purse. A bag holding a boombox, with a recording of *Flight of the Valkyries*, that he played when his dachshund army took to the skies. I couldn't have made this up if I tried.

"Here you go," Ax thrust a handful of papers at me. "I found them on different days. Sometimes they were in my mailbox. Other days they were on my front door or stuck into the crease of a window. It all happened over the past month. I don't know why; I'm not unlikeable."

My heart clenched a little at the distress on his face. "No, you aren't. Harpies aren't the nicest of creatures. I'll see what I can find out," I reached forward and patted the back of his hairy hand.

"Thanks. Money is no object. Not when it comes to keeping Waffles and my little army safe," Ax sighed out happily.

"May I ask why you have an army of dachshunds?" I felt compelled to ask.

"Security," Ax stated thoughtfully. "My kind have been hunted for years out in the non-magical areas. There are some places out there that I can't resist going to and spending some time in that amazing nature. I want to be able to do it without fear of getting captured, injured, or killed."

I nodded. "That makes sense."

"We've been training to drop bombs strategically

on people that are acting out of line," Ax boasted. "My little friends are getting excellent with their aim and being able to produce on command. Admittedly, it went a little haywire when one ate some human food, and it was more liquid than solid. Oh boy, was that ever a lesson."

I should receive an award for keeping a straight face during that. "I imagine the helmet wouldn't help much in a liquid napalm version of shit." Damn, my tongue got away from me.

"No," Ax agreed solemnly. "No help at all."

I quickly stood up and grabbed a contract from my drawer, and handed it to Ax. "I'll have you fill out the information on this contract, and then I can get started investigating. My fees are outlined here and here," I pointed out to him and plopped down on the floor.

Ax didn't hesitate in filling it out and signing his name with a flourish. "Thank you! Would you like to meet them? It might help you in your investigation."

"Uh, sure." What could it hurt? "They are here?"

"Oh, dear, no. You can come by; I was assuming you'd want to see the areas where they train and the layout of the neighborhood," Ax cited as he planted his hands on the floor and pushed his massive frame up.

I got to my feet rapidly, so I didn't crane my neck looking at him. "Okay, sounds good. How about tomorrow morning?"

"Perfect!" Ax's smile lit his face. "I'll have coffee ready for you."

Chapter Three

Risa, I know you are in there, open the damn door," Danny's voice came from my front door.

Damn, I was hoping to avoid this scene. I didn't move for a few more seconds, let out a hefty sigh, and yanked the door open.

"Hey, Danny! How's it hanging? I was about to leave and head to my new client's place. What brings you by this early?" I babbled, knowing he would see right through it.

"Okay. I figured you'd freak out after the weekend, though I didn't expect complete silence from you," Danny pushed his way in and set his hands on his hips. He was doing that sexy, assertive thing again. "You weren't leaving yet. Not in only a T-shirt."

My spacious living room felt a lot smaller now, and his posture and tone were making me hot. Danny's reddish-brown hair appeared as if it were glowing, and I leaned to the side to see if the lamp he was standing in front of was on or not. Nope, not on. That meant he was leaking magic.

"Calm down," I held a hand out towards him. "I don't want all my light bulbs to explode again."

"Then explain to me why you can't return a phone call?" Danny began to pace. Until I saw Ax, I'd considered Danny tall at six-foot-four. He still cut a good figure and filled out those jeans wonderfully. Heavily muscled, tattooed, and sexy as sin.

Whoa, my brain derailed, and I fluffed my shirt away from my suddenly sweaty chest. "What?"

Danny paused, flicked his eyes over at me, took two steps in my direction, and pinned me with a kiss that deprived me of all oxygen. Ax could wait. I needed to get Danny out of his pants. I didn't understand what was happening when he backed away from me.

"No, Risa, I want you, but I want more than this only when you're turned-on shit. I want the bad stuff too," Danny huffed out. He adjusted the noticeable bulge in his pants and ran a hand through his hair. "That came out wrong."

I felt the spark of my magic and temper at the same time. "You think I'm bad?"

"No. You know I didn't mean that. I mean, I want the good and the bad, not only sex when the mood strikes either of us," Danny fidgeted nervously. "I'm aware that your past relationships were rocky, but you don't even consider giving us a chance, and I want to know why? Am I not good enough?" His voice had taken on a steely tone by the end of his question. It was scorching hot.

I think I was emitting electricity because my blond hair was standing out around my face like a frizzy cloud. "I'm a chicken shit!" I shouted. "It has nothing to do with you not being good enough. It's me that's not good enough for *you!*"

Both of us fell into shocked silence at my admission. That predator thing that Danny does so well to make me pliable happened, and he held me against the wall. His lips skimmed my neck, his tongue flicked my ear, and my knees began to quake.

"Darlin', you are more than good enough, and chicken shit is not words anyone would ever use to describe you," Danny's hot breath tickled my eardrums. "I'll accept that you're scared. For now. We make sense, and we work."

Danny bent forward and hooked his arms under my knees, giving me an assist to wrap my legs around him. Oh, yeah. We excelled at this. Grateful that I had no pants on, I moaned my agreement and lost my mind to the rhythm of my hips slamming against the wall. Worth it.

I wasn't in a relationship; I repeated to myself the entire drive to Ax's place. I wasn't even able to convince myself. Rolling my eyes, I took notice of the neighborhood as I drove through. I didn't know which house was the councilwoman's, and I made a mental note to ask.

The houses were slightly larger than mine and well maintained. The neighborhood was large and dead-ended in a cul-d-sac before circling back to the entrance. All were similar in style and color, each blending in an array of sameness, making it so that I didn't understand what drew Ax to this place. It was a magical *Stepford Wives* thing.

I shrugged it off, pulled into the driveway, and killed the Jeep. I cracked the window open to keep the air flowing through so it didn't get hot and stuffy, also to see if I could hear the music playing that signified flying dogs. Hearing nothing, I got out and made my way to the front door.

Ax met me there, the barking I now heard giving my presence away. The second the door opened, the overwhelming smell of dogs assaulted me. It made me think of dirty Frito's. I seriously needed to be nominated for an acting award for not showing my dislike on my face.

Ax gifted me with a bright smile. "Coffee's ready!" he declared happily.

"Oh, great," I smiled back. I couldn't help it. Ax was likable if a bit strange. "I didn't get a cup this morning, and I require caffeine."

"My pleasure, Risa!" Ax held the door wide open

for me.

I can't say that I had any preconceived notions of what I expected his house to look like, but I was surprised. I didn't expect designer luxury in rich earth tones and artwork of gorgeous old-growth trees that looked like they could house an entire pixie clan. The couch was leather, the most delicious chocolate color, and sasquatch sized; I wanted to sink into it and take a nap.

"Have a seat," Ax swept his hand out to the immaculate furniture. Not a dog hair in sight. Yet the smell gave away their being there. Well, so did the clickety-clack of their nails on the dark hardwood floors. "I'm going to go grab you a cup of coffee."

I sat in a buttery soft, light brown recliner and almost groaned. How did a reclusive sasquatch attain this level of luxury? Whatever, it wasn't my concern as long as he paid his bill. I couldn't help but feel a little bit jealous that he was living so much better than I was, but it was fleeting.

Ax came bustling back in with a stack of papers and a steaming cup of coffee in a large artisan type mug that smelled heavenly. "I didn't know if you took cream or sugar. I apologize for failing to ask."

"Ax, you're fine. I take it black. Actually, I take it any way that I can get it. I'm easy," I blurted out, reaching for the cup like a dehydrated desert dweller.

"Here are the letters that I was left," Ax thrust the stack of papers at me before going to sit down on the oversized couch.

I rifled through the stack, noting that there were several, many more than I thought there would be. "Other than Malevolent Mercy being who she is, do you have any proof that it's her doing this?"

"No," Ax admitted sheepishly. "But that's why I hired you. I don't want to accuse her publicly if it isn't her."

Go back to the woods where you belong, so we don't have to smell you; one of the notes said. Mean, but not life-threatening. Also correct; Ax had a distinct smell to him. In my opinion, the dogs smelled worse. The notes were all typed and printed from what looks like a standard laser printer. I didn't sense any magic on them either. Plain white paper, nothing special; the font was large and bold, but not an uncommon one that I could tell.

Leave now and never come back, or you will get a wax job with boiling wax you won't recover from in this lifetime; read another. Creative.

Your ass will get put into a press and end up looking like a real waffle; was printed on another. That could be taken as a threat to Ax and his donkey.

You are invited to a hotdog roast in the swamp house as it burns down around you and your zoo. Wow. These letters are pretty directed and hate-filled. I didn't need to look at any more of them to get the gist.

The more I thought about them; the letters could have been written by anyone, though it did fit with Mercy Kane's attitude. I'd need to look at the other neighbors to keep the investigation fair.

"Have the letters increased lately?" I asked, setting them down on the coffee table in front of me. I should have looked at them yesterday when he handed them over the first time.

"They have indeed," Ax nodded his head vigorously, his shaggy hair flopping around. "I want it to stop."

"I bet," I murmured, wondering why the dogs weren't out here with their fearful leader.

"How's the coffee?" Ax asked, distracting me. "You haven't drunk much of it."

"Letting it cool off," I told him. "Where are the dogs?"

"Oh, I have them contained in the back, so you

didn't get swarmed. Do you want to meet the army?" The grin that split his face was blinding.

"Sure," I committed myself to a dachshund invasion.

Ax practically pranced from the room. The sound of a thousand scurrying rats headed towards the biggest smorgasbord they've ever seen filled the air. Fifteen wiener dogs wearing camouflage doggy sweaters came running into the room, tails wagging furiously. Reddish-brown, black and tan, long-haired, short-haired, and even a black and gray one filled out his dachshund army.

If I hadn't been sitting there and seen it with my own eyes, I wouldn't have believed it. The doggy sweaters were a bit much, and I found myself stifling an incredulous laugh as they all jumped at my legs, begging for attention.

"Wow," I finally managed to say as I patted each of them.

"Come on," Ax begged excitedly. "I'll show you how they fly."

I stood as Ax whistled, and all the dogs fell into line behind him, tails at attention now. Before I made it two steps, a donkey came trotting down the hallway and took up the formation's end position. I needed to watch my step.

I followed off to the side, so I didn't step in a steaming pile of dung, and we marched behind Ax's house into a forested area. We wound through some dense trees and came to a clearing where several landmines were in plain sight.

When the music of *Flight of the Valkyries* filled the air, my jaw dropped open and hysterical laughter bubbled up from my throat. Fifteen wiener dogs jumped into the air like Santa's reindeer delivering presents on Christmas Eve. Only these gifts were smelly, hot, and unpleasant to have dropped on your head.

"It's something, isn't it?" Ax whispered in awe. He didn't wait for me to answer, thankfully. He let out a shrill whistle, and the dogs moved into a circular formation. At the sound of two sharp whistles, one-by-one, the dachshunds dove down and dropped a shit-bomb.

I'd seen everything.

Chapter Four

After leaving Ax's house and the doxy demonstration, I wandered through the neighborhood, talking to other people out walking their dogs. I asked about Ax, his flying wiener dogs, donkey, and any other issues they thought the neighborhood had. All but one person complained about Malevolent Mercy.

"That woman is a saint," one guy told me. "She's turned this neighborhood into a safe haven, except the nuisance of the sasquatch."

"Why is that?" I wondered aloud.

"No one wants doody on their head," he told me with a sneer. "Gross."

"Has that ever happened to anyone?" I pushed him for some solid proof instead of the opinion of one councilwoman.

"Thank heavens, no," the guy who I thought might be a shifter of some sort sighed.

I thanked him and kept walking to the end of the street and began to smell a strongly scented magic in the air. My skin prickled with the power of whatever spell was hanging in the air. I was in front of a well-manicured lawn, perfectly aligned flowers in accenting colors to the shutters on the windows.

I'd almost believe the illusion if I couldn't feel the

magic and the danger that lurked underneath it that was stirring my muddled powers to react. Whoever lived here didn't have good intentions. I noted the address and texted it to Danny to find out who owned the property.

Two more steps and a bolt of electricity blasted me off my feet and threw me ten feet backward. My head thunked the pavement, and the momentum tossed my legs over my head into a somersault. Pain radiated through my body as recurring little jolts continued to zap me.

I swear I saw surfing rats riding a tsunami while chewing on turkey legs. I rolled to the side and finally came to a rest outside of whatever strike zone I had been in if there was one. I didn't need Danny to tell me who lived in that house. I already knew. I'd found Mercy Kane's residence.

That spell fit her personality. It often felt like being electrocuted when you talked with her about anything with which she disagreed. Mercy was a piece of work, and I was a little irritated that no one told me about the magic that surrounded her house. That was a rude awakening.

With scraped elbows and a throbbing head, I got to my feet and squinted my eyes at the house. Cursing my failed magical defense, I trudged back towards Ax's to get my Jeep and start digging into whatever is driving this bitch of a harpy into trying to run Ax out of his house.

Climbing into my Jeep, I glanced at my phone as a text buzzed it and scowled at the reply from Danny that I'd already figured out. I wasn't responding because whatever I would say wouldn't be nice, and he didn't deserve that. It wasn't his fault my ass got handed to me by a spell.

I headed to Glimmering Rock's version of a city hall to dig through some records on that neighborhood. Ax had resided there longer than the harpy had, and that meant something existed about the land or property in specific that she wanted to own.

It always boiled down to Mercy being more powerful or having it all. She was greedy. For power, for money, for class, for the position; you name it, she wanted to one-up whoever she could. I needed to figure out which aspect of this the torture of Ax fell underneath. I no longer had doubt Mercy was behind this.

I was going to start my search with Ax's property. There had to be something about that place in specific that was making him a target. I couldn't see it being his personality. He was a nice guy if a bit odd. The dogs and donkey weren't offensive other than to your nose at first until you became accustomed to it.

Though, on the other hand, I *was* talking about Mercy Kane. She needed no reason to hate or torture anyone, and she frequently had several victims at a time. She's hated me since the day she arrived in town for no reason other than she didn't like the way I took no shit from anyone.

Maybe it was my own need for revenge on her for continually trying to ruin my life that made me focus on her as the culprit, but let's face it, a spade is a spade. Mercy Kane was evil in spades, gotta call it like I see it.

I pulled into the city hall lot, parked, and made my way to the entrance. There was a spell over the door that stripped magic from you when you entered. Many years back, someone had gone in there and went apoplectic on an employee for authorizing repossession of land due to non-payment and released lethal magic on several people.

I could understand the reasoning, but it was disconcerting to feel something forcibly removed from you that was a part of your very essence. Even if it wasn't something that I had control of, it still left me feeling oddly empty and unnerved.

I approached the counter and saw an old acquaintance of mine from way back in the day, one of the elves I used to run with between Gavin and Gage's birth. He still had that elvish beauty going for him, but his eyes were hard and had a cold glint to them that wasn't there before.

"Hey, Clive, how are you?" I asked with a smile.

There was a marginal brightening of his eyes before they dimmed back to ice. "Risa, it's good to see you. Tell me you ran over an orc in the parking lot, and my day will be a lot better."

I snorted out a laugh. "Sorry, buddy. No vehicle assaults today. Someone giving you a hard time?"

"No more than usual. If I had your fighting skills, it wouldn't matter that I had no magic," Clive chuffed. "Regardless, what can I do for you?"

"I'm working on a case and would like to see any information you have on this address," I slid a piece of paper with Ax's address scrawled on it.

"Did you know Mercy Kane lives just up the street from there?" Clive asked as he processed my request. "That's another one that needs to get run over."

"Popular opinion on that one," I retorted quickly. I gave Clive the rundown on the spell that attacked me without divulging any details on the case. Clive was smart; he'd guess that our esteemed councilwoman was involved.

Clive began writing something down on a piece of paper while surreptitiously looking around him. He'd glance back at the computer every few seconds, make something print, and go back to writing. I wasn't entirely sure if our conversation was over or not, so I kept quiet, not wanting to interrupt whatever he was doing.

A few minutes later, he stopped, gathered up the printed papers, fastened them with a paperclip, and looked at me. "That will be three dollars," he said with a friendly tone. "That last page has some interesting information for you. Hope you figure your case out."

I slid the cash through the window with a puzzled

frown. "Thanks, Clive. Appreciate the help. We'll need to catch up soon," I finally said as the papers came through the slot.

"For sure," Clive responded with a smile and a nod. The sudden professional attitude told me that there was someone within listening distance. I grabbed the papers, waved, and headed back to my Jeep.

It wasn't until I was in the front seat with the doors locked and windows up that I shuffled through the stack he'd given me. There was information on several addresses in a pile, as well as the information on Ax's. The last page was his handwritten note.

She's up to something, Clive had written. *The other pages are the addresses that Mercy has been asking about, same as you. She's been in here frequently over the past month, and I don't trust her one little iota. It can't be a coincidence that you ask about an address in her neighborhood and not have her involved. Crucify the bitch.*

I chuckled. Clive didn't mince words. I wadded up the note and crammed it into a half-full water bottle that was still in my Jeep and watched until the paper disintegrated. The spelled-paper was a wonder in instances like this one.

I tucked the pages into my folder and drove to the library to look up any news articles written about that neighborhood or Ax's property specifically. Something would come of that search with any luck and would aid me in looking through these properties that Clive added.

Chapter Five

"om! What the hell happened to you?" Jameson demanded when I walked into my house.

"What? What are you doing here?" I paused and wondered what he meant.

"You have bruises and scrapes all over your arms and weird splotches on your face," Jameson rushed over to examine me.

Damn that harpy. I calmly told my youngest what had transpired and watched Jameson's face morph from concern to anger. His magic flared brightly, and I felt the healing powers inside him work on my injuries that I'd forgotten about; no wonder the people in the library had been giving me side looks.

"This is a case for the crazy, smelly, hairy guy that was outside talking, isn't it?" Jameson asked as he pulled his hands away from me.

"Yes. I can't really give you any case information, but if you have time, you can help me look through these pages and see if something common sticks out to you or something odd that would make that bitchy harpy sit up and take notice." I waved the folder with the stack of papers in there, along with the few articles I'd printed out.

"Sure. Tell me this, what was that guy?" Jameson followed me into the kitchen.

"Sasquatch, and he isn't crazy. Eccentric is what I'd call him. Genuinely nice guy," I added for extra benefit.

Jameson looked at the folder I'd set on the table. "The Doxy Proxy?" he asked with raised eyebrows. "Never mind. Confidential information."

"You didn't answer my question," I reminded my son. "What are you doing here?"

Jameson shrugged with a guilty expression written across his handsome face. "Hiding from Gavin. He's driving me nuts right now. He won't look for me here because he won't risk you cornering him on what he's doing and for who."

That much was true. "Okay," I accepted Jameson's answer without further questions. He'd tell me when he was ready to talk about it. Jameson wasn't good at keeping secrets from me. I crossed the kitchen and opened up the freezer. "I've got frozen pizza, want that?"

I got another shrug. "I can order us something healthier than that, but if that's what you want, it's fine with me."

I rolled my eyes and pulled out the frozen pizza just to make a point. I don't know what that point was supposed to be, but I'd think of something if Jameson asked. It was apparent that Gage had put a bug in Jameson's ears about my eating. Groceries are expensive, and at the bottom of my list below the essential bills that keep my water hot, electricity on, and rent paid.

Once the pizza was cooking, I gave Jameson the stack of the other addresses in the neighborhood and kept Ax's to myself. There was something else going on here that I was trying to figure out. Jameson was unquestionably a momma's boy, though he didn't ordinarily come by this much.

"How's work?" I innocently asked as I sat down.

"Slow. We are waiting on the materials to arrive.

One of the architects ordered some super fancy high-end marble that is getting imported," Jameson offered up.

Okay, maybe it wasn't the job thing that was bothering him. It also semi-explained his involvement with Gavin on the potion thing. Jameson didn't like downtime any more than I did. The firm he worked for was an all-in-one type of business. People hired them to draw up blueprints for custom buildings, and then they had the workers to make it a reality.

Jameson was good with his hands and could build anything. He had an innate ability to see on the plans the parts that wouldn't work and offer up workarounds. Jameson made his way through the ranks from general laborer to foreman with a crew of his own. Jameson was my saving grace with my house.

He frequently checked out the things I complained about, fixed them, and then went around to look for any other potential issues. Sometimes when they had leftover materials, he would gather them and replace things. He'd redone the floor in the kitchen with beautiful hardwood.

"I'm looking for odd things, right?" Jameson asked as he perused the stack of papers, then laid them out on the table in a line and began studying them in earnest. It became clear he didn't expect an answer from me.

I plopped in the armchair and draped my legs over the arm while I read through Ax's property information. The property he was on dated back to long before the neighborhood was even there, and judging on the last name attached to the deeds, it was all in Ax's family. That explained how he was able to afford the luxury, family money.

What it didn't explain was why Mercy Kane would be interested in it. Nothing the property assessments yielded showed anything powerful or magical on the land. The tract itself was the largest by far of the neighborhood, which could be a draw in my humble opinion. It didn't feel right that the answer lies in the property size, though.

"Do you have a map of the neighborhood, Mom?" Jameson interrupted my thoughts.

"Mmhmm," I murmured and passed the plotting map over to him.

"I was right. Look at this," Jameson poked me in the leg. "All the properties on these sheets butt up against the woods. If Mercy is behind something, she's methodical about it. I would guess that these other three properties are on her intended list if what she is looking for is in the woods."

Jameson tapped the plots on the map and gave me a questioning look. I stared at the map so hard I expected it to burst into flames. One of the properties was the Mercy fan. I'm guessing she wouldn't need to target that one since that guy was already in her pocket.

I tossed a highlighter to Jameson. "Highlight those for me, please."

"One other thing is two of these properties," Jameson pointed to them, "have ties back to before the neighborhood existed. They own plots of land that extend farther back."

Interesting. Same as Ax. My focus needed to be on the woods if the attacks on Ax weren't personal. I made a mental note to ask Danny if he could search on that wooded area for anything that stood out. Something anomalous had to exist out there.

When the timer dinged for the pizza, I heaved myself out of the chair and went to grab some plates. Jameson gently pushed me out of the way and took over. He'd make a good husband and father someday.

"Mom, are you happy?" Jameson asked after he finished eating. He pushed his plate away and gave me one of his dead-serious looks that always made me want to laugh.

"I'm happy," I declared. "Why would you think I'm not?"

"How do you feel about Danny?" Jameson zeroed in on me.

Damn. "Why do you ask that?"

"I ran into him earlier, and he asked me for advice about you. I didn't know how to answer him without feeling like I was betraying you. All I could come up with to say was to follow his heart, which is cheesy as hell. But it did make me think and wonder if you were happy. I want you to be glowing with life how you are right now, only, all the time. If Danny doesn't make you feel that way, then end it with him," Jameson expelled in a rush of air.

I wanted to be mad. I truly did. Yet, I couldn't muster the energy to lash out. Jameson was right to call me out. I raised them not to be that way with people and didn't live by the standards I set for them. He also had a point to question if I was happy or not with Danny. I knew I was; hell, I think Danny knew it, too.

"Did he tell you he cornered me about that this morning?" I hedged. Jameson might be a momma's boy, but he was also not one to rat out someone else on a personal conversation.

"He did. I wouldn't call it cornering you, though. I'd say he was standing his ground and letting his feelings known," Jameson calmly stated. "Don't let the past chase away a future. Danny's not like any of our fathers."

My son spared no punches. "Understood," I nodded my agreement. We parted ways for the night after that.

Chapter Six

When my alarm jarred me awake like a firehose on full blast the next morning, I reached for my phone and groggily called Danny. "Hey," I greeted him when he answered. "Did I wake you up?"

I heard Danny laugh. "No, but it sounds like you aren't there yet. What can I do for you?"

I grunted, sitting up. "A search."

"Elaborate on that a bit more, babe," Danny chuckled. "Have you had any coffee yet?"

"No," I groaned out while I stretched. "You were my first thought."

I almost shit myself when I realized what I had said. I fell silent, and the air felt pregnant with unspoken feelings. Damn my brain and its disconnected tongue. What was it about this man that made me forget I'm not ready for a deeply committed relationship yet?

Danny's voice had taken on a husky tone that set my lady parts into a frenzy. "What should I be searching for, babe?"

"Uh," I scrambled, thankful that he'd let my slip of the tongue go without comment. "The forest. Hang on." I shot to my feet and ran to the living room to grab the papers with Ax's address. I recited it to him and explained that I was looking for an anomaly in the woods behind that location.

"Alright. Let's give it a couple of hours to come up with something," Danny replied. I could hear his fingers flying over his keyboard.

"Thanks. You're the best," I told Danny with sincerity. "I'm going to go back to the library and search for mysteries in the woods on the microfiche."

Danny let go of a belly laugh. "No need, beautiful. The computer will do it for you. It's all been digitized. Save yourself the effort and go drink some coffee."

Not that he could see me; however, my eyes still rolled hard in their sockets. "Thanks. Talk to you soon."

I took my time in the shower, pondered the conversation with Jameson and the one with Danny that happened yesterday morning. I knew I wasn't ready, yet my psyche kept getting in the way of logic. I switched gears to think about Ax's situation, and my anger at Mercy and her unnecessary attacks surfaced.

My temper can trigger my magic at times, depending on its ferocity, and this time was no different. Waves of elemental power shot out from my body, causing a surge of water to explode from my shower head, popping it right off the pipe coming out of the wall.

The blast of water caused me to stagger backward, and the showerhead beaned me right in the forehead. It was a domino effect that sometime a few hundred years in the future, I'd look back on and laugh. My feet flew out from under me, kicking up into the faucet and dumping me on my ass in an almost full bathtub. Cavorting dolphins would have made less of a mess.

It became a mad scramble to get the water turned off, mixed with brief thoughts of being glad the magic hadn't been ice or fire and trying not to slip on the tile floor that was now soaked. Throwing practically every towel I owned on the flooded floor, I dried off with the remaining towel and ran for my phone.

Magic caused a flood in my bathroom. I could use help if you are available. I hated to think of what Jameson would think of that, but I knew I could count on him to help.

On my way, Jameson's response had been almost immediate, and I hurried to get dressed before he got here.

With my bra halfway over my head but not on, I decided to call Ax. "Hey, Ax," I greeted when he answered. "Are there any stories you can remember hearing about the woods behind your house? Or legends that your family liked to talk about?"

I cradled the phone between my ear and my shoulder and tugged the bra down over my exposed chest, and finished getting dressed. Ax was humming while he thought about my question, and I yanked my jeans on and rooted in my dresser for a pair of clean socks.

"Not off the top of my head. Let me dig around in some of the journals that previous family members have left behind and see if there is any mention. I'll call you back," Ax promised and hung up.

It didn't take long for Jameson to arrive, and I wasn't sure where he was when I had texted. He only pushed past me to assess the damage and set about putting things right. Bless the boy. He didn't ask me what the hell I did and didn't request any help. When it came time to clean up, he wordlessly handed me the wet towels, which I promptly threw in the washing machine and ran the load.

"Thanks, baby." I kissed his cheek, and he glanced at my forehead. Seconds later, his healing magic once again traversed my injuries and mended them.

"Not asking," Jameson returned the kiss. "Talk to you later, Mom. Stay whole and go wash the blood off of your face."

I hmphed out a scowl at his retreating form. I think this haphazard thing was a phase I was going through. I walked back into the bathroom to look at my face and winced at the ugly bruise that had formed in the center of my forehead with blood streaks trailing from it. How had I not known that was there?

I finished drying my face when my phone rang, showing Ax's name on the caller ID. "Hey, Ax."

"Greetings, Risa. There are some references in a few of these journals that date back several years to some plant that grows out in the forest that is valuable. It appears that some of my ancestors may have run into some trouble over it. I haven't seen the name of the plant yet, but is it possible that what you are looking for information about is this?" Ax rushed out.

A plant? "It's not out of the realm of possibility. You didn't find anything magical? No fountain of youth, portals, mushroom rings, wormholes, or an undiscovered race?"

Ax chuckled, "No. Do you think this is about the property and not me?"

"I do. Do you mind if I grab the journals to look through them myself?" I wondered.

"I'm heading out. Would you like me to drop the books off at your office?" Ax volunteered. "It wouldn't be a problem."

"Perfect. I'll wait for you there," I told Ax, grabbing my purse and keys.

I wondered about the plant and if this could be the answer to everything the entire drive there. I guess it depended on the plant's uses and how it would tie into Mercy Kane. I couldn't rule it out. Intuition was telling me to dig deeper.

By the time I pulled into my parking lot, my brain was a jumbled-up mess of possibilities and things that would require a lot more thought than what I had put into it during the drive to my office. I was missing vital information that would link the disarray of thoughts befuddling me.

Besides getting to the bottom of what was bugging Jameson, I had no other case that I was working. That meant I could devote the rest of my day to these journals and trying to find the link that connected it all for me.

No sooner than I had made a bargain with my chair not to toss me on my ass, did Ax walk into the door. Yeah, I said that right. He walked into the door instead of through it. Maybe the sasquatch needed to get his eyes checked.

"Oh! Good heavens! What happened to your forehead?" Ax asked, rubbing his head.

"Magic mishap in the shower this morning. The shower won. I'm okay. My son healed me up; the bruise is just the remnants of that," I replied reassuringly.

"Did you know your shirt is on backward and inside out?" Ax wore a puzzled expression.

"Oh, yeah. It's all the rage these days," I lied. Guess the showerhead hit me harder than I thought.

Ax shrugged, accepting my answer. He dropped a stack of six hardbound journals on my desk. "These are the years that the forest is mentioned. I tried to mark the pages, but Petunia didn't like the bookmarks too much. Every time I looked away, she would pull them out."

"Petunia?" I could have sworn Ax said he was single, also that his one-time pet chicken was named Petunia.

"Petunia is the general," Ax supplied with a grin. "She was leading the pack."

Right. I can't believe I forgot that bit of information. I was too dazzled by flying dachshunds to remember their names. "Got it. Thanks for dropping these by; I appreciate it. I'll make sure they get back to you with no harm."

"No worries. Waffles and I have an appointment

today, so we were headed this way. There is an alchemist not far from here that has a perfect potion for fleas," Ax filled in. "Gotta run!"

Another tidbit of information I hadn't known. I'd file that away for later use if I ever needed a potion for fleas.

Chapter Seven

Four hours into reading the journals Ax had brought to me, I knew far more about his family than was socially acceptable for a non-relative. Also, no further information on the plant than I had to begin with before opening the books.

A couple of obscure references that Ax had told me over the phone, and no more. I did see a particular location that Ax's family mentioned a lot, but always in terms of a place where they felt calm and safe.

Maybe that plant had a calming effect on sasquatch, and that's why they wanted to protect it? I stood and stretched, cracking my neck a few times and rolling my shoulders. I'd been hunched over my desk too long, and there were still more journals to go through. I was determined to get through them before I left today.

Another hour crept by like an injured snail pulling a recreational vehicle through a tar pit when I finally found something searchable. The plant wasn't native to earth and only grew in three spots in that forest where a magical influence dwelled deep in the ground. They called it Squatchgold. Indeed, it did have a medicinal calming effect on sasquatch.

I glanced back at the cover of this journal to see what year this was and found it dated back to the mid-eighteen hundreds. My mind started spinning through everything I'd read, and I remembered a couple of references to Squatchgold.

I grabbed my phone like it was trying to run away from me and shot a text to Danny. *Search for references to Squatchgold.*

Okay, but your fee for this will be a date, came the return text from Danny. *A real date, not a "nearest surface will do" session.*

My heart began to beat out an odd rhythm. *Deal;* I had hit send on that text before my brain even registered that I was agreeing. I positively wasn't thinking that I was capable of falling in love again. Nope. I didn't believe that at all. I sighed at my own stupidity when my heart went erratic once more.

Focus, I told myself. I dialed Ax's number and impatiently waited while it rang. When it went to voice mail, I requested a callback and recited my number, then disconnected. I hadn't even realized my foot had been tapping restlessly.

To stop that, I stood up and paced the length of my office while my thoughts spun like an out-of-control Ferris wheel. I wondered if Ax had ever seen this plant and could describe it. What would Mercy Kane want with a plant that calmed sasquatch? That didn't fit.

I marched back to my desk and flipped through the books until I found the places that mentioned the locations and wrote them down. I needed to see with my eyes this Squatchgold. If I could find one, I could have someone analyze it and tell me the effects of this plant. My gut said the plant is the reason for all this, but I didn't know why.

I glanced at the time mand decided that the visit could wait until tomorrow, and I could bring the journals back to Ax at the same time. It was getting close to dusk. I didn't want to be traipsing through the woods in the dark.

Mind made up, I picked up my purse, phone, and keys and headed out. Locking the office up, I saw one of the other tenants doing the same. I got a cordial nod and tentative smile before he made his exit. He was a squirmy accountant man that always set my teeth on edge, and I may have threatened to remove his balls when he asked me out a few years ago.

I was so lost in thought as I walked outside, I didn't notice the luxury car parked across the street with the customized plates displaying *MyMercy* until it was too late. A tornado-like wind picked my ass up and flung me around like a ragdoll that lost all its stuffing before slamming me into the side of my Jeep with enough force to leave a dent.

The act left no question that the harpy was involved in whatever was going on, and my mission just shifted from helping Ax to bringing down Malevolent Mercy Kane in a spectacular fashion. Her little stunt with the wind was going to leave my back bruised all to hell and back.

My neck was screaming with pain, and my shoulders were answering the scream with noise just as loud. My body protested each movement as I righted myself. There were things you didn't do, and an open unprovoked attack on me was one of those things.

I looked around for my purse that had gotten ripped out of my hands. I found it over a hundred yards down the street, thankfully still intact. I dug around for my phone and dialed Danny.

"Hi babe, what's up?" Danny answered.

"Mercy just assaulted me outside my office. Can you file a complaint with the council for me and look at the security footage from that camera you installed? It was a wind attack," I rushed out, the anger starting to take over my voice. I gave him the necessary details and trudged back to my Jeep.

With hands that were shaking violently, I tried to

start the Jeep and kept missing the keyhole. Belting out an aggravated yell that startled Danny silent, I jammed the keys into the ignition with a force that caused one of the keys to slice open my hand.

"Babe, why don't you come here instead of going home," Danny suggested gently. "We can go over the search results together."

"No. I'm not good company right now, and I'd end up taking it out on you, and that isn't fair. Email them to me, please. I'm going to lay on a hot pad and maybe drink myself stupid and do some laundry. I'm going to sue the harpy bitch for dry cleaning fees if this blood doesn't come out. These are my favorite jeans," I growled with menace.

"Whoa, wait. Blood? Risa, babe, what's bleeding?" Danny's concern was mounting fast.

"My hand," I told him. "They're shaking, and I couldn't get the keys in to start the Jeep."

There was a silence, and through the phone, I could hear Danny typing. "It's indirectly her fault, so I'm adding it to the injuries sustained. It wouldn't have happened if she hadn't come after you like that."

I was *not* falling in love; I reminded myself. "Okay. I'm going to hang up now."

"Text me when you get home so I know you are there and, relatively speaking, safe," Danny instructed.

Warmth flooded my chest, and I refused to acknowledge it, like a petulant child. Yet, I agreed to let him know when I was home because it was nice that someone other than my children cared about me enough to worry.

The ride home was best not to have been heard by children's ears. My temper was flaring brighter than the sun in the midday heat in the middle of the desert. This case gave me a headache in more than one way, and it was all the harpy bitches fault.

My empathy for Ax went through the roof. I swore I'd kick Malevolent Mercy's ass all over the town if she hurt Waffles or any of the dachshund army; those poor animals were innocent. Though the idea of buying them a lifetime supply of dog bones had merit if they shit on her head.

I'd pictured Mercy getting shit on in so many scenarios that by the time I got home, I was laughing at it and begging karma to work her magic. I was also going to research what gave dachshunds diarrhea and consider feeding it to them before having Ax play his music, so they took to the skies. Was I awful? Possibly. Did I care? Not in the slightest.

I sent a quick text to Danny letting him know I was home and was digging out my hot pad. I warily eyed the shower and sighed at the thought of the steam and heat soaking in, but the memory of the showerhead pelting me was fresh enough to keep me out.

The couch it was. I plugged in the hot pad, got it situated, and before laying on it, I went to get some first aid supplies to clean up my hand while I lay there. Ready to be soothed, I plopped on the sofa and let the soothing heat soak into me. That was all she wrote.

Chapter Eight

I woke with a jolt sometime before the sun rose. At first, I thought someone was in the house with me, and I fell utterly still to feel the air currents and listen for the faintest of sounds. When I felt reassured that I was alone, I took stock of what could have woken me up that way.

Landing on dreams, I paused and tried to recollect the ambiguous visions that had been playing out in my mind while my body tried to heal itself. The memories were elusive and playing hide and seek with me, adding to the mounting frustration.

On occasion, my dreams were warnings or foretellings. I wasn't clairvoyant. I attributed that little gift to the lucky leprechaun blood that kept my ass out of the fire more often than not. It wasn't looking like this was going to be one of those days.

Grumbling, I got up to use the bathroom and check the time. Four in the morning. Gross. I couldn't believe I'd fallen asleep on the couch of all places and slept the entire evening away. I guess that explained the gnawing pain in my belly.

I glanced at my phone and saw several text messages from Danny, Jameson, Ax, and Gage. The only one of those that would possibly be awake at this hour was Gage, and that was if he had a morning shift or was baking.

I wasn't going to risk waking any of them up by calling or returning a text.

I made myself a pot of coffee and settled in at my computer to go through the research that Danny had emailed me. That would occupy me until a decent hour to reach out to Ax to arrange a trip out to the woods.

A familiar tingle raced along the surface of my skin, and without forewarning, my desk chair shot backward as if shoved by a giant. I ricocheted off the chair in the living room, which jarred the chair under my ass enough for it to dump me unceremoniously on my hardwood floor.

"What the actual fuck is going on with my life?" I shouted to the empty room. "Not cool, magic!"

I pushed up to my feet, rubbing my hands over my derrière and groaning at the ache. I retrieved my desk chair and flung it back towards my desk with some anger behind it. I was beginning to feel like a punching bag, and it wasn't all that great of an experience.

"Is this some type of fucked up magical menopause or something?" I mumbled while contemplating putting wheel chocks behind my chair to keep it in place.

When I touched the backrest of the chair to sit down, a violent shock sparked and had me fumbling around while shaking the life out of my hand and cursing until I ran out of air. Damn, was I going to have to find a rubber outfit to wear now?

Muttering a final expletive, I tentatively sat down and opened my emails. I dove into reading everything Danny sent me and lost track of time. Over half of what I read was irrelevant until I stumbled on a hiking blog about those woods.

The hikers made references to a teal-colored flower that had a gold powder that fell from its petals if shook. They asked several questions about if anyone heard of it and if it were poisonous, a drug, or in any way harmful since it had gotten on their skin.

Unsurprisingly, no one knew what it was, at least on this hiking blog, but it did come across that these two hikers were heavily into recreational substances, and a lot of comments dismissed them as hiking while high. Unfortunately, no pictures accompanied the post, though the description of the area matched the geographical location mentioned in the journals. I printed that page out and kept reading.

A couple of other blogs from nature lovers mentioned that forest, but no plant. Numerous creepy things had happened to them, which I was sure was caused by protective wards that Ax's family had placed around some of the areas to keep people out. Non-magical humans who wandered into those would probably feel watched, have that creepy-crawly feeling come over their skin, and felt compelled to leave the area.

I found myself snickering at one mention of a hiker believing they saw Bigfoot. No doubt one of Ax's family watching over their land. I swear, the non-magical government should hire sasquatches to do their spying. Out in their natural and mountainous habitat, no one would ever see them unless they were unnaturally lucky.

I jumped when my phone chimed its low battery warning and plugged it in while I perused the rest of the information from Danny. Vague references to the forest being a weird place by the non-magical people. More directed statements about the same area being a well-protected tract of land by magical people. A key message from an alchemist searching for the plant to learn what alchemy components are useful as the little bit he had encountered seemed to affect magic.

I sat back in my chair and looked up at my ceiling, my brain spinning a web faster than a cracked-out spider could. The two most helpful elements of these search results had been the plant's description and that it affected magic.

Doing simple arithmetic told me that the magical part held Mercy's intent to obtain the land and the plant. Now I needed to figure out what the plant could do besides calm a sasquatch. If it gave power to the magic that already existed, that would be a massive boon to Mercy Kane, who was mediocre at best.

Malevolent Mercy was only in her position because the clamor of harpies voted her in before Mercy ran them all off after they began to see her true colors and tried to oust her from the council. She's retaining the seat she holds because Mercy bends the ears of whoever possible that she has the majority vote of a race that is almost non-existent in this area, and they deserve a voice.

I checked the time and saw it was after eight; I sent a text to Ax asking if he was awake and available for a walk in the woods, or at least a guiding hand to show me which direction to go. I then responded to Danny, letting him know my plans and that I was okay. I answered Jameson's query about my health status and then confirmed a dinner date with Gage later in the week.

I performed a quick internet search for alchemists in the area, wrote their names in my notebook, and then shut my computer down. I wandered into the kitchen in search of sustenance other than coffee and stuffed my face with a sliced-up apple and made some toast. Not gourmet cooking, but it would give me some energy.

After slathering some peanut butter on my toast, I grabbed my purse and headed out to the Jeep. If I hadn't heard from Ax by the time I reached the turn for my office, I'd go there instead and pace the room until he responded.

The information I had uncovered felt to me like I was on the track of solving this. The plant *was* the key, and how it affected magic in some way. It fit; I only needed to prove it and Mercy's involvement. I wasn't sure how to do that yet, but it would come to me.

Three seconds before the turn to either go to my office or Ax's, he called. "Greetings, fellow early riser. I am indeed awake," Ax jovially spoke as I answered with a gruff hello.

"I'm on my way there," I told him, turning my Jeep at the last second and making my tires screech. "I'll fill you in when I arrive." I hung up before he could respond, which, admittedly, was rude of me. The rate at which I was processing information was too fast for me to drive, hold a decent conversation and continue to think. Sad, I know; at least I'm aware of my shortcomings.

I made it there in record time and heard the chorus of excited barking as I exited the Jeep. My mind split on asking them to join us if Ax accompanied me out to the forest. I couldn't shake that feeling like I was walking on an edge and about to slip on some black ice.

The door opened, and I was looking at Waffles, who I could swear was smirking at me. I wasn't entirely sure that miniature donkeys could smirk, but anything went at this point. The sasquatch had flying dachshunds.

Behind Waffles, I could hear Ax telling them to move so I could come in, then his face appeared above the donkey, and the clip-clop of hooves on his beautiful wood floors sounded. The screen door opened with his giant arm span, and I grabbed it and waited while countless little doggy nails clicked in their happy dance to have a visitor again.

"Sorry," Ax apologized as I entered. "We don't get a lot of company, and I think they remember you."

I smiled in return. "All is well, Ax. Like I said in my message, I need to go out into the woods to the place mentioned in these journals." I handed the stack of them back to Ax, happy I remembered to bring them with me.

"It's a beautiful morning to go for a walk if you'd like company. I have an extra helmet you can wear, and we can let the army do its training exercises. Waffles needs to get out and work off some of his laziness, too," Ax spoke gently but firmly directed towards the still smirking donkey.

"Great. Let's go," I replied adamantly.

Chapter Nine

I wasn't a fan of helmets. My hair was going to look ridiculous for the rest of the day. The conglomerating sweat on the top of my head made me want to scratch my scalp with a wire brush. For added protection, I put on a garbage bag over my clothes; I wasn't conspicuous. Looking at a piece of paper that shows a plot of land is different from hiking through the area and precisely seeing how large it was.

Don't get me wrong, it was beautiful, and I could see why the hikers posting about it had been so exuberant about the area. I also felt the wards and set magic prickling my skin like little electrical volts zapping me to remind me not to step foot out of bounds.

Eerie was an excellent word for it, I decided. I kept sensing that someone was watching me, too. It was that danger warning that set off the red flags in my mind and kept my magic uncomfortably close to the surface of my skin, reminding me of the edge I was skirting.

We passed through a thicket of trees that appeared to have arthritis in all their limbs. The leaves were dancing in synchronicity with each other with no wind. Petunia let out a small growl that had her soldiers trailing after her go razorback with their hair. The wiry tails all sprang to attention, becoming rigid and pointing straight up.

I wasn't about to ignore that sign and loosened my body to ready myself for an attack. I'd explained what I'd figured out to Ax, described the plant that the hikers had found, and he was looking around, the same as I was.

"Here, Risa. We are approaching the clearing the Doxy Army uses, and just beyond that is the space discussed in the journals. It is a very serene area for my kind. More powerful wards protect that land than what we have walked through already, and you'll need me to enter. I don't want you to get hurt," Ax advised me with a solemn tone.

"Got it," I answered as my eyes swiveled in their sockets, watching for signs of danger.

Ax gasped and paused his steps. "Risa, the ends of your hair changed color."

"Is magical menopause a thing?" I blurted out. "Too many odd things are happening with me lately. What color is it?"

"Kind of orangish," Ax grew quiet, and his expression was concerned. "Are you feeling okay?"

"Fine," I snapped, irritated.

Waffles brayed and reared up on his hind legs. His eyes bugged out, and *Flight of the Valkyries* started blaring. I ducked to avoid getting hit with doggy paws and quickly made sure that my helmet covered most of my head. I frantically tried to tuck up the exposed hair because I didn't want to have to wash a dog shit bomb out of it.

Ax had a hand on Waffles to soothe him while he issued visual and verbal commands to the flying pups. I watched, amazed, as they moved into formations and took up a watch over the woods while moving in odd patterns.

"Can anyone enter these woods?" I asked, moving under cover of one of the arthritic trees for added poop protection.

"Yes and no." Ax waved his hand around again, and

the flight of the doxy army became erratic. "If you have magic, then it's relatively easy to get around those wards on the property line. It will cause mild discomfort, but they could use a spell to help alleviate that if they intended to enter. If their magic is weak, it will repel them. But a non-magical will feel creeped out, as they say. The wards won't hurt them unless they intend to harm. If that's the case, magical or non-magical, the wards will cause pain."

"Is magic able to travel through those wards?" I asked, looking to the sky. "An attack from above isn't unheard of, and your cute little army is up there flying around and putting themselves in the line of fire."

"They have magical protections, but you are correct," Ax looked worried. "They want to be useful, and it was their decision to make. I am but a humble servant to them, and their devotion to me is unwavering and firm."

"Lead the way," I gestured to the land with the mysterious plant.

Crossing the field had me tucking my arms inside the garbage bag and moving as swiftly as possible. I shivered at the feel of magic that pressed in on me from all sides. The urge to duck and roll struck me hard, and I dropped, using all my available strength to yank Ax down with me.

A blast of wind sailed through the place we'd been standing, and through my peripheral vision, I saw all the dogs get scattered out of whatever formation they'd been using. Like clockwork, brown bombs began falling from the sky and landing with a messy splat.

I rolled farther away from the strike zone. A quick glance at Ax confirmed he was alright. "Roll this way. We need to get into that space and find that plant," I hissed.

Ax army crawled to me, creating a humorous spectacle that almost had me giggling because of his size. However, I got to see some of the sasquatch abilities manifest in the way he blended with his surroundings as a chameleon does.

"Take my hand," Ax commanded me and held his hand out.

I didn't question him and silently grasped his hand. I got hauled to my feet the moment Ax stood up simply because of the size difference. He took two giant strides and brought us through the magical barrier that had me wanting to flee in terror.

A second later, silence settled on my senses, and I felt compelled to be as still as the air. A calm feeling came over me that I had to fight against because there was someone out there flinging magic on the dachshund army and wanting to attack us.

"Snap out of it," Ax shook me before releasing my hand. "That's the magic working on you."

I shot a nasty glare at the sasquatch and began my search for a teal flowered plant. I encountered several alien-looking plants, and I was sure it was an alchemist's dreamscape in here. Yet, I wasn't finding the plant we sought.

A couple of fireballs slammed into the clearing, breaking my concentration and making me worry about Petunia and her followers. A secondary thought of Waffles hit me.

"Where's the donkey?" I yelled at Ax, looking around with a sense of urgency.

"I sent him home," came the utterly composed answer as he continued his search. "He will be safe. Thank you for asking."

I shook my head at his demeanor and tried to control the magic that was trying to burst free from me. I returned to moving logs, rocks, and long grass, searching for the elusive flower that dropped gold dust with magical properties.

"Will magic penetrate the wards around us?" I

hesitated before asking.

"Only powerful magic," Ax replied with a tranquil tone. This plot of land indeed was an insular, serene place for him and his kind. He was utterly Zen. It was unnerving me since we were in a precarious situation, and his little friends were flying and trying to defend us against a harpy bent on harm.

Somewhat mollified, I searched with more confidence that I wasn't going to get jumped from behind. I halfway expected to turn around and see Ax taking a nap with his head resting against a log. I was happy to see that wasn't the case when I came around the tree's backside that I had been looking around the base of for the Squatchgold.

"I think I've found it," Ax's softly spoken words hung in the motionless air. "I want nothing more than to lay down here and watch the sky move."

"Not the time for that," I admonished him and moved to inspect the plant. "Can we pick it?"

"I don't see why not," Ax agreed. "There are several more hiding under the thorny bush right there." His tone was dreamy, and it was a bit alarming. "Let's make sure that we dig up the root as well. If there are magical properties to this beauty, there might be something special in the roots that can be utilized for medicinal purposes."

I was a surprisingly lucid thought, given the expression on his face and the tone of voice. "Agreed. I'll do it. I don't want you falling asleep or into a trance."

Ax produced a bag I hadn't even noticed he was carrying and retrieved a plastic bag. "Place it in here, and I'll carry it out with me. I think the wards might prevent you from doing so."

Chapter Ten

I had carefully dug a hole with a branch and flat rock deep enough to get the roots of the Squatchgold out intact and placed it into the open bag. Ax looked about ready to drift off into a wonderland in his mind, so I sealed the bag quickly.

In moving the flower into the bag, the gold dust had fallen onto my hands, and it caused a surge of magic to jolt through my body and propel me backward into a tree. A curious reaction, and I had no idea what it meant.

The sudden movement had Ax widening his eyes, and he quickly dropped the flower into his bag and put it back on his shoulder. Amazing. I couldn't even see it. I righted myself as Ax slowly stood at a leisurely pace.

"Are you going to be okay to get out of here? I don't think dawdling will do us any good?" I voiced my growing concern.

"I'll be right as rain once we pass through to the clearing. It's the effect of this place on me. I am worried about what the dust did to you, are you injured?" Ax asked melodiously.

"No, I'm not hurt. It reacts with magic, for sure," I replied, studying the skies where the doxy army still flew. They didn't look any worse for the wear. The clearing, however, wasn't so clear; we'd be dodging land mines.

"Oh, dear," Ax moaned, looking perplexed for the first time since we entered this little sasquatch oasis. "Waffles didn't listen. Will he be in danger?"

I didn't want to answer him, nor did I want to lie. "The possibility exists," I finally spoke, hedging my answer as much as I could. "Let's hurry back and get them all out of harm's way."

Ax grabbed my arm with a death grip that I swore was going to snap my bone in half. His hand was more sizeable than my head, and my arm felt like an itty-bitty twig under it. Before I could tell him to loosen up a little, he had yanked me through the ward and was half dragging me behind him with his six-foot strides.

I winced, seeing the doggy bomb remnants smearing all over my shoes as I scrambled to keep up with the sasquatch. About the only good thing that came of the situation was I made a lot smaller of a target next to Ax. Not that it would matter if we got hit with magic.

No sooner than I had that thought we got blasted with hurricane-force winds. I don't know how Ax didn't go surging into the air the way I did, but I was airborne in a hurricane of dachshund shit bombs. Terrified to open my mouth and scream, I tucked my head as far into my chest as I could. Then, as if it were nothing at all, Ax plucked me from the funnel cloud and set me back on the ground with his meaty hand on my head, holding me down.

"Thanks," I dared to mutter, hoping the excrement on my face didn't fall into my open mouth.

"Move," Ax ordered me, applying pressure to my head.

His tone wasn't friendly, and I now had the pleasure of witnessing an outraged sasquatch. Pit me against a bitchy harpy any day. Angry Ax was intimidating and frightening, and somewhat sexy.

That led to thoughts about Danny being dominating

with me, and that had chain reactions that were not appropriate for this run for your life scenario. I scooted out from under Ax's hand and turned to face the clearing.

My feet almost instantly left the ground; I wished my magic would work and I could block it. The same moment I was thinking about a shield, a fresh steaming bomb caught the airwaves and was headed straight for me.

Simultaneously, Ax yanked on my shirt, pulling me back to the ground as I threw my hands up in front of my face. I don't know what happened or how. The shit splattered against some invisible wall in front of me, and the wind died down to almost nothing.

"Petunia," Ax barked. "To me!"

The scattered flying wiener dogs fell into line and immediately returned to Ax, who then sent them deep into the cover of the trees headed back to the house. Grateful the little guys were okay; I didn't see the next attack.

I felt the impact of Waffle's hooves on my back, and I went sprawling face-first into the shit-covered field. The air over my head whooshed with intense heat, and the ground behind me went up in flames. Waffles brayed again, and Ax was screaming at him to move.

"Thanks, Waffles," I called out weakly. "You saved me. Ax, get going."

"I can't, in good conscience, leave you here," Ax declared. "The orange part of your hair is changing colors. Are you okay?"

"Go call for help," I insisted. I didn't have time to worry about color-changing hair. "You hired me for this."

I could see the sasquatch move farther into the tree line through the flames, but he didn't retreat. "I didn't hire you to get hurt. I hired you to find out who was sending me threats."

"It's part of the job!" I yelled and motioned him away. Water magic would come in handy right now. I didn't want the field to burn down and take the forest with it.

I waved my hands again and water sprayed from them like I was holding a fire hose. I was so startled that I turned my hands to look at them and doused myself, causing shit water to flow into my gaping mouth. Sputtering and spitting, trying not to puke, I re-aimed my spouting water hands at the flames until they were smothered and pushed to my feet.

"As you can see," I coughed out more septic water, "I've got this handled."

Right. I had no idea how any of that had happened, and I clenched my fists closed until the water stopped its wild spurting. Ax looked entirely unsure of everything, understandably, but he finally nodded his agreement and ran off into the woods with Waffles trotting behind him.

"Okay, Malevolent Mercy, show your hideous harpy self," I yelled to the sky. "I know it's you."

It took a few moments, but the brown-gray- sludge wings came into view. Mercy Kane was in her proper form. Long talons with wicked sharp claws were prominently displayed, and with the sight, I knew she wanted to tear me into tiny little pieces. Her claw-like fingernails were clicking together as if she were counting seconds until they embedded in my flesh.

Her hair was flat mud-brown and matted, breasts were saggy, deflated water balloons, with her ribs showing beneath. Wrinkled skin and ugly mottled feathers covered the rest of her and her lady bits, thankfully, and her black beady eyes fastened on me.

"You haven't aged well," I fired off, mentally planning out how to save for a plastic surgeon, so I never looked like that. Her breasts alone were going to give me nightmares. "You have chicken legs."

"Give me the flower," Mercy squawked, her nails clicking faster. "I'll own these woods one day. Your repugnant pissant genes will help me do it, too."

I'd examine that statement later because if she were talking about my kids, I'd kill her here and now, screw the consequences. "You'll own none of it. It's private property and not for sale. Cease and desist in your threats against my client, or we will press charges and drag your name through hell. Oh wait, you're a harpy; hell is your happy place—scratch that. I'll just drag you through a shit covered field; how's that? Come on down here," I smiled sweetly.

A wall of wind rocked me off balance, but I didn't fall. I needed to watch my tongue; Ax wasn't here to pull me from the currents of a hurricane again. I also knew she possessed of spells because she didn't have fire magic. Either that or she had someone else with her that I couldn't see.

I guess there was a lot I didn't see because a spear appeared a few feet in front of me, and before I could register what it was, a draft of air carried it right into my side, piercing through my skin. Without a second thought, I ripped it from my body, screamed, and heaved it back at the flying bitch. I wished it was on fire.

I staggered to my knees, trying to control the pain that was wracking my body, and got knocked flat by a blast of wind. An unearthly shriek filled the air, and I opened my eyes to see singed feathers and an ugly harpy dive-bombing me.

How did she get burned? Did this magical menopause only need me to wish for things to make my wonky magic function? If that was the case, why wasn't I rich? I had but a few seconds to react, and I imagined that I had a rope I could swing like a lasso and bind her wings. I used to be pretty good with a lasso back in my youth.

To my utter shock, Mercy's wings folded in on themselves, and she plummeted from the sky;

unfortunately, right on to my prone and bleeding form. Talons impaled my thighs, and I screeched and flailed around, trying to dislodge her.

"Risa!" I heard my name being shouted. Danny? What was he doing here? Was I hallucinating? This fight was no place for a computer nerd.

I shoved against Mercy with all my strength and sent her careening into a pile of dog shit that matched her feathers. It smelled better than she did too. Using my elbows to prop myself up and suck in a painful breath, I took stock of my various injuries.

"Why do you want that flower?" I managed to ask through my teeth.

"How are you doing this?" Mercy bellowed. "You have no magic to speak of, you mutant."

"I'm the mutant?" I scoffed. "For your information, I have plenty of power." I left it unspoken that it was mostly useless to me. Regardless, she was the one bound and on the ground by something I'd done with that unmanageable magic.

"Give it to me, and I won't call you up on charges with the council," Mercy seethed. "When I own his town, you'll be evicted, and I'll never have to deal with you or your kind again."

My kind? Was the harpy high? Whatever. She'd given me enough information to hang her with already. "Keep dreaming."

"Risa? Holy shit, are you okay?" Danny screamed, skidding to a halt next to me and seeing all the blood. He gave a passing glance to Mercy and helped me up. "Ax saw it all. Malevolent Mercy will be imprisoned, run out of town, or executed. Police are on their way."

"Mom!" Jameson's voice came from the forest.

"What are you doing here?" I asked Danny, confused at the sight of him.

"When you texted that you were coming out here to look for the Squatchgold, I got dressed and left. No way should you be out here alone. I contacted Jameson to join me because I had some disturbing dreams about you getting killed," Danny confessed.

My previous night's dream warnings flitted through my mind, and I looked over at the bound harpy. "You were going to kill me?"

"I still will," Mercy promised.

Danny shifted, forcing my body to move, and I almost crumpled at the pain ripping through my wounds. A sheepish look came over his face as a loud rustling sounded from behind where we were standing. "No, you won't," Danny answered.

"Mercy Kane," Penelope Pine's strong dwarven voice called out. "You are hereby unanimously voted off of the council and will be brought up on charges of attempted murder, theft, assault, and espionage."

"You don't have the power," Mercy cried out with fury at the turn of events.

"Babe, Jameson can't heal you until the police take stock of the injuries, pictures and get Ax's statement and yours. Do you think you can stand on your own for a moment?" Danny's gentle voice spoke directly into my ear.

"I've got her," Jameson declared with a hard stare at Mercy Kane.

Danny let go of me and removed some cuffs from his pocket, and further bound the harpy. "Have you always had those?" I asked, more than a little turned on now, despite the pain.

"Mom," Jameson groaned. "Time and place."

Chapter Eleven

It took a week for everything to settle enough for me to have a few hours of quiet in my office. It hit me now that some of my children were involved in whatever Mercy had been trying to do, which was apparently taking over the town.

Jameson had taken possession of the plant after the police had taken Mercy away. He promised Ax that he would run some tests on it and determine what the plant was capable of with the right spells. I haven't seen my youngest son since then.

Jameson's involvement with spells was the result of Gavin dragging him into something. The way the pieces were shaping up, it looked like Mercy, or someone working with her, hired Gavin to procure or create a spell that would allow her to take over the town.

I knew it had to be more complicated than that, and somehow Braxton became involved, and that was something I'd have to figure out later down the line. No one even knew what that plant could do yet, besides turning a sasquatch into a marshmallow.

A knock sounded at my office door, and I called out, "Come in."

Ax poked his head in with a shy smile. His hair was all combed down, and he wore what looked like new clothes. "Greetings, are you busy?"

"Not at all, Ax. I still don't have a chair large enough for you," I said with an apologetic tone.

"I don't expect you to. I wanted to make sure you were okay and to pay you," Ax ducked and came in. "Waffles sends his regards."

I smiled at that. "I'm super glad that none of the animals became seriously hurt by all the hullabaloo."

"Only minor bruises. Petunia would like to say something," Ax grinned and looked back at the door. The general of the doxy army pranced into my office and nudged the door closed. "She says thank you for getting beat up for me, Ax, and protecting her master. She wishes to call you an honorary member of her squad."

"I wasn't," I started, then paused. "I didn't," I stopped speaking again. "I—uh, okay. I got my ass handed to me. You're welcome, Petunia, and I'd be honored." I felt like an idiot talking to the dachshund. Her little tail was wagging furiously, and her tongue was hanging out of her mouth. It was adorable.

"I hope that you can consider us friends," Ax went on. "I don't have many of those, and I feel that you went the extra mile for us. Not only that, but the whole situation got me a date. How do I look?" Ax twirled in a circle for me.

"Fantastic," I couldn't help but grin. "Also, of course, I consider you a friend. Petunia, and Waffles, and all the rest included. Who is the date with?"

"Ms. Pine," Ax's smile dimmed a bit. "She asked me out. Is that strange?"

I stifled a laugh. Penelope Pine was one of those women who saw what she wanted and went after it with a passion that I admired. "No, Ax. You should be flattered." The height difference would be interesting.

"Phew!" Ax swiped his hand against his forehead. "I was so surprised I thought I was going to swallow my tongue. Glad I didn't. I might fancy a kiss. Anywho, here is your payment, and thank you for taking such good care of us." Ax slid a sealed envelope across the desk to me.

"Thanks, Ax. I wish all clients were this prompt in payment. Good luck with your date. You might get a call from me asking for details," I waggled my eyebrows at him.

Ax blushed bright red and got flustered. "I don't know what to say."

I let out a belly laugh at his expression, "You don't have to say anything, Ax. I was joking." Kind of; my dirty mind was running wild with trying to picture a sasquatch and a dwarf. "Go on, don't be late and make Penelope seek you out."

"Oh, one last thing before I go. I heard from an arcane master. I reached out to him to ask about magical menopause," Ax whispered the menopause word. "He said there is no such thing. He *did* tell me of cases where people who have various races in their genealogy have what is considered a coming of age or awakening. He said that might be what is happening with you."

I snorted. "Coming of age? I'm almost four hundred years old," I blurted out.

Ax gave me a gentle smile. "For some, that is a teenager, Risa. Don't discount it. I see your hair is back to blond now, too. Maybe it's something to consider given everything you experienced."

With a bow, Ax and Petunia left my office. I sat there with an open jaw, and I ran through all the mishaps that have been taking place—magical puberty, not menopause. I'm not sure which is worse.

Book 3
You're the Tits

Chapter One

I walked into the club Gage sent me the address for and looked around for my middle son. As a supernatural or paranormal private investigator, this type of place wasn't on my list of usual haunts. I felt out of my element and drastically underdressed.

My black leather jacket was vintage. Of course, I'd bought it new back in the 1950s, but these young people wouldn't know that. Most of them were non-magical. I sported fashionably ripped blue jeans, but I hadn't bought them that way; they became that way after some rough cases. I did wear a nice shirt, at least. It was silky and red and hugged my feminine curves the right way. Okay, fine, my boobs.

A few of the well-dressed younger men at the bar gave me some appreciative glances that not too long ago would have had me sidling up and asking for a ride. Now that Danny, who I used to refer to as my booty call, had me on a precarious edge of a relationship, I kept my libido tamped down. It helped that I had just come from his place. I snickered like a teenager at my pun. Danny would have laughed at the I had just come statement.

I finally spotted Gage at a table near the stage area the club had set up. He had invited me here to listen to his new beau play piano and meet him. I remembered his last love interest well, a succubus who had more curves than should be allowed. She left Gage satisfied, but her attitude was awful, and she whined about everything. Gage is lucky I didn't strangle her.

I reviewed my last week as I wound my way through the crowd, shifting chairs and not well-placed tables. I had finished my previous case with a sasquatch and town council member less than a week ago. My business, I S.P.I., had been placed into the spotlight because of it. My three sons from three different baby daddies had been fussing over me since.

I was still trying to unravel whatever Gavin had tangled Jameson up in; my oldest son, Gavin, and youngest, Jameson, were somehow involved with a potion that Mercy Kane contracted them to procure. Gage had been pushing for me to meet the new love of his life. A satyr, at that. Gage was part Selkie; it was an adventurous mix, much like the pairing with the succubus had been. Oh well, here I was, in a club in Branstone, the non-magical city that hid the magical town of Glimmering Rock.

Out of the corner of my eye, I spotted Wiley, the new resident in Glimmering Rock. Something was off with that man, and I hoped he hadn't seen me. I quickened my step towards my son. A few weeks back, after a cow trafficking case that I had worked on, Wiley had tried to hire me, and I was beyond rude to him in response.

Gage stood, "Mom!"

I motioned for him to sit down and hush up. Finally reaching his table, I kissed his cheek. "Hi, honey."

"Who are you hiding from?" Gage slyly asked me. "Another bad date?"

"Wiley," I spoke quietly in his ear. "I don't like him."

"Move to sit on this side of me, then. My body will block you, and you'll be able to see if someone is approaching us," Gage instructed me and shifted his body without further question. "Did you color your hair?"

Crap. "No, when I left home, it was blonde, as it always is," I replied with a scowl.

"Did someone paint your hair on the way here? The ends are a magenta color," Gage fingered my hair. "It's pretty."

Magical puberty at its finest. "It will go away. Most likely, it's a reaction to Wiley."

Ax, my new sasquatch friend, had asked his friend what he knew about magic suddenly manifesting. Ax asked about magical menopause, which I had assumed is what was happening because I couldn't come up with any other reason for the strange things that were happening.

His academic friend told him there was no such thing as magical menopause but that it wasn't unheard of for people with various magical races in their bloodline to develop at a slower rate than others. Translated, that meant magical puberty.

Saying my ancestors were of mixed races was an understatement. Yet, I couldn't deny that something was happening with my already muddled and wonky magic. The latest being when I was in precarious situations, where my magic used to show up but be unmanageable and unpredictable, it suddenly changed to me wishing for something, and it happened.

Since that last case, I'd been doing my best not to wish for things, especially in a predominantly human non-magical club. The results would be disastrous. My magic tended to go pear-shaped rather quickly.

Now that I changed seats, I could watch the rest of the crowd, and Gage was right; his larger body blocked mine. "Swanky club, son," I spoke while people-watching.

"Zhor plays here three times a week. The crowd is huge because he's popular. Wait until you hear him sing, Mom," Gage breathed out dreamily.

"Zhor, like Thor, but with a 'Z'?" I asked Gage, unsure if I had heard him right.

"Are you making fun, Mom?" Gage sounded disappointed.

"No, honey. I was making sure I heard you correctly. There's a lot of noise in here, and I don't want to call him by the wrong name," I quickly replied, covering my childish amusement at the satyr's name. "Don't be a Zhor loser."

Gage rolled his eyes but chuckled at my stupid pun. "You'll never change."

"Nope. Better to love me as I am than expect me to be grown-up," I grinned.

Gage leaned over and rested his head on my shoulder. He was always the tender one of the three. "Stop, Mom. You are grown-up. You just have a warped sense of humor. You've raised three drastically different children and run your own business with danger lurking around every corner. If you want to make bad jokes to relieve the strain of your aging life, then don't let anyone stop you."

I threw my head back and laughed. "There you go. That took longer to surface than it usually does."

"It's not every son that can say he has a pubescent mother," Gage went on.

I knew I would come to regret spilling that to him. "Zip it." I patted his head, "Tell me about this Zhor guy so I can judge him before I meet him."

Gage shook his head with a grin. "You're incorrigible. I met him in the restaurant here in town; you knew that part. We hit it off right from the start, but it took a couple of weeks before we went out. He was in a relationship with someone else at the time. She was with him the night we met, and boy did they look unhappy. Anyway, he took me out for a romantic picnic, pulled out a guitar, and sang to me. It was the tits."

"It was the tits?" I echoed stupidly. "What the hell does that mean?"

"For a female in puberty, you sure aren't up with the jargon. It means it was beyond great," Gage explained.

"Cut the puberty shit, or I'm going to embarrass the life out of you," I warned my son.

Gage caught the tone and snapped back into his story. "Zhor is quite musically talented. He has a dreamy voice, can play the piano, and he classically trained. He taught himself the guitar, and he plays the flute, too. He writes his own music, and I've been helping him record some of it."

"Got it, he's a one-man band," I quipped. "Do you have anything other than sex in common with him?"

"No complaints in that department," Gage grinned at my wince. "You brought it up. Yes, in answer to your question, we have things in common."

Right then, the lights dimmed, and Gage's head whipped towards the stage. "I guess this means he's about to go on," I mumbled. Gage's attention was held rapt.

It dawned on me that the rest of the club was the same way. It had fallen quiet, and all eyes pointed to the microphone sitting over the piano bench. Curious. I didn't sense any magic in the air; maybe Zhor was just that good.

Chapter Two

I would agree that Zhor had a natural talent for music. When the lights brightened, the club burst into a flurry of activity with waitresses flitting around and serving drinks. I narrowed my eyes and studied the crowd, coming to the conclusion that the owner of this place must be magical and is using Zhor to boost alcohol sales.

The satyr had a sensual voice that drew you in, and Zhor threw a lot of emotion into his performances. It was arousing and had me covertly sexting Danny from under the table. Put that element into a setting where people usually looked to hook-up, making for some big liquid courage sales. Smart.

Motion caught my eye, and I spied a buxom brunette with red tones in her hair headed towards us. I automatically assumed she was coming to hit on Gage and dismissed her outright. Gage was handsome and had an alluring personality; there was no reason to think anything other than my assumption. So when she looked directly at me and addressed me, I was startled.

"Risa Sanders?" she spoke my name as if it were a song and with a slight Mediterranean accent.

I blinked in surprise and found myself short of a voice for a few seconds. Gage nudged me, his eyes wide and nervous looking. "Uh, yeah. Do I know you?" I finally replied, wondering what was wrong with my son.

"No. I'm sorry to approach you here, and I have to admit I followed you and was shocked to find you coming to this place." She nodded politely to Gage. "No hard feelings, I swear," the mystery woman spoke to him.

"What the hell are you doing here?" barked a new voice that had me swiveling in my seat.

Zhor stood a few feet away with an angry, stormy expression on his devilishly good-looking face. I guessed they knew each other. It took me a few seconds of frantic thinking to put together the situation. This woman must be who Zhor was dating when he met Gage. Awkward, and why was she following me?

"She's looking for me," I spoke up before things got heated and my magic reacted. I also didn't want to draw Wiley's attention in this direction. I glanced back at the woman, "I'll be with you in a moment." I held my hand out to Zhor, "Great performance. I'm Risa, Gage's mom. It's nice to meet you."

The handshake I got was limp and unimpressive for a creature that's known for its erections. The hardened expression didn't leave Zhor's eyes, though he gentled his tone when he spoke to me. He wasn't chalking up a lot of points.

"Zhor, the pleasure is mine, Risa." Zhor released my hand and turned his attention back to the woman who made her untimely appearance. "Don't stir things up that should be left alone."

I raised my eyebrows at that. "Enough. The lady was looking for me. Gage, I'll talk with you later. Excuse me," I stood up.

"Mom," Gage rose and hugged me. "He's not normally like that," Gage whispered in my ear.

"I'll take your word on that. I'm going to see what the lady needs," I released him. "Have a good night, honey."

I gestured at the beauty to leave, and I followed. It was easy to see why the female had captured Zhor's attention, and what was with the voice thing? We wove our way out of the club and stood on the sidewalk under a streetlight.

"Did you want to talk here?" I asked her.

"I'd prefer more privacy," the woman responded quietly, her voice still melodious.

"Your car? My car? My office?" I suggested. I figured if she'd followed me, she had to have driven. "By the way, what is your name?"

"Wylene. Could we go to your office? I realize it's after hours, but I would like to hire you, and to come to see you during the day is harder since I'm at work," Wylene requested.

I shrugged, "Sure. I'll meet you there." It would be another payday, and I couldn't turn those down. Unless it had something to do with Zhor, that would strain my relationship with Gage, and I didn't want to do that.

Wylene nodded her agreement and hurried off around the back of the building. I hadn't known there was a parking lot back there, or I would have utilized that instead of parking at a pay lot three blocks down.

I texted Danny to let him know that I wasn't returning to his place because something came up with a potential new client. That thought gave me a moment of pause. I'd come straight to the club from Danny's, which meant she was following me from Danny's house.

An irrational stab of jealousy tore through me that the beautiful woman somehow knew Danny. Damn it! That was precisely why I didn't want a relationship. Things had a way of getting messy without reason. My brain immediately jumped to the conclusion that she knew Danny instead of the more logical answer that she had followed me from my office to Danny's.

I let out a growl of frustration with myself and climbed into my Jeep. I didn't care; I wasn't in a relationship, I reminded myself. The lie didn't roll easily, and I did my best to ignore it. I knew I'd have to face it eventually but now wasn't that time. Work beckoned me.

I drove faster than I typically did due to my irrational pubescent train of thought. Phew, this phase needed to be over soon. I was annoying myself. Honestly, I wasn't confident that's what was going on, but no one could deny that something was changing. It might be time to check-in with my parents and see if they had ever experienced anything like this before.

It didn't take me long to arrive at my office, and to my complete surprise, Wylene was already there, sitting on the steps waiting for me. Brave woman to be sitting out here in this area alone. I quickly exited my Jeep and made my way toward the mysterious woman.

"Hope you haven't been waiting long," I called out while flipping through my keys, looking for the one to open the building.

"Nothing to worry about," Wylene stood as I approached.

She was taller than I was, and it could have been the fashionable knee-high boots she was wearing, but I doubted it. Not with those long legs. She appeared to be feminine in all the ways I wasn't, and I began to feel inadequate as a female. I wasn't usually a jealous person, so I didn't understand these reactions I was having.

Jamming the key into the lock, I shoved the door open a bit more forcefully than I should have and moved to hold it open for Wylene to enter. I closed and locked the door behind her to keep any unsavory sorts from dwelling in the building overnight and turning my office building into a criminal hangout.

As Wylene seemed to float past me, I realized something was alluring about the female that had me paying attention to curves, smells, sounds, and the way she moved. When I was more cavalier with my habits in my younger days, I'd have probably hit on her. I'd only done that once, and it had been interesting.

Shaking my head, I followed her swinging hips to my office, unlocked that door, and let her waltz on inside. It had to be the effect from Zhor's singing that has my libido in an uproar. It's not like I hadn't gotten laid in the past few hours.

For the sake of safety, I locked my office door behind me and saw Wylene raising her eyebrows at me. "I'm not kidnapping you," I blurted out. "It's a safety measure since this is a seedy part of town."

Wylene nodded, looking tired all of a sudden. "I understand."

"Take a seat," I gestured vaguely at the orange plastic chairs and moved around my desk to close the blinds. I didn't want to advertise that someone was here, even though my Jeep was a dead giveaway. "Tell me what made you seek me out?"

"I need help," Wylene began, not wasting any time. "Someone keeps possessing me, and it's having a domino effect on the rest of my life."

With that, I plopped down into my faulty office chair, temporarily forgetting its penchant for tossing me on my ass. There was no exception this time, and it shot out from under me, crashing into the wall behind me this time, ricocheting off it and back into my body with a painful whack.

"Oh, wow. Are you okay?" Wylene stood and peered over the top of my desk down at me.

"Yeah," I muttered. "Nothing new. That chair has an attitude, and I think it's telling me to go on a diet."

"I doubt it. You are beautiful," Wylene scoffed. "And your ass is perfect."

Using the desk as a counterweight, I heaved myself to standing, kicked my chair into place, and slowly lowered while trying not to blush and turn my head to look at my ass. The validation was nice.

"Well, thanks," I drawled out. "Let's get back to what's going on with you and how I can help."

"I'm eidetic," Wylene continued after nodding her acceptance of my gratitude. "I'm also a medium, with a bit of precog."

"What race are you?" I interrupted, fighting against the dazzle effect she brought on.

"Siren," Wylene said on a sigh. "I promise I'm not using my voice. It shouldn't work on a female anyway."

"I'm not falling in love with you," I reassured her and understood why I was feeling these things. "However, your voice still has a mesmerizing quality to it." I shook my head again. "Also, it could be the singing that Zhor was doing that still has me out of sorts. You believe something is possessing you, and with the eidetic memory and medium skills, that makes for handy skills at remembering everything and communicating."

Wylene nodded, "It does. Yet, there are times it feels like I am this man or that I am the woman he's stalking. It doesn't make sense, and it's getting hard to keep things straight. I am almost certain that the memories getting embedded in my mind are his, but sometimes, I swear I can hear her voice. The strange thing is," Wylene looked down, and I saw the red tint to her cheeks. "Sometimes his thoughts are so sexual that I find myself taking care of the issue when I wake up. Shouldn't I be aware that I am doing that?" Wylene asked in a whisper.

I snapped my jaw closed. "You wake up alone or with someone?" I asked to clarify.

"Alone. I'm not ashamed of masturbation, but I do think I should remember starting it," Wylene answered with a tinge of anger. "What if something happens with this guy during the day? What if I turn on the siren's voice while I'm at work? They might frown on me devouring my male co-workers."

I coughed and cleared my throat. "Has that ever happened? The siren's voice coming out when you don't intend to use it, I mean. Not the devouring of males."

"Not since I moved here," Wylene replied adamantly. "I don't want it to, either. That's why this is so concerning to me. I'm old enough that I've gotten used to talking with spirits, but I moved here before this town existed to escape the ways of devouring besotted men simply because I could. I knew there had to be more to life than that. I know it's part of who I am, and I can't lie and say there isn't something satisfying in it, and not to mention the sex, that's fabulous." Wylene fanned her hand in front of her face.

I had to smile at that because I could only imagine, and if I kept thinking about it, I would be uncomfortable and distracted. "Those are conversations that we should have over drinks once this gets solved for you. What are you hoping I'll be able to do?"

"Banish this guy or something. It feels like he's attached to me, or, and I have only entertained this thought a little, the woman might be attached to me, and that's why he is doing what he's doing," Wylene told me in a rush. "I knew her," came the harsh whisper.

"The woman who's getting stalked?" I asked, confused.

"Yeah. Not personally. I knew who she was. Her murder happened right after I moved here," Wylene closed her eyes. "It could be either of them or both of them, but I need it to stop. The sexual urges drive me nuts, and this town doesn't need me to be the top story on the news for ripping men apart and feasting on them. Or worse, as a person that didn't stop a murder from happening."

I pulled open my drawer and slid out a contract. Pushing it across the desk, I told Wylene, "Look over the contract and the fees. If any of it is questionable, let's talk it out before you sign."

Chapter Three

Wylene was reading the contract word for word while I fretted about the possibility of any of my sons becoming a sex doll and meal for this woman. I'd do the work for free to keep that from happening. I wasn't going to tell her that just yet.

"I don't have any questions, but I did read the whole thing to do my due diligence," Wylene began filling in her information on the form and signed it. "I'm not overly worried about the fees either. I'm quite successful at my job. I sell insurance."

I did laugh at that and felt terrible. "I apologize. That was unprofessional of me."

"No worries. The job is laughably easy for me. However, the flip side is I do get to help people," Wylene shrugged and stood. "I have to work in the morning, but I have time to show you the last memory that plagued me, and it makes me think a girl is in danger. We can meet Friday evening, and I can give you others."

"Show me?" I asked stupidly.

"Yes, show you. As part of my medium abilities, I can touch you and show you thoughts or memories. Like transferring the data from one hard drive to another," Wylene held out her hand to me.

Reluctantly, I stretched my hand out to grasp hers.

It was cool to the touch, but Wylene's skin was silky and had the smell of vanilla wafting to my nose. The moment her hand closed over mine, I transported into her memory. It was like I was watching a movie, only I was there.

The wind whipped her hair around in random bursts of temper. The sky rippled with shades of gray clouds that blended into the horizon, swallowed by the dark expanse of the ocean. The roar of the waves drowned out her naturally low and quiet voice. The only artificial sound she heard was the music that was a part of her playing in the earbuds in her ears. It was a nightly routine—music, and ocean under cover of night, rain, or clear skies alike. Someone once asked her what does she see looking out in the dark. Endless possibilities was her reply. The land here knew her presence, accepted it even. She was a fixture in the landscape every night.

How did I know this? I've kissed the salty spray of the sea from her lips. I've warmed the cold rain-soaked skin. I've loved her since I met her, and now, even in death and all her reincarnated forms.

I jerked my hand back out of Wylene's hold. A man spoke that memory in a voice that was distinct and clearly communicating with Wylene. "That's here. That's now. I recognize that girl."

Wylene nodded. "Do you see my problem? What if this is a way that I can see who is going to die next? It's not just me that is in danger, and that is my true fear. I can't get prosecuted for being a siren and doing what is natural to me; the laws protect me from that fate, but I can be run out of town, and I love it here."

I glanced down at the signed contract, silently vowing to do what I could to help the siren. "The relationship with Zhor?" I couldn't help asking for Gage's sake.

"Happily ended," Wylene filled me in. "The sex was

good, but we had little else in common. I'm not too fond of horse meat, so there wasn't too much of a chance I'd eat him, but Zhor did have good oral skills, so it lasted longer than it should have."

I snickered. "Understandable. Those skills are hard to pass by, I know."

Wylene nodded sagely. "They are rare. No worries, I won't interfere with your son's relationship with Zhor. The man is an asshole and a mistake I don't want to repeat."

I was sure Wylene made that statement to make me feel better, but it didn't. If Zhor were an asshole, Gage would get hurt whether Wylene was a part of the picture or not. I kept my mouth shut, though. Gage was an adult and had to make his mistakes to learn.

I nodded my acceptance to Wylene. "Okay, the first order of business is for me to find this girl, make her safe, somehow, and then meet with you tomorrow night?"

"Not tomorrow, Friday night. We can meet here or somewhere else. Would you like to write down the dreams or rather I show them?" Wylene stretched, and it was then that I saw her wings.

"Whichever works better for you," I mumbled distractedly. "You flew here," I stated dumbly. "That's how you got here so fast."

Wylene stretched glorious black wings that had a magnificent iridescent green sheen to them. They were stunning. I reached out to stroke one of the feathers, and Wylene stepped out of the way. Shaking myself out of the daze I was in; I looked up at her.

"Sorry, when people touch them, it sometimes has a sexual reaction. It's been a while since I ate as sirens eat, and when those flames light, I get hungry," Wylene explained with a blush.

Note to self, don't touch wings and turn on hungry sirens. "Got it. Let's meet here Friday at six?"

"Sounds good. I hope you can find that girl," Wylene held her hand out for me to shake.

I shook it and followed her out, locking up as I went. I watched in fascination and envy as she took to the skies with an ease that I wished I had. Hell, I wished I had her wings. My tiny little wings were nothing compared to those.

I got in my Jeep and started to brainstorm about how I would find this girl and tell her she was getting targeted by a stalker spirit. The location of the scene Wylene showed me was well-known to me. If all else fails, I could go there and simply wait for her to show up. Maybe I'd even spot the spirit.

My decision made I stuffed my headset into my ear and called Danny. "Hey," I greeted him when he answered. "How do you feel about an excursion to the cliffs above the sea at Nymph's Point?"

"Right now?" Danny asked distractedly.

"No, not right now. I was thinking tomorrow," I replied with an eye roll I was sure he could hear.

"Babe, I'm sure I'd go just about anywhere you asked me to," Danny told me, his attention now on our conversation. "What's the reason for this impromptu adventure?"

"A case I signed on for," I admitted. "Sorry, it's not romantic, but you know I won't turn down some treasure hunting inside our pants."

Danny barked out a laugh. "Treasure hunting? I've already found the treasure, babe. Plus, it's still time with you, and I'll take it. What time?"

"I'll come to get you," I told him, feeling a bit on the twitterpated side after his comment. "Probably around eleven or so."

"How about I come and pick you up? We can take the truck, and that way, no one driving by will know it's you out there. You'll be incognito," Danny used that practical tone that made me roll my eyes again.

"Okay, whatever. You can pick me up," I agreed. "We might need to be there until after dark."

"We can do treasure hunting at any time of the day," Danny growled.

I almost turned my Jeep around right then and there. The man's tongue should be licensed as magic all of its own, not to mention the rest of his equipment. Jeez, I was terrible. I did my best to tamp down the irrational lust this man ripped out of me at every conversation. I needed to focus on Wylene. "Are you willing to do another search for me?" I changed the subject.

"Nice brakes, sweetheart," Danny groaned. "What's the subject?"

"Banishing persistent spirits. How many ways are there, what's the most effective manner, and is it permanent? I need a crash course on all of it," I listed off, thinking.

"Can you see ghosts?" Danny asked incredulously.

"Always have been able to. I can't always communicate with the spirits; that's more touch and go. I want to be prepared, though," I told the man I was trying my best not to fall in love with, somewhat unsuccessfully. Not that I would admit that.

"Is this going to put you in danger?" Danny's question was hesitant.

"Every case has that possibility," I hedged. "You know I can't divulge the particulars."

"Cut the shit," Danny replied with a soft tone. "I watched you almost get killed on the last case, and that sticks in my head. You matter to me, Risa."

If the roles were reversed, I'd feel the same way he did, but I was terrified to admit that to anyone, even myself. "Let me do my job, Danny. I'm good at it, and I'm not helpless. I ask you for help, and you come through each time. Can that be enough for now? I won't give up my business because it makes you uncomfortable."

"I wouldn't ask you to, Risa. I know better than that. I guess I was only hoping you could tell me a little so I know what to expect if things happen. Seeing you hurt tends to make me lose control of my magic," Danny softened his tone.

"I'm going to be looking for a girl I saw in a vision that my client and I believe might be in danger. I couldn't say what kind of things we can expect since this will be my first time investigating a spirit in this manner," I relented and told him more than I wanted to.

"Thank you. I won't ask for more," Danny promised, sounding contrite. "Are you on your way home now?"

"Yep. I'm tired. Gage's new beau is quite the singer and was also my new client's ex-girlfriend," I told him randomly. "Made for an interesting moment when she appeared."

Danny made a humming noise. "Have you considered adding me as an employee to your contracts? That way, we can discuss cases in more detail."

"I can't afford to pay you," I argued, ashamed I hadn't thought of that.

"The terms of my payment aren't necessary for client contracts; it merely lists me as an employee of yours and becomes understood that you would be sharing information with me to help you solve the case. I'd work for dates; no physical form of money needs to change hands," Danny explained, heat coming back into his voice.

"You are going to prostitute yourself out to me?" I asked jokingly.

"No money is changing hands," Danny chuckled. "I think the proper term would be ho'ing."

Chapter Four

After I woke up and emptied my bladder, the first thing I did was head to my office. Once there, I pulled the contract that Wylene filled out, opened my e-mail, and began to write out a message to her. I explained that I had an employee who helped me out with aspects of cases and that I would be rewording my contracts for future clients. I made sure to add in the verbiage that he would be bound by the same confidentiality that I held myself accountable to and asked if she would mind if I enlisted his help.

Once I sent the e-mail, I refiled the contract and checked for any new voice mails. Before I left the office, I had Wylene's reply stating her agreement and printed it, filing it with the contract, and smiled. Paid or not, it appears I had hired my first employee.

I headed back home to pack up a few snacks for Danny and me to munch while surveilling the cliffs. While I was thinking about it, I tossed an extra set of clothes into a backpack along with some shoes. I grabbed my rain jacket and stuffed that in too. I knew Danny was a warlock and could cast drying spells, yet I wanted to prepare for other eventualities.

I filled up a couple of metal bottles with some water, one of them a strikingly similar color to the green in Wylene's wings. The woman was appealing; there was no doubt about that. Wylene had an intelligence to her that carried through in everything she did and humor and beauty. Her movements were grace personified, and well, then there was the voice.

Mental note, keep Wylene away from Danny. I couldn't compete with that, even if I did have a perfect ass. *Wait!* I wasn't in a relationship; why was I having this train of thought? Scowling, I dropped the snacks, water, and backpack at the front door and stomped back to the kitchen to gulp down some coffee.

Not wanting to be on that train of thought, I went back to Wylene's case. She'd said she moved here before this town was a town; that made her more senior than me. Not by a large margin, just enough to make me smugly happy that the woman was older than me. My scowl came back when I realized that I looked older than her.

Moving on, I reminded myself. I wasn't used to comparing myself against other females, and the whole thing was throwing me off balance. I genuinely like this woman; this destructive thought process I kept engaging in wouldn't help either of us. I recognized that I needed to address this on an internal level and yet felt compelled to ignore it.

I began to pace my hallway between the kitchen and the front door, and my reflection caught my eye. My hair now sported dark green ends. I huffed out my frustration with the magical puberty, and my best guess was this was my magic's way of telling me I was infected with jealousy.

It should have served as a warning for me to change my attitude, considering I had no idea what I could do in this state. Instead, it only fueled me to act out even more. Damn. I *was* in puberty again, if this was any sign. I was ridiculous.

I heard Danny's truck pull into the driveway, and I

yanked my purse over my shoulder and stomped like a child back to the front door, snatching the bags I'd dropped there. I slammed the door behind me, locked it, and huffed over to where Danny stood gaping at me and holding the passenger door open.

"Whoa. Is this magical, or did you color your hair like this?" Danny dared to ask with a smirk.

My feet chose that moment to upend me, and I landed directly in Danny's arms like a helpless damsel in distress. It pissed me off something fierce. Wisely, Danny righted me and said nothing, but the smack on the ass he gave me didn't help matters.

"Don't push it," I snarled as I climbed into his truck.

"Got it. Magical," Danny chuckled as he closed my door and rounded the truck to get in. "I won't ask."

"Good move," I snapped and bit my tongue. "I added you to the contract this morning."

"No shit?" Danny's eyes went saucer-shaped. The man had no bad look, and it didn't help the jealousy running through me.

"The client agreed, and your suggestion made sense. I figured if you knew the background of the cases instead of the little tidbits that I feed you, your searching expertise would better help me since you think of things or see them in a way that I don't," I rationalized, only halfway doubting my decision.

"I'm honored, Risa. Thank you. Do you want to tell me about this case on the way to Nymph's Point?" Danny's tone was soft and decadent, and my lady parts all woke up in a blaze of fire.

"The client is Wylene," I started and paused as Danny broke out into a coughing fit.

"Wylene Silla?" Danny managed to get out, his face a curious shade of red.

I froze and stared at him, willing an answer that

defied my thoughts to fall from his plump lips that I felt tempted to rip off his face because I already knew where this was going. "You dated Wylene," I stated instead of asked.

Danny nodded, "Years ago, before I knew you. I'm sorry to hear she is having trouble. Wylene is a fantastic person."

Oh yeah, *that* helped with the jealousy issue that was rearing its head. I didn't care if it was a hundred years ago; if she was with Danny, that meant she'd slept with him. Wylene knew what he looked like naked. At that thought, the conversation about oral skills leaped back into the front of my mind.

In that split second, my magic roared to life. Which bloodline produced an ability to call birds, I couldn't say. However, I was positive that it was my magic that made the largest flock of birds dive-bomb Danny's pretty truck and cover it with shit. Hey, at least it wasn't flying dachshunds.

Danny slammed on his brakes to avoid hitting the unwilling avians, and well, because he couldn't see through the windshield anymore. As quickly as the magic flared to life, it died, and insane laughter bubbled out of my mouth.

"What the—shit?" Danny cried, appalled at the sight of the white and dripping display on the windshield. "Risa! Was that you?"

I couldn't stem the laughing. We were stopped in the middle of the street, blocking traffic, in a now bird shit white-colored truck thanks to the jealousy that fueled that crazy burst of magic. If that didn't accurately describe my life now, I don't know what will.

Danny muttered something under his breath, and a torrential downpour cleared the remnants of the birds excreted lunch from the windshield. The look he gave me had no accurate words to describe it, and I sobered as our drive continued.

"Let's not revisit that, please," Danny finally managed to say with no humor in his voice.

"I'm sorry," I tried to say without laughing. The attempt wasn't successful.

"Try telling me about the case again, minus the bird involvement," Danny groused and resumed driving amidst the honking cars that were swerving around us. "I'll cuff you if I have to so your magic doesn't drown us in shit."

Hello, libido. "Well, now that you mention it," I purred and turned in my seat to face Danny.

"Damn, woman. We aren't going to make it to the destination if you keep that up," Danny's voice turned husky. "The case," he reminded me.

Right. Danny's ex-girlfriend, my client. I felt like this was some extensive cosmic test that I was failing grandly. I took a deep breath and began to explain everything from the moment I spotted her to the second she took flight, and I developed a girl crush.

Danny let out a small laugh, "I don't know that I can add a lot about Wylene in a historical sense. I do know that she arrived here maybe a couple of years before it became a town. Branstone was a fresh new city at that time, and the area where Glimmering Rock is was nothing but a wasteland, according to the mayor of Branstone."

I knew that part of our history, and I wanted him to talk more about Wylene. "Did she play a part in it?"

"In Glimmering Rock becoming what it is?" Danny glanced over at me. "No. Wylene avoids politics. She's a generous person, kind to a fault, funny, and smart. Yet, she stays away from conflict. Wylene never talked much about her past to me, only that she left the Mediterranean suddenly to start a life somewhere new."

As curious as I was, I had no intention of asking Danny about his relationship with the woman. I wasn't sure I could rationally handle that information. Given that he didn't elaborate, I assumed he understood the results would be questionable.

"We are going to Nymph's Point to look for the girl that you saw in Wylene's vision? How do you plan on convincing her that she is in danger without sounding like a nut job? What are your plans if that stalker ghost shows up? Do you have any idea who he is?" Danny fired off a round of questions at me.

"I don't know to all of it," I answered and shrugged for emphasis. "Wait, except, yes, we are going to see if we can find the girl. If I have to stalk her to keep her safe, then I will. Did you do any research for me on the banishing stuff?"

Danny nodded in response. "I should be able to perform it, but we'll need to get a circle up for protection. I read that some of these spirits that linger like this and affect the living can still have access to the magic they might have had while alive. We'll need to figure out what race he was and go from there. If Wylene knows who he is, that helps too. I might be able to do some digging and find out more."

"Also, I'd like to know who is being stalked," I added, tapping my nail against my teeth.

"Wylene said she knew who it was and that she was murdered not long after she arrived? That should be easy enough to figure out. A ton of the history is online, and I can set a bug to search with those parameters," Danny offered.

Okay, so maybe adding him as an employee has benefits I hadn't considered. "You might end up being the employee of the month."

"Awesome. You are the dessert I get to eat as a prize," Danny gave me a sultry look that had me squirming in my seat.

Memories of his tongue doing what it did so well

had me feeling like it was on me already; they were so vivid. I rolled down the window and stuck my head out like a dog to try and cool off. I was going from one extreme to the next today, sheesh.

The sound of Danny laughing had me pulling my head back in and glancing over at him. "What?"

"No need for a metal detector to find treasure. I've got iron in my pants," Danny informed me with a grin.

He didn't need to point it out; it was obvious. I reached over to fondle him, and the truck swerved violently. Danny cursed loudly but didn't stop me. I wasn't going to stop either. I wanted to make sure the only one he was thinking about was me when his Iron Man came out to play. I had no idea who I was anymore.

By the time we arrived at the cliffs, Danny was panting and had broken out in a light sweat. His magic filled the air in the cab of his truck, my pants were no longer on, and I was hauled right over the console onto his lap. I've been in worse places.

Even mindless with need, he took care of me before he let go of the rigid control he was maintaining. I swear rainbows burst from the windows of his truck as my ass honked the horn to the cadence of his pleasure. Don't judge; it was music.

"Damn, darlin'," Danny sighed in my ear. "No one will ever exist for me the way you do."

Oh, hell. "I'm in a relationship, aren't I?" I mumbled into his neck.

"With me," Danny clarified. "Say it. Say I'm yours."

Okay, the fact that he didn't say I was his made me stupidly happy that he wasn't all macho and possessive in a bad way. "You're mine," I agreed. "I'll be your girlfriend," I added as a little extra benefit. The scorching kiss I got in return made me forget I wasn't sure I was ready for that title.

Chapter Five

I paced the cliff's edge and wondered briefly how many people had fallen from here and landed on those giant rock's way down at the bottom. Scratch that, I didn't want to know. Based on the watchful gaze of Danny on me, he wasn't going to look it up either unless I moved away from the precipice.

Danny was on a bench about five hundred feet back from the ledge and searched for me on the murder that Wylene referenced. So far, there had been no sign of the girl or any spirits that I could see.

That was a fact I found strange considering this place was steeped in legends. Whether they were true or not, I had no idea. I suppose I could ask Wylene since she was here. Regardless, I figured at least that a few non-malicious ghosts would be fluttering around watching the scenery if nothing else.

It was a beautiful place, and if I could sit still and relax, this would be the place to do it. The beach was at minimum a hundred and fifty feet below me, strewn with large jagged rocks and waves that crashed up against them, trying to beat them down into grains of fine sand.

Up here where we were was grassy hills that led to the precipice I was wandering, and farther south from me was a forest that ended ten feet from the cliff. Some of the adventurous types secured their lines to some of the trees and repelled down to the bottom. A few said there were some caves partway down. I believed them and wasn't going to check it out for myself.

"Risa, come here," Danny called me back.

I frowned at him and turned to walk to the bench. I figured he was calling me to get me away from the ledge. Haphazard things happened to me, but not from clumsiness on my part. I wasn't going to fall off the cliff. I rolled my eyes when I got closer to him.

"I found some history here I think you might be interested in," Danny explained and semi-turned the laptop so I could see the screen when I sat next to him.

"Tell me," I demanded, not wanting to read. I might have wanted to hear Danny's voice reading to me. I wouldn't tell him that though, no need for his ego to inflate anymore after declaring I was his girlfriend.

"Long before this place was thought of or discovered, a sea nymph lived here named Halia. It's believed she is the granddaughter of Nereus. Instead of calling herself a nereid for a short time, she would call herself a haliae, which, I guess, would be correct given her heritage. She left the Greek islands, by her own account, to find love without interference. Halia was described as tall, fair-skinned, with long dark hair that glimmered in the sunlight and eyes as deep as the ocean. It doesn't list a color," Danny read.

"I've never heard the term haliae before," I mused.

"It describes daughters of Nereus and Doris," Danny explained. "Halia began to call herself a nereid after that, then finally just a nymph. Guess where her dwelling was."

I looked over at Danny's handsome face and couldn't help grinning back at him. "Well, let's see, we are at a place called Nymph's Point, so my guess is here."

Danny tapped me on the nose. "Good guess. Halia is

described repeatedly as stunningly beautiful and often sought after for attention by various men, which she turned down time and time again. Because she was looking for the deep love that she had heard Poseidon talk about, he declared this cove as Halia's. There's an oddly blank time span, then Halia is mentioned again, this time with a beau named Cato."

"Cato?" I echoed, the name feeling sour on my tongue and my face involuntarily wrinkled.

"There's an excellent chance that Cato is the spirit that is stalking women," Danny continued with a worried expression. "Cato was a centaur that had been sent away from his homeland for breaking some laws. The retold story goes that he came across Halia dancing along the cliffs and singing songs of her people, and he fell in love in an instant. Cato pursued her with a passion that borders on crazy and eventually earned her attention. There are side stories that he used magic potions to make her love him, and when they finally wore off, she was outraged, and they fought. Halia found another love and lived happily for a while, and there are accounts that she had some children. The story gets muddier here, some say hooves crushed her, others say she threw herself off the cliffs to return to the sea, and the last theory is that he, Cato, beheaded her and buried her head here; so she could never leave him again."

Horrified at the thought, I stood and paced in front of Danny. "What happened to Cato?"

Danny did a bit more typing and fell silent for a few minutes while he searched. "He was killed by settlers. That's all I could find, but that happened here in this area as well. The other disturbing thing is that several women who all bear the same general description as Halia have died in this place. Most of them thought to be suicides, though a few were considered murder and never solved."

Guess that answered that question I hadn't spoken

aloud earlier. "Wylene's description matches Halia's as well. So does the girl we are looking for today. Who was the father of Halia's children?"

"Not one mention of his name, or the children," Danny replied as he looked up from his computer. "You haven't seen any spirits at all around here? I figured there'd be a lot of them after reading that."

"Nope. Though Cato's name makes my tongue feel like I stuck it in a lemon," I shuddered.

Danny laughed, "That explains the pinched look on your face. After Halia's death, the newly formed town dedicated this coastline and the cove to her and named it Nymph's Point."

"Tragic," I mumbled as I faced the sea again. "Halia, are you still here?"

"There's one account by a hag that said since Halia was killed before her time, she would be reincarnated throughout the years until she found the love that brought her here," Danny relayed as I resumed pacing.

"If Cato is still here, then he's killing all these women, so she never finds that love and is stuck here for eternity with him," I snarled and shivered as a cold draft went down my back like an icy finger on my spine. "Other than appearance, is there anything in common with all the women who died?"

Danny went back to typing, and I headed toward the cliff face to see if I could communicate with Halia if she were still here. Something had to be here to make me feel like that when I spoke or heard Cato's name.

"Halia?" I whispered into the wind. "I want to help."

The sea crashed loudly below me, the salty spray reaching me on the top of the cliff. Halia was here. I guess it could be Poseidon, which was a way scarier thought. I turned back to face Danny and was in time to see him shoot to his feet, his computer forgotten as horror crossed

178

his handsome face.

"Risa!" Danny screamed as my skin began to itch painfully.

I took an involuntary step backward as the transparent figure of a centaur appeared before me. It had to be Cato, and he was furious. Front legs came up and slammed into my chest with enough force to crack ribs and, unfortunately, launched me right off the precipice I was standing on.

So many things happened at once. I couldn't process anything other than the thought of wishing a trampoline was under me instead of the rocks I was going to be broken and dead on soon enough. A wild scream tore through me as my limbs went flailing in all directions like a drunk windmill.

I plummeted like a rock tied to an anchor. I felt Danny's magic brush my skin, and my own burst out of me in a desperate attempt to keep me alive. Tornado-like winds spun me in a circle, slowing my descent marginally.

I tumbled crazily through the air, and the sea below me surged at least fifty feet up, and I prepared to drown. The next moment I was bowled right out of the magical wind funnel and surrounded by cowny black feathers with a green tint. However, we were still on a downward trajectory, and a wave slammed into us, almost smashing us into the face of the cliff.

I had half a second to see that there was indeed a cave there before we started to rise again, and my magic interfered once more when I felt the oily presence of Cato coming at us. A pocket of wind came up under us and lifted Wylene and me high in the air when I felt Danny's attempt, bringing us back like a magical lasso.

We crashed down on the grass with a bone-cracking oomph and tangle of wings, limbs, and arms. My face was the only thing that had a soft landing, and when I opened my eyes, I saw why. My head had gotten sandwiched between two luscious boobs.

"I've never motorboated anyone before," I groaned as I tried to move.

"You still haven't," Wylene muttered. "Next time, if you ask nicely, I might let you."

"You can honk mine if it makes you feel better," I told her with a sniff as I flopped to my back on the grass. "Just don't touch Danny's, and we're good."

Chapter Six

Once I had caught my breath and Danny had checked every inch of me and helped me up, we hobbled over to the bench and huddled together for warmth while Danny ran to get a blanket and some towels from the truck.

"How did you know to come?" I asked through chattering teeth.

"Halia told me the sylph was here and in danger," Wylene's teeth clicked when she answered.

"She's the tits," I tried the saying again. Sylph?

"It always comes down to the tits, doesn't it?" Wylene shot off. "What is the fascination with them anyway? It's not like they are fake. Your face was there, you know." Wylene squeezed her boobs for emphasis.

I burst out laughing. I couldn't help it. "I don't care if you've touched my boyfriend's junk. I like you."

"Oh, you and Daniel are an item?" Wylene looked surprised for a moment, and then her face broke out into a beaming smile. "That's good. I can see how that would be an excellent match. He deserves someone good like you. I'll admit, his junk is pretty great."

My laughter immediately stopped, then started again. "Yeah, it is. I agree."

"Were you jealous?" Wylene asked suddenly. "No reason to be. The sex was good, but we weren't a good match. I think he had to work too hard at it to have his happy ending with me. Did you color your hair last night?" Wylene fingered the ends distractedly. "Wait, it wasn't this color when you went over the cliff."

I glanced down at the tendril in her fingers and sighed. It was yellow, green, and purple now. "I believe my hair is a magical mood ring. Why did Halia say sylph?"

"I don't think she knows what you are, only that she thinks you have magic related to hers. I believe you have strong elemental magic," Wylene shrugged.

"That's the fairy blood in me," I told her. "Halia shouldn't feel bad; I don't know what I am either."

"Elemental, like I said," Wylene cocked her head to study me. "Not a fairy, though they are similar. Regardless, it doesn't matter. I knew she meant you. I left work immediately and flew as fast as I could. You haven't seen the girl yet?"

Danny walked up and handed us each a towel, motioned us to stand up, and wrapped the blanket around us both. Once we sat back on the bench, he dropped to his knees and rested his head on my legs as his shoulders shook. It took me a hot minute to understand he was crying.

I snapped my jaw shut before I said something to make the situation worse or downplay his emotions. Instead, I wound my fingers through his hair and let him have his moment. It didn't take long, and soon he stood and sat as close as possible to my side.

"Wylene, thank you," Danny said sincerely. "It did me wonders to see my girlfriend motorboating my ex."

Wylene and I both snorted out laughter at the ice breaker Danny offered up. He filled her in on the research he had done and the history we had learned while we sat there and dried in the waning afternoon sun. Not one of us noticed the girl we'd been looking for sitting in the trees watching us.

"I can't fill anything in on their lives. I can confirm the history of this town, the naming of this place, and the rumors. I can tell you why it's named Glimmering Rock, and I can ask clarifying questions to Halia. I cannot guarantee she will answer. It's only sometimes in my dreams that she comes through, and I suspect that Cato is suppressing her in some way," Wylene explained.

When she stiffened and swiveled her head around, I went on alert. I raked my eyes over the area looking for signs of danger. I swept over the girl twice, and it didn't register that she was what had drawn Wylene's attention. At least not until Wylene spoke.

"The girl is here," Wylene said softly, making Danny jolt. "Danny, plug your ears, please."

Oh, Wylene was using that siren power to entice. I felt the presence of Danny's magic settle like a blanket over my skin, and I couldn't help but note the familiarity of it. That's when it struck me that he had help getting us back on land. I'd felt more than his magic.

Wylene's song drifted on the air like the sweetest lullaby, and my body relaxed into the sounds. I wasn't under a thrall like when Zhor had been singing, this was more soothing, and I still had a functioning brain. I mean, I still wanted to crawl on Danny's lap and make a sex tape, but that was normal.

The girl materialized out of the woods and began to walk towards us as if she were floating. I didn't know if she was naturally that graceful or it was Wylene's song that was causing her to move that way, but it was enchanting to watch.

"You can stop singing now. I'm here," the girl spoke softly. "I'm happy you are both okay."

"Did you help?" I asked her gently. I was afraid she'd melt back into the trees.

The young girl nodded at me hesitantly. "I've seen you around before. I don't know what hit you, but the air around you shimmered with something that made my blood react." She held out her hand to me, "I'm Hallie."

"Risa," I responded, shaking her hand. "Are you by any chance related to Halia?"

Hallie nodded slowly. "Why do you ask?"

"When you saw me go over the cliff, it was because of Cato. Do you know about him?" I was trying so hard to be gentle with this. I didn't want Hallie to get scared off, yet I also wanted her to feel the situation's seriousness.

"Cato was Halia's captor," Hallie answered firmly. "He's here?" Her eyes flicked over Danny for a moment.

I bit back a snicker when I realized he still couldn't hear us. I tapped my ears for him, and he let go of the deafening spell he'd been using to block Wylene's song. He gave me a wink and rested his hand on my hip in that possessive way that did things to my lady bits. The sex tape was still an option.

"Yes," Wylene answered Hallie. "Cato is here, and he wants to hurt you. I've been having visions of you, and I wasn't sure if you were in the present or something from the past. Risa told me she recognized you, so she came here to warn you. Cato tried to kill her for it."

Hallie slid her gaze back to me, then Wylene. "Can he be stopped?"

"That's what I intend to do," I told both the women.

"How will I know when I'm safe?" Hallie fixed her eyes on me this time. "His reign of terror on my family needs to end, and I'm not looking forward to being next on the list to perish."

"You can leave your contact information with me, and I'll let you know when it's over," I offered. "I intend to have this wrapped up in the next couple of days. My partner here will be helping me," I gestured at Danny.

"Cato made a bargain with something dark," Hallie told me with a tint of anger that colored her tone. "That is the legend that has passed through my mother's line over the years. It's how he had power over Halia and how he still has power. I didn't believe any of it until you told me Cato is here."

"Something dark?" I repeated, my mind spinning. "Demons?"

Hallie shrugged. "To my knowledge, it's never been named, only that it's dark in nature. I do know that if you don't stop him, Halia's line ends with me. I'm the last," she admitted sadly. "That's a lot of pressure on me. The nymphs of my bloodline seem to all die early, before reproducing."

Wylene sniffled, "I'm going to help Risa make sure that doesn't happen. Halia wants you to know that you are beautiful and destined to have a long and happy life, and she's proud of you."

I understand why Wylene relayed the message; however, the sappiness was getting deep, and my need to spout off sarcastic comments to lighten the mood was overwhelming. I was feeling the pressure Hallie mentioned. Only I needed to save her, Wylene, and the future of the sea nymph race that carried Halia's blood, banish the evil spirit and hopefully release Halia in the process.

"Do you have a safe way to get back home?" Danny interrupted my thoughts.

Hallie nodded. "I live close to here. We always have." Hallie turned and pointed to a house I hadn't noticed when we pulled in.

I reached out and patted her hand. "Then I'll knock on your door when things are safe."

"Stay inside, and don't let anyone in. Hunker down with whoever else lives there," Danny suggested. "Do you have enough food in there to last you a couple of days?"

"No, probably not. Money is tight," Hallie said with shame.

"I'll fix that. Come with me," Danny stood and gestured with his arm for Hallie to follow. "You two, please, stay out of trouble for a bit." He fastened his eyes on me, "I can't watch that again, Risa. It felt like my heart was ripped out."

I didn't know how to respond to that. "Thank you for taking care of Hallie," I whispered in his ear when I stood up. "I'll have Wylene show me the rest of the visions while we wait for you."

Danny latched his arms around me before I could move away. "Never have I felt this way about anyone before. I mean it, Risa, be safe. I won't say the 'L' word because I know it will freak you out. However, it's there."

I gasped as Danny melted the skin off my bones with one of his kisses. When he stepped away, I was sure I was about to slosh into a puddle, like the one inside my pants. Damn. That man was lethal.

Chapter Seven

Wylene and I were on the third vision when she abruptly pulled away, and her eyes glazed over. It was a stark reminder for me that Wylene was my client and not Hallie. I needed to free her from the spirit of Cato. Hell, I needed to free the land from the dead, overbearing centaur ghost.

This case was shaping up to be more difficult, dangerous, and profound than the last few I had worked. It was a nice change of pace, though I preferred not to be a hairs width from meeting death. I observed Wylene for any signs that she was in distress and became more aware of my surroundings. I also couldn't help wrapping my arm around the back of the bench for an anchor in case we got tossed again.

I was so intent on Wylene that I didn't notice the man sneaking up behind us. I couldn't begin to imagine the state Wylene was in, only that at some point, she had become aware that we were in danger and her eyes focused to an intense emerald color, and I swear they glimmered. Her jaw opened, and she began to sing.

Three notes in, and I saw Benji Brown, the famed most wanted in Glimmering Rock for burglary, grand theft auto, and assault. What surprised me most was that he was no more than six inches from me, and he was armed.

Benji was a threat to everyone in the town, and our law enforcement was under the belief that he had fled the area to avoid being stripped of his magic and imprisoned for life. He was a bad man, and I had been once more knocking at death's door.

As Wylene continued to sing, I saw the gun drop to the ground, and I leaped over the bench to snatch it up, using the towel, so I didn't get my prints on it. I wrapped it up and tucked it under my arm. Benji was under Wylene's thrall, and he stood pliant before her. I didn't want to watch, nor could I look away.

Wylene began stripping from the waist down, and Benji followed suit, and to my satisfaction, he was far below average in the size department. Wylene's movements were sinuous and mesmerizing. I didn't understand the words to what she was singing, for which I was grateful since I knew what was coming.

I closed my eyes when Benji began to pleasure Wylene and silently cheered the siren on for getting some in public, even if it was from a criminal. I can't lie; something in the song turned me on the same way one look from Danny did.

When the sounds changed to flesh-ripping, I opened my eyes to see Wylene tearing his arms off, along with little Benji. The man hadn't stopped doing what he was doing either. He didn't even flinch. That siren song was impressive. Not many men would be able to keep going after having their Richards torn off.

I closed my eyes again before I saw Wylene eat the flesh because gross. I heard the flutter of feathers, boots hitting the ground, more ripping sounds, and the smell of blood struck me hard. When everything went silent, I cracked open my eyes to a gruesome scene.

Blood spatters marred Wylene's beautiful feathers, her clothes, mine, and the ground around us. Benji's head sat a few feet away from her, staring into the afterlife with cloudy eyes. I saw the bird-like legs that always hid under her knee-high boots with bits of flesh clinging to them. My stomach rolled.

"God, I was hungry," Wylene said. "His skills were greatly lacking, but at least my hunger is satisfied, even if the rest of me wasn't."

I half-snorted, not wanting to puke at the grisly mess. I was immensely delighted that Danny hadn't been here, both for his sought-after oral skill talent and not having to resist the siren song. I turned my back so she could dress and clean up however she saw fit. "I'll check with Danny to see if he has a friend on the force we can notify."

Sirens now topped my list of savage beauties that made me happy I wasn't a man. That was one woman no one should mess with; the woman was lethal. I texted my request for a friendly cop to Danny and waited for Wylene to finish.

"What happened? How did you know?" I finally asked, my curiosity brimming over and out my lips.

"Cato was doing his thing and making those sexual cravings surface, and when I caught movement behind you, I sang out of instinct. Cato was cackling and jerking off, and it nearly distracted me. He's a sick fuck," Wylene growled.

I grimaced. "Uh, maybe you should go home. I'll do my best to take care of this," I waved my hand at the severed head.

"No, you won't. I didn't hire you for that, and it's my responsibility. I won't go to jail for that," Wylene promised. "Hopefully, they won't run me out of town."

I chewed on my lip as I waited for an answer back from Danny, praying he had a friend on the force. I was also contemplating how much I would relay about this. I wasn't sure about his reaction to me being in danger so quickly after the cliff thing.

"Don't lie to him," Wylene said quietly behind me. "That man is head over heels in love. Respect his feelings."

"Are you a mind reader too?" I snapped, spinning around.

"No. I'm not blind. It's ludicrously easy to see how Daniel feels about you. Daniel is a good friend, I'd like to think you will be too, and I don't want to see either of your hurt. There is baggage on both sides, and I can see that too. Believe me when I say that Daniel doesn't show emotions often, and today he's run the gamut with them," Wylene lectured me.

I silently fumed because I knew she was right. I was also secretly pleased that she wanted to be my friend. I didn't have too many female friends, and a siren as a friend would be badass.

"What does magenta mean?" Wylene asked me, her voice tinted with humor.

"Huh?" I raised my eyes to hers.

"Your hair," Wylene pointed. "It really is like a mood ring. I thought you were joking."

"I was," I mused, tugging on some strands to see the ends now a magenta color. "I have no idea what that means."

"Well, what were you feeling?" Wylene pressed for an answer.

"Irritated," I rolled my eyes.

Wylene broke out into delighted laughter. "I think you're tits."

"*The*," I snickered. "You're *the* tits. Otherwise, you are just calling me a boob." I was guessing. Gage hadn't totally explained the statement's nuances to me, but being called a tit was still amusing. I would probably never grow up.

Chapter Eight

I expected some reaction from Danny; however, screeching tires and his truck slamming to a stop in the parking lot with him beelining for me, wasn't it. His eyes were wild with panic as he took in the bloody head and our clothes.

"What the fuck?" Danny barked at us, his eyes swinging between Wylene and me.

"You didn't respond," I pointed out. "Do you know someone on the force?"

Danny cocked an eyebrow at me and gave me a scrutinizing look as he analyzed the situation. When his gaze finally switched back to Wylene, who was picking chunks of Benji from her teeth, I almost lost control and broke down into hysterics. Almost. I don't think he would handle that well.

"That guy was going to shoot Risa, so I sang and ate him," Wylene answered and spat out a bone fragment.

I lost it. I bent at the waist and slapped my thighs while peals of laughter erupted from me like a pressurized volcano belching its lava. The bone fragment did it. "I think I love you," I managed to get out between painful breaths from damaged and smarting ribs.

There was an extended silence from Danny, then a pregnant sigh. "In answer to your question, yes, my friend

Travis is on the force and is on his way here. I'm gonna end up owing him, aren't I?"

I straightened up and tried to calm myself. "Probably. After Travis leaves, we need to make your banishing circle because the dude's gotta go. I can't unsee any of that."

Danny's facial expression was priceless and indescribable. He was saved from speaking by the shrieking of a police siren as the car presumably, Travis, drove slowly and casually into the parking lot. It was as if he were only using the obnoxious sounds to be dramatic.

"Yeah, um, I'm going to try to explain this before he walks up on a severed head," Danny turned and headed towards the cop, just opening his car door.

"That was a first for him," Wylene told me sincerely. "Daniel handled it better than I thought he would."

"Severed heads might be a first for a lot of people," I quipped, tossing a glance over my shoulder at Danny. "Is Cato still here, and can he hear me?"

"He's still here, yeah, because he's trying to lure my siren song back out," Wylene admitted sheepishly. "I also want to climb that cop like a tree."

I snorted and took a closer look as the two approached. Travis was tall, beefy, bald, with a close-shaven beard and ink-covered arms; Travis filled out that uniform well, I agreed. My eyes were still drawn to Danny, though, and the irrational part of my brain was irritated with that.

"Looks like Danny is explaining the situation," I remarked, watching Danny's body language.

"I agree. Daniel would probably bargain with the devil if it meant keeping you safe," Wylene agreed. "It's sweet."

I rolled my eyes and glared at her. "Enough."

"You don't hold the patent on jealously," Wylene

snapped. "Before you jump to conclusions, I'm talking about having someone love me like that, not jealous that Daniel isn't with me."

Oh. I'm big enough to admit I had indeed jumped to the wrong conclusion. Right as I was about to apologize, I saw Wylene's eyes glaze again, seconds before they turned to emeralds. I didn't think. I dove at Danny and boxed the hell out of his ears, causing him to drop painfully to his knees with his hands clamped over his ringing ears. Hopefully, it was enough to block the song that Wylene released.

I watched, stunned as Travis looked at all of us in confusion and started moving his hands around frantically. It took me a moment to understand he was signing. The only sign language I knew other than my middle finger was the deaf sign, which I made, and Travis slightly nodded before he moved to Wylene and put his hand over her mouth.

The touch snapped her to attention, and I helped Danny stand, his moves sluggish. He leaned on me a little before dropping to the bench and handing something to Travis. It clicked when I saw him place it in his ear; hearing aids. Travis was a perfect man for Wylene, and bonus, she was attracted to him.

Travis let go of Wylene's face when he was confident she would remain quiet and not sing. He moved around her and pulled a plastic bag out of his back pocket, and, without touching the head, scooped it up.

"That effectively closes this manhunt," Travis smiled at me. "Dan and I go way back. I'll mention that you found the head in the park and we'll leave it at that. How does that sound to you?"

"Works for me," I agreed.

"I'm Wylene," the siren interrupted and held her hand out to Travis.

"Travis," he gripped her hand and shook it gently. "How about I give you a ride home?"

Wylene looked over at me with a slight frown. "Do you need my help with banishing Cato?"

Danny shook his head in response. "I've got that. Go ahead and go with Travis, and thanks again for keeping Risa safe."

"Be careful," Wylene warned me. "Cato is imbalanced, and he's burning through a ton of energy, which makes him unstable. Oh, and yes, he can hear you if he listened. Cato is far too narcissistic to pay attention to what you are saying. He's more likely to listen to Daniel than you."

"Cato as in the centaur who is rumored to be the stalker of the nymph who lived here?" Travis asked, fascinated.

"The very same, I'll tell you the story," Wylene hooked her arm through his and led Travis back to his car.

"Oh! Damn. Danny, this is the gun that Benji was going to shoot me with; I didn't touch it," I held it out to Danny. He grabbed the gun from my grip with a frown and ran after their retreating forms.

I turned back to face the cliff and the raging sea below while keeping my distance. The space in front of the bench was the best place for a circle to be. That carried risk since it wasn't far from the edge I'd already gone over. The rest of the area was hilly and could work, yet it would be more difficult. I'd let Danny be the final say in that since he would be performing the magic necessary.

I turned to see Danny hugging Wylene and tucking something into his pocket. Remembering her earlier comment about jumping to conclusions, I pulled back from overreacting and waited patiently for Danny to return where I'd grill him. Damn, I needed to snap out of this jealous streak.

I walked around and kicked debris out of the way where I suspected Danny would place his circle. I didn't need the malicious ghost to have more weapons to use against us. While I was doing that, my phone rang, causing me to jump a bit. I was surprised the thing still worked.

"Yeah," I answered without looking at it.

"Mom," Jameson said in my ear. "I think I might have a way to use the Squatchgold in a potion that will help you control your magic."

I paused my pacing. "Is that what you've been doing?"

"Not directly. I've been working on the formula that Mercy was trying to have Gavin make. From what I've been able to find, that exact recipe would drain a person's magic and make it transferrable. If I tweak it a bit, I believe that it will give you the ability to direct it to benefit you," Jameson explained excitedly.

Interesting. "Okay, honey. I'm on a case right now, so we'll talk about that later," I told Jameson distractedly as Danny walked up on me.

"Be careful, Mom. Love you," Jameson chirped and hung up.

"We might want to lock our electronics up in the truck. There's a good chance this magic could fry the electronics," Danny addressed me quietly.

I didn't question it; I just handed him my phone without argument and watched as he ran back to the parking lot. A sense of unease settled on my bones. I didn't know if it was due to the banishing spell that Danny had to perform or a danger warning that my instincts were trying to send me.

I examined the feelings more closely as I watched Danny returning, his face a morose mask of seriousness that bothered me. I missed his fun smile and genial attitude. Maybe bringing him on the case was a mistake.

"I need a favor, darlin'," Danny told me, circling his arm around my waist and squeezing gently. "Would you be willing to go up to Hallie's house and ask her for some blood? I'm hoping to add it to the magic to help break the spell or curse on her bloodline. It has to be that," Danny mused, thinking. "There's an attachment there, and if Cato bargained with something dark, chances are there is a blood link."

"Creepy," I muttered. "You want me to go knock on Hallie's door and ask for blood. What's she supposed to put it in?"

Danny pulled a small vial out of his pocket. "I got some from Wylene too, and I'll need yours to ensure nothing attaches to you. The circle is going to take me a couple of hours to create to make sure that we are both protected, and it can hold Cato."

"It's not a ploy to get me out of here?" I asked carefully. I didn't doubt his motives. My question was more directed due to past experiences, not Danny specifically.

"No, Risa. That was a genuine request, and if you aren't feeling up to the walk, I'll do it myself," Danny dropped a kiss on the top of my head. "Thanks for clearing the area."

Not one hint of deception or condescension existed in his tone. "Will do. Watch yourself. My instincts are tingling. Be a shame to ruin this nicely shaped ass," I retorted with a pat on his firm backside.

"Happy to see your priorities haven't changed," Danny chuckled, pulling a spade from his pocket, and he squatted and got to work creating a circle.

Chapter Nine

It had been stupidly easy to get blood from Hallie. All I had to do was ask, and she cut her finger right open and bled it into the vial. The young girl needed to ask more questions before giving her blood to a virtual stranger. I sighed as I reminded myself it wasn't my problem and made my way back to Danny.

My ribs were aching something fierce, and I longed for a hot bath. I pondered over Jameson's phone call as I trudged along the dirt path. I thought about Wylene and her struggles in her relationships and how this possession thing with Cato affected her life. I wondered about the future and if there was one that had Danny and me together. In short, my thoughts were all over the place to distract me from the building pain.

I wasn't used to spirits fighting physically; in all my dealings with them before, they were annoying. Moving furniture around, appearing in the least desirable places, and sometimes I could hear them, and they never shut up. That was rarer, though. Cato was a new experience and one I didn't care to repeat. I wanted this wrapped up, for Wylene's sake, Hallie's, and the town.

I hadn't been gone but half an hour, and already Danny had the circle drawn into the earth, and he was carving runes. Whatever their meaning, it was reacting oddly with my magic. Not in a wrong way, just a different feeling than usual. Not that anything about my magic was normal.

"Hey, you better keep this for safety reasons," I called out as I walked up to Danny and held out the vial to him. "You can give me the one for mine too, and I'll get that done."

Danny stood, stretched, which lit my ovaries on fire and sauntered over to me. "Let me have a finger," he held out his hand.

Automatically my hand went to his. It was like my free will disappeared around this man when he used that tone. "I was capable of doing it myself," I replied snidely.

"I know. This way, I can make sure your perfect skin stays intact," Danny kissed my fingertip.

I never even saw the knife or felt the poke. I saw the vial get filled, and then my finger was in the wet heat of Danny's mouth as he sucked on it. "Good god," I moaned. "You're going to kill me."

"We might have time for a treasure hunt before we summon the asshole," Danny whispered in my ear. "There's about an hour and a half before the sun sets, and Travis is going to keep people out of here for us so we'll be alone. Being buried inside you is the holiest experience I've ever had. We can call it the worshipping hour."

I laughed. "Call it whatever you want, as long as it happens. How can I help?" Danny made a low growl in the back of his throat as he closed the space between us. His hard body met my softer one. "I meant how can I help finish the circle. I know how to take care of that already," I grinned and rubbed him through his jeans.

Danny cleared his throat and stepped away. "Right. Yeah, you know how to take care of that," he agreed. "I need an inner circle inside of this larger one. Leave about twelve inches between the two."

"When you say twelve inches, do you mean by a male scale or an actual twelve inches?" I asked teasingly, holding my hands apart dramatically.

Danny grinned and resumed his work while I used a branch to carve out an inner circle. I kept glancing his way every few minutes because it was easy for me to forget that he was a powerful warlock since I usually saw him in his non-magical element of a computer genius. The man was a complete package of yum.

With both of us working, the circle took less time than Danny initially thought it would, and we carefully stepped out and sat on the bench to watch the sunset. I jumped up, remembering I'd brought food for us.

"I have food in the bags I brought," I told him excitedly.

Danny grabbed my hips and brought me down on his lap. "I brought food for us too, and it's right here in this bag. Stay put."

Not one to listen, I shifted and straddled him. "You brought us food?"

Danny groaned long and low. "Are you planning on being my meal?"

"There's merit to that idea," I replied coyly. "However, I need real food and real energy. Also, my ribs hurt like a bitch, so that means I'd need to be on top, and I don't think we should provide sex education for Hallie."

"You'd better stop teasing me then," Danny growled. He lifted me off and set me gently next to him, and he pulled out a bag of food that bore Gage's restaurant's name. "I know this woman who has connections to one of the best chef's around."

I didn't even care what was in the bag. I knew it would be good. "I'd be jealous, but I'm too hungry. You were a busy boy this morning."

"I needed to make sure I was taking good care of

my girlfriend," Danny smiled.

My mouth didn't know whether to go dry or water, and the fluttering in my belly was of indeterminate origin. "Feed me," I requested when I couldn't think of anything else to say.

Danny pulled out two gourmet sandwiches and salad combos and let me choose which of the two I wanted. I figured this would be our last peaceful moment of the evening, knowing that I ate slowly instead of scarfing my food down. I didn't even argue when Danny handed me ibuprofen and had me take those.

Then my mouth happened. "Don't think because I'm not putting up any arguments and letting you tell me what to do that I'll be a docile girlfriend. It's not in my blood. I won't ask permission before I do things."

Danny belted out a laugh. "I don't want docile. I want you."

Huh. I guess that was a good answer. "Okay," I replied lamely. "How's this going to work?"

"Well, I'd think we become exclusive and not see other people. Spend time together, maybe sleep at each other's houses, plan activities to do together. Things like that," Danny gave me a strange look.

I giggled. "I meant the spell." I stood up and gingerly stretched until I felt the twinge of pain that told me to stop. "Cato is messed up in the head. Some of those visions that Wylene showed me, both from his perspective and Halia's, were flat out wrong. There's a line between obsessed and passionate. He was fully on the obsessed side and not seeing things clearly. It wouldn't have surprised me to learn that Halia killed herself to try and escape him; she was that miserable."

"Do you think that's what happened?" Danny rose and stared out at the fading sunset with me.

"No. I didn't get that sense at all from what Wylene

showed me. We might not ever know unless Halia decides to show someone. I got a sense of happiness from the visions where she was with her family. I don't think she would have left them voluntarily," I responded truthfully.

"Tell me," Danny spoke hesitantly. "I know you have another witch, mage, warlock contacts. Would you have sought their help with this instead of me?"

I gave his question serious thought before answering, and my delay in speaking made a crushed look appear on Danny's face. "Don't jump to conclusions. You know I won't pull punches. There is a part of me that says I would have. The reason for that would be to keep you safe and away from the danger I am sure is lurking nearby. The other part of me says that I don't trust others the way I do you. It's a toss-up, but standing here with you, I can honestly say I am glad you are here and not them."

"I'll take it," Danny whispered and gently cupped my face, brushing a tender kiss over my lips.

Chapter Ten

ere's how I envision this working," Danny began once the sun entirely disappeared from the night sky. "I want you to stand in this outer ring here," Danny pointed. "It should keep you safe but separate from being in the ring with Cato because everything we've learned about him says you will be in more danger than I will be. I know that probably rubs you the wrong way, and you will have to deal with it. I'm going to want to keep you safe always."

I sighed, "It doesn't rub me the wrong way. I do want to point out that I want to keep *you* safe as much as you want to keep me safe."

Danny's eyes softened. "Noted. I'll be in the center," he continued. "I'll say the incantation and drop one drop of each of our blood for the protection portion, and the earth magic in your blood should react and light the ring up. I'll move into the summoning chant. That should pull Cato directly into the circle whether he wants to or not, and the circle will lock him in. After he's in with me is when things will get risky. We know he's vengeful and angry and not right in the head. I expect some retaliation. I need to be in the circle with him to perform the ritual where it cuts ties from Wylene and Hallie. Once that is done, I can move to the outer ring with you and do the last part, which is banishing him from this realm."

"It sounds so easy when you say it like that, and I know the reality is much different. I'll follow your lead," I promised and meant it for once. I was out of my element with this. "Please keep yourself safe, Danny."

"I'll keep us both safe, babe," Danny assured me. "You ready to start?" He waited until I nodded before moving next to me. "Give me a kiss for good luck."

It was a request I couldn't deny. I planted a smoldering kiss on Danny's lips and let myself drown in it for a moment before pulling away. "Let's do this and kick the hell out of that bitch."

Danny gave me a goofy grin and saluted. "Got it, boss."

Well, at least he knew who wore the pants in this relationship. I nodded and took my place, where he pointed. "By the way, nice call on the deaf cop thing."

"In this case, it had its advantages," Danny said with a laugh. "Get ready. I'm going to start."

I took up a wide-legged stance and braced for an impact of some sort seeing as how Cato already knocked me off the cliff. I was sure I looked ridiculous, and I didn't give a damn. I wanted this case over with already, and I couldn't believe this had gone on as long as it has, with no one else being the wiser.

I studied the ground closely as Danny chanted in a foreign language, and when I felt the pull in my gut, I didn't fight it. Blazing white light erupted from the earth along the drawn lines of the circle. I almost gave out a victory shout and figured distracting Danny at this critical juncture wouldn't be helpful.

The spoken language Danny was using now sounded different from the first incantation, and the air around us shimmered with a dark hue reminiscent of a portal. My instincts screamed at me to move away before I got sucked into another abyss, and it took every bit of will I had to remain in place. I had zero shame in admitting that air scared the hell out of me.

Hooves thudding over the ground sounded all around me, followed by the bellow of a wretched spirit that made the hair on my arms and neck stand at attention. Whatever Danny was doing was working. The ground shook under me as if a stampede was headed right for us at high speed.

A few seconds later, the massive centaur materialized from the shimmering air and looked dead set on flattening my new boyfriend. It didn't make me overly happy, and my magic reacted accordingly. Beams of fuchsia-colored light shot from my palms, sending me reeling and almost out of the circle.

It wasn't anything Danny had said, but something I already knew. I could *not* break the circle. It would have dire consequences for both of us if that happened. I fought to regain my balance and closed my fists, trying to control the magic and keep it contained.

It had the effect of a charging bull on Cato. He aimed directly for me now, and my eyes bugged out at the sight of the spirit creature galloping toward me. That's not what had my body springing into a rage, though; that would be the sight of Luca, Jameson's father standing in the background calling to Cato.

"Stabit, Cato!" Luca shouted in a Latin command. Dark energy surrounded him in a swirl.

If I hadn't been worried about distracting Danny from doing what he needed to do, I would have roared and unleashed every bit of magic that I could feel gathering under my skin. Instead, I silently waged war on my ex and ducked so I didn't get a centaur dick in my face as Cato sailed over my head, something scratching me.

Danny kept on chanting, but his eyes were bouncing between Cato, me, and Luca in the background. It was easy to see he had about a thousand questions, and now that he was trapped in a magical circle with Cato, there was little he could do about it.

Danny shifted to Latin, the same that Luca had been using, and I knew the cheating, lying bastard of a hybrid demon angel could understand what was about to happen. If Luca is who Cato called upon to help him in his twisted games, I hope the severing of their connection would hurt.

"*Nolite nocere illam Catonis,*" Luca called out again when Cato zeroed in on me.

I knew enough to know Luca had been telling Cato not to hurt me, and the concession did nothing to stem my anger. It did nothing for Danny's state of mind either as he quickly realized that Luca knew me, though he didn't know the extent of that familiarity yet. I hadn't ever taken Danny for the jealous type, and it became evident that the emotion existed within him.

With my attention divided between Danny and Luca, I missed the strike leveled at Danny until I heard the oomph sound and pivoted to see Danny doubled over. He never stopped the chanting, and while he was bent over, I saw him spilling the collected blood onto the ground. That was when all hell broke loose.

Whatever was released blew me back into an invisible barrier that crackled against my skin. I was trapped between two unseen walls and wasn't able to sink to my knees. My movements felt restricted, and my magic was going haywire inside my body. My skin felt like it was peeling apart with the building energy.

Inhuman bellows came from inside the circle and what sounded like a stampede of rhino's, and all I could see was blinding white light. I didn't know if releasing my magic would hurt the process Danny was following or if it would blow-back on me and disintegrate me; it was so strong.

I felt violently sick and like my tongue was sweating something sour when the noises in the circle changed. Now it sounded like a professional boxing match going on in there with the constant sound of blows hitting flesh. I hoped Danny was kicking Cato's ass. That was the last coherent thought I had.

My bones felt like they turned to liquid, and I melted down onto the ground in a hazy cloud of dizziness. I saw Luca standing a foot away with a growing look of concern on his devilishly handsome face. Then there was nothing, only pain and darkness and brimstone cupcakes.

Wait. That wasn't right. Who made cupcakes out of brimstone? That would taste awful. Wherever I was hot enough to produce brimstone. Shit. Did I die and go to hell? There wouldn't be cupcakes in hell, would there? Why was I stuck on cupcakes? I wasn't even hungry.

Though I was getting sleepy listening to the song that someone was singing. It was relaxing, and whoever was touching me was lighting fires in parts of my body that I liked having flames. I began to wish that whoever was caressing me would take my clothes off. Damn, it was hot.

A jolt of searing pain shot through my body like I was being tasered or got struck by lightning. Neither option was high on my choice of things to experience, and it felt like I was going to swallow my tongue. I could feel my body flopping around like a fish out of water, trying to dance to salsa music.

Through the buzzing and static sound in my ears, I heard Danny shout something, then what felt like hooves doing jumping jacks on my belly. I wasn't having a good day. Maybe it was a nightmare, and I just needed to wake up, and then it would all stop. That would be the ideal outcome.

Another blast of what I could only describe as raw electricity shot through me, and this time I know I screamed. Nope, it wasn't a dream, and I still couldn't see.

"Open your eyes, babe," Danny's voice felt like a sensuous sin on my ears. "Look at me, Risa."

All I could do was incoherently mumble, which meant I wasn't dead. I felt my eyelids pried open and saw Luca's face poised above mine. That did it. My eyes flew open the rest of the way on their own, and I tried to sit up. That was when I realized I was cuffed.

"What the fuck?" I yelled, assuming the worst.

Danny made a shushing noise and shoved Luca out of the way. "It's okay, sweetheart. I used my cuffs on you to stop your magic from lashing out. It's out of control," Danny explained gently.

I calmed marginally. "We're using these later for different reasons," I croaked, my throat feeling raw and like I'd eaten sandpaper. Or brimstone. I turned my head to glare at Luca. "If the taste of brimstone is in my mouth because you did something to me, I am going to castrate you."

"Brown hair doesn't look right on you, beautiful," Luca reached out and fingered my hair. "Now shut the fuck up, behave for once, and let me heal you."

Irrational, insane rage bubbled up out of me, and my innate mixed-blood strength kicked in, and I broke free from whoever was gripping me. "Put your hands on me, and I will feed you to a siren."

"Relax, beautiful, I've already had my hands on you, and your clothes were disappearing," Luca sneered. "Just like old times."

"Another comment like that, and I'll take those cuffs off her and vouch for whatever lie she tells the cops when we report your dead body," Danny growled menacingly. "Babe, you have some type of poison in your blood from the scratch that Cato gave you. This asshole is going to heal you, then disappear before I permanently remove him from existence."

That idea sounded appealing to me. "Get it over with," I demanded. "If your hands roam, you will regret it."

Chapter Eleven

A week later, Danny and I sat in my office waiting for Wylene to show up. It had taken me a week to get over whatever had been introduced into my bloodstream, and just as long for Danny to get over the experience of banishing Cato, meeting one of my exes, and nursing me back to health. We did have some fun with that last one.

To my surprise, Wylene walked in with Travis, and I wasn't sure what to think about that. Danny got up out of the chair and moved to stand behind me, leaning against the wall while Travis and Wylene sat down.

"I thought since he was there that night, he could hear what the wrap-up would be," Wylene offered up the explanation. "I'm glad to see that you are okay. I was worried."

I frowned, puckering my lips, "I remember hearing singing. Were you there?"

"Only at the end when they were trying to heal you. I sang to relax you because Danny was on the verge of a mental break seeing you in distress like you were," Wylene smiled gently at me. "So what happened? They were all fairly tight-lipped with me on details."

That made sense. "Danny would have to tell you most of the details. I can tell you that who Cato made a bargain with was one of my exes, half-angel, half-demon, and father of my youngest."

I didn't need to turn and look to know that Danny tensed up. He'd gotten that way every time we discussed the details of that night. He'd given me enough information to know that Luca had been running his hands over my body in ways that belied his claims of searching for injuries and using his demon magic to seduce.

Danny cleared his throat and began to give Wylene a rundown of the night after she left and the steps he took to sever the connection Cato had made to her and Halia's bloodline. He described the process in a way she understood, which I thought was a nice touch. I'd seen him use terms no one understood when he was irritated and wanted the conversation over.

"When I arrived, you were pretty beat up yourself," Wylene stated. "Are you healed now?"

"I am. Thanks for asking. Risa's son came over and took care of me," Danny shifted behind me.

"You never did tell me how Glimmering Rock came to be," I reminded the siren.

"Oh, I was going to do that, wasn't I?" Wylene hesitated only a moment. "You know the rock out in the cove at Nymph's Point?"

I nodded. "The one that the waves break on."

Wylene nodded. "The waves breaking on it aren't what gives the town its name," she bit her lip. "The name happened not long after they created the town and were calling it Haven. I was fresh from Scylla, the island in the Mediterranean, and not over my old ways quite yet. A pirate had anchored off-shore, and his crew was rowing them in. I could hear their conversations about finding women to have their ways with since they'd been at sea for so long. Nothing wrong with that in the grand scheme of things if they were looking for willing partners. However, the talk was not geared that way. I landed on that rock and began to sing. You saw what happens when I do that. It was my last great feast, and I painted that rock red with their blood. When the sun started to lower in the sky, it glimmered off the rock and cast a lovely glow that captured some town folk's attention. Thus, the name changed from Haven to Glimmering Rock to serve as a warning to those who wish harm."

I gaped at the women. "You are my hero. No, wait. You're the tits." I was determined to get that phrase right and in the proper context.

Travis's eyes fell to Wylene's chest at the comment, and Wylene flushed.

"In my opinion, you two have gone above and beyond to solve this. I can't tell you how happy it makes me not to feel violated by Cato's thoughts and having the urges to masturbate or strip down and climb someone at the most inopportune times," Wylene breathed a sigh of relief. "It's nice to feel my own urges," the siren said with a glance at Travis.

I grinned and fought the instinct to ask how he was; it wasn't my business, even if I was curious. "I'm glad we could help, and I can easily admit I couldn't have done this case without Danny. Though, I can freely say that I could have done without knowing you've, uh, touched his junk."

Danny coughed, and Travis raised his eyebrows. Wylene quickly asked for the bill, passed me her credit card, and then asked if I wanted to meet for dinner later that week as friends this time. I agreed, and then she rushed Travis out the door.

Danny prowled around my desk and locked the door, then gave me that predatory look. Instant reaction. "I agree that flat brown hair isn't your best look; however, this red and black you are sporting right now is hot."

"Sex and power," I quipped automatically.

"Yeah," Danny moved towards me. "We've had fun in my office. I think it's time we broke yours in."

"Wait," I held up my hand. "Am I going to run into any more of your ex-lovers?"

"Am I?" Danny fired back, not slowing until he was inches from me. "How about neither of us answers that right now, and we cross that bridge if we come to it."

The heat coming off his body was distracting. I could live with those terms since I was sure I had more of those annoyances that had seen me naked than he did. "Yeah, okay," I relented. "Watch out for that chair. It's evil."

Book 4
Cop Out

Chapter One

I had just wrapped up two cheating spouse cases this week, and I appreciated their simplicity after the case with my new friend Wylene where I almost kissed my ass goodbye a few times. My bank account had money in it; my sex life was flourishing, my sons were all happy, life was good.

None of that explained why I was restless and undressing with my eyes, every man I saw. I factually knew it had nothing to do with this magical puberty thing Ax, a former client and now friend, had planted in my mind. I think it was more that I was reacting to being in a relationship. Something in my brain rebelled against that thought, and, for the lack of a better term, I was eye-fucking every male specimen that crossed my sight and some females to boot.

It was completely irrational and childish. Another fact I knew. That was why I was on my hands and knees scrubbing my office floor as if I were about to perform surgery and needed a sterile environment. I'd already organized my files, cleaned out my desk, balanced my books, and followed up with potential clients.

I'd started to look at my desk chair to see if I could fix it, but I swear that piece of furniture was sending bad omens at me if I dared to touch it. It wasn't healthy to have a fear of your chair, was it? I had considered moving it to be a client chair; then I thought about a new client getting launched across the room, and I saw lawsuits, so I left it alone.

I looked at my watch for the fourth time in two minutes. I despised cleaning like this. My preferred way was to have someone else do it while I did literally anything else. Yet, it was working at keeping me from doing something stupid.

I've been a supernatural/paranormal investigator for over a hundred years now, you'd think I have seen everything there is to see, yet in the past month, the weirdness level has gone through the roof. My youngest son Jameson believes it's because my magic is awakening, and I can handle another level of what the hell.

That reminded me, I needed to call my parents and see if they knew anything about this and if Ax and Jameson were correct. Honestly, it was a reason to get off the floor and stop cleaning. I'd deal with a phone call to my parents to get out of that. My magic should be a priority, right? So why was I still on my knees cleaning the dingy floor?

Probably because avoidance should be my middle name, I love my parents; I do. I was happy that they lived far away from me in some magical commune living their hippy lifestyle and not telling me how to live my slightly more organized life. The possibility existed that I wasn't ready to admit that I was in a relationship either.

It wasn't that I was ashamed of Danny; that wasn't the problem at all. It was more I was afraid to lose something that I valued. If I kept it quiet, maybe the fates wouldn't learn of it and snatch it away from me. My grandpa told me that if love didn't scare you, it wasn't really love that you felt. It meant you needed to get laid.

Losing—or potentially losing—Danny scared the gallivanting cloven hooves in my chest right out. That scared me even more. I never felt this way about any of the three fathers of my children. It was that reality that had me down on the floor scrubbing as if I was trying to wash the devil out of existence. It wasn't working.

All that I was doing was making my hair expand with the humidity I was creating. That was my polite way of saying I was sweaty and gross feeling. Huffing out a puff of air to get the hair out of my face, I sat back on my heels and surveyed the floor. No amount of scrubbing was going to make this dump shine. A polished turd was still a turd, as my father liked to say.

I could do with a break, so I stood and stretched, then sat on the corner of my desk, balefully glaring at the chair that hated me. With a heavy sigh, I reached for my desk phone and punched in the number I'd had memorized for years and rarely used. Lifting the receiver to my ear, I listened to the ringing.

It was probably wrong to hope no one answered, and I was sure it painted me in a bad daughter light. The truth was, I missed my parents. However, I didn't like hearing about their sex life or telling me each human ailment they were sure they had contracted. I don't know when they turned hypochondriac, but I wasn't too fond of it.

"'Ello," my dad's voice floated across the line.

My throat seized up for a moment. I cleared it with a croak. "Hi, Dad," I got out. "How are you?"

"Peanut! Is that you?" my dad crowed. My childhood nickname hit me harder than the sound of his voice had.

"Yeah, Dad, it's Risa," I chuckled, reminding him of my name. He was eight hundred this year; it was just as likely he had forgotten my name.

"Honey! Our baby is on the phone!" my dad yelled excitedly. "Peanut, I'm going to put you on the speaker thing!"

I couldn't help the smile that spread across my face. My dad's exuberance was contagious. "You don't have to yell, Dad. I can hear you fine. How are things over there? Are you and Mom living your best life?"

"Oh, we sure are," my dad yelled like he was trying to be heard without the phone. "Your mom and I took up strip poker."

I slapped the heel of my hand into my forehead and wrinkled my face. "Boundaries, Dad," I tried to remind him. "A daughter doesn't need to hear those things."

"I spanked him, honey," my mom, Cimi's, more reasonably volumed voice came next. "Literally and figuratively."

I groaned and shook my head. "I'm glad to hear you all are doing well. The boys are fine. I'm good."

"The boys all call us, so we knew they were okay," my mom's tone changed to slightly accusatory. Not that I didn't deserve it.

"I know, I'm a shit," I confessed and rolled my eyes. "I've got a family history question I need to ask."

"Ask away, Peanut," my dad shouted.

"Zeke, lower your voice," my mom tried. "Risa can hear you fine. You're going to make my ears bleed."

"Sorry, Cimi," Zeke quieted his tone. "What's going on, Risa?"

"This is going to sound odd, but did anyone in our family develop late?" I asked slowly, unsure of how to word the question.

"I'm assuming you aren't talking about boobies," my mom sounded confused.

"I doubt it, honey; Risa developed those quickly. Can you give us more to go on, Peanut?" Bless my dad and the fact that he is half a world away from me.

"I meant magic," I clarified. I shook my head at myself for not specifying that in my original question. "I have odd things happening. For example, in a couple of cases, I've wished for something, and my magic made it happen. Plus, my hair is changing colors with my moods."

"Wow," my dad exclaimed. "I remember my grandma having something similar but it was her fingernails, and not her hair."

"Me too," my mom added. "It was my grandpa, though. He didn't have anything that changed colors, but his magic developed later in life, and he was quite powerful. I always knew you'd grow into it, Risa."

"Even if she didn't, it doesn't matter, Cimi. Peanut is skilled in other ways. Speaking of skills, Gage told us you were in a relationship," my dad teased.

"Dad," I groaned again and rolled my eyes. "If I don't want to hear about your sex life, that means I am not willing to discuss mine. Yes, I have a boyfriend. His name is Danny."

Whatever was happening on the other end of the phone, I heard my mom squeal and giggle. "That's great news, Risa."

"Go do whatever made mom make that noise, just hang up the phone first," I pleaded. "I'll talk to you guys later. I'm going to go enjoy my magical puberty."

My dad laughed, "Nice name for it, Peanut. We'll talk to you soon. Please don't wait so long between calls, daughter. We miss hearing your voice."

My mom let out another sound that told me my dad was getting frisky with her. "Okay, Dad. Love to you both. Take care."

I couldn't hang up the phone fast enough. It was time for me to return to cleaning the floor to get those sounds out of my mind.

Chapter Two

There were three inches left of floor to clean when my office door burst open and smacked me right in the ass. "Hey!" I cried out without turning around. "If you are going to spank me, then at least pull my hair and tell me to ride like a cowgirl!"

"I can provide the cows," a male replied from behind me with a laugh.

I dropped my chin to my chest. "If it isn't my favorite non-mistake. Hi, Ivan. What brings you by?" I sat back on my heels again and looked over my shoulder.

"Can't a guy drop in and say hi to a beautiful woman on her knees?" Ivan joked. "Half the work is done already."

I belted out a laugh at that. "Well, you aren't my client now. However, Danny might not be so happy about that."

Ivan grinned, "No. He wouldn't be. Congrats to the happy couple, by the way. I stopped by to introduce a friend who is looking for some help. I'll be quick with the warning since he's on his way inside. He was on the phone when I left him in the lot. He suspects about your world but doesn't know for sure."

"Got it. Thanks for the referral. I'd say I owe you one, but given my situation with me on my knees, you could take it the wrong way," I told Ivan with a wink.

Ivan held his hand out and helped me to my feet when his friend walked in. If not for Danny, this guy would be the mistake I made after Ivan. He filled out his police uniform nicely, and I wasn't nervous about letting my eyes roam. To be fair, I usually wasn't shy about that.

Ivan held back his laughter. "Your secret is safe with me. Chad, this is Risa, the private investigator I told you about that helped me recover my missing cows."

"Hi, Risa. Ivan speaks highly about you. He failed to mention how beautiful you are," Chad smiled and held his hand out for me to shake. He was a charmer.

Soft skin, clean nails, a few scars, and a firm grip without being overpowering. "Hi, Chad. If frizzy, sweaty, big hair is your thing, then I guess I fit the beautiful bill."

Ivan chuckled again. "Tell Danny I said hi." Ivan patted Chad on the shoulder and walked out.

Wanting to keep some distance between us, I moved around my desk to sit down. I logically knew that the reason my hormones went all out of control was my brain was trying to rebel against my relationship status. I could look, though, and if the desk were between us, it would be harder to touch.

There was something to be said about a man in uniform. The same could be said of a man out of uniform, too, I decided. I tamped down the need to ask him to take it off so I could verify and lowered myself into the despicable chair without a cautionary thought.

Instead of depositing me on my ass in some embarrassing fashion, the dreadful thing catapulted me forward like I was in a slingshot. I landed half on my desk and half-almost in Chad's lap with the items on my desk scattering in every direction while the chair sat there looking innocent.

"Damn! Are you okay?" Chad jumped to his feet and tried to help me back up.

"Fine," I grumbled. "I might have a bonfire later with that chair."

"It could be a bad cylinder," Chad peered around me and told me with a helpful tone. "Would you like me to see if I could fix it?"

"No, that won't be necessary. I'll fix that bastard right up, one of these days," I mumbled and began picking up the things from my desk and unwittingly presenting my ass to Chad.

Chad cleared his throat, "Well, I can't say I mind the view, but would you like some help?"

I righted myself and noticed a red-tipped strand of hair falling in my face. "No. Keep your cute little ass right in that chair and tell me about yourself."

"I have a cute ass, huh? It's the uniform, isn't it?" Chad asked flirtatiously. "Ivan told me you don't sleep with clients, but he did say you can dish it out with the best of them. I'm not disappointed. Okay, about me. As you can see, I'm a cop for Branstone. I moonlight on the side as an adventure guide for the weekend warrior type of tourist. Kayaking, hiking, snow-shoeing, rappelling, or rock climbing, that sort of thing."

"Wow, okay, one-stop shopping, I understand," I replied, checking him out again as I put stuff back on my desk. "My curiosity is getting the best of me. What brings a cop to a private investigator?"

Chad started to fidget in his chair like fire ants were biting his nuts. "This is confidential, right?"

I nodded slowly. "If you hire me, the only other one that will be privy to information is my partner. There's a confidentiality clause written into the contract. Aside from that, technically, there is nothing to keep me from speaking about this visit if you don't hire me. That said, I don't operate that way. I don't spread information. I seek it."

Chad coughed into his fist. "I'm a skeptic about

anything paranormal, as some say. A skeptic might be putting it mildly, but there you have it. Yet something happened on my last adventure gig that I would get laughed out of the department for bringing up. I don't do the woo-woo stuff."

Not wanting to get relaunched across my desk, I sat down slowly this time and vowed revenge on the demon possessing that chair if something happened again. When all I heard was a squeak, I relaxed.

"Okay," I returned my attention to the cute cop. "What happened?"

"Uh, it's like this. Adrenaline, nature, and accomplishing something tends to have an effect on females that put them in a mood," Chad blushed a little. "Usually, they hit on me afterward, like at the top of a hike, and I'm not one to turn away a good time. It's all consensual and above-board, and I nicely turn down the married ladies. I'm not a jerk."

I bit back a laugh. "Got it. Man-whore adrenaline junkie that likes to get it on in nature. I'm going to assume that's not the problem that brought you in here."

Chad chuckled and grinned, "No. Man-whore might be stretching it since it's not every time I take someone on an adventure. I mean, dudes hire me too, and that doesn't interest me. Though, Ivan was right about your sense of humor. I like it. Okay, anyway, last weekend, I took two females out to Shadow Mountain. There is a nice rock face for beginner climbers and a cave at the top where you can light a fire and roast a marshmallow, and the Widow's Waterfall is close. So close you can see the edge of it from the cave's mouth."

I knew the place that Chad was describing. "You call that a beginner climb?"

"It is. There are a lot of holds, and the way the waterfall comes down leaves that section of the cliff dry, so there isn't a lot of risk of slipping and falling from wet rock," Chad explained. "Regardless, these two had enough experience that it wouldn't be an issue, and the view is unbeatable up there. I've been up there tons of times and never had anything weird happen."

Widow's Waterfall was rumored to be haunted by the woman who murdered her cheating husband and threw him from that very cliff. I didn't tell Chad that, but I wondered if the legends were true if something happened.

"Things were starting to heat up with these ladies," Chad went on. "They stripped down and were on the ledge rinsing off with the spray from the waterfall. They wanted me to join them, but the water was a bit cold, and they'd already voiced their request for some side action. Cold water would have slowed that down, you know?"

I snorted and tried to cover it up. "Nothing weird, so far."

"Not yet. I leaned against the opposite side and watched, safety reasons and all that," Chad added quickly. "I was in their sight the whole time, and they were putting on a show for me. When we moved back to the cave, their clothes were gone. That was the first weird thing. I've searched that cave, and there is no way out or any other access to it. Where did the clothes go?" Chad shrugged.

"Interesting. Is that all?" I leaned forward with my elbows on the desk, wanting more details.

Chad cocked an eyebrow at me but continued. "We had free-climbed up, and they wanted to rappel down. Cool, right? I had the equipment strapped to me; no big deal. The gear was untouched, but the clothes were gone. They thought I was playing around with them and blew it off, but I was perturbed. They distracted me fast enough with the offer of a three-way, and I lost focus for a while. Well, not lost focus but instead had my focus shifted to more entertaining avenues. That is until something snapped the back of my nuts."

Now my eyebrows raised. "I'm going to go out on a limb and guess it wasn't one of the women."

"Correct," Chad confirmed sarcastically. "Their positioning made that impossible. I swear I heard someone cackling when it happened too. That brought my focus back to the missing clothes, and that made sense to me that someone else was up there because where else would the clothes have gone? Regardless, my attention diverted off that thought in a matter of seconds as things came to a happy conclusion for all three of us. Then we noticed that my clothes had disappeared too."

"Now all of the clothes are gone?" I had completely forgotten to take any notes on this. I was too busy trying to picture the scenario.

"All of them. Yet the gear remained, and it had been sitting on top of the clothes. It makes no sense. I grabbed my headlamp and wandered back into the cave to see if someone was punking us or something, which would have pissed me off, but we would have our clothes back. I found nothing. Shit wasn't funny anymore. I've done a lot of things, a lot of stupid things too, but I've never rappelled naked with my junk dangling from a harness. The only positive is that I stow a backpack at the bottom that has extra clothes in it, and I wanted to get to it," Chad told me emphatically.

I was picturing Danny rappelling naked. Talk about distracted. I blinked slowly and remembered that I was supposed to be taking notes. I grabbed my notepad, wrote down the missing clothes, and injured nuts details along with the location.

Chad's eyes darted to the notepad, and he winced a little. "It wasn't until I was helping the women strap their harnesses on that they noticed the welts on my back. They thought it was from them, and then I remembered something hitting my nuts, and I somehow think they are related, but I can't figure out how or where the clothes went. Anyway, I went over the cliff first because they wanted to make sure the rope wouldn't break. Once the women saw all was good, they passed me and, despite being naked, were hooting the whole way."

Oh, how I wished Danny and I had been out in nature that day. I would have recorded that spectacle. I so badly wanted to laugh and secretly planned a way to get Danny naked outside and then hide his clothes.

"I was almost home free and able to get to the backpack when the line broke," Chad relayed. "Only mine. It was a brand-new line, too—no reason for it to break. I've used more frayed lines on sharper rocks and haven't had anything happen. I damn near shit myself when I was suddenly free-falling to the ground, naked. In that span of a second, I covered my junk and hoped for the best. After I landed, the rope and the carabiner came down and landed on my chest."

That told me that someone had indeed been up there with them but not visible. It could be a ghost, but I wasn't leaning that way. "Were you hurt?"

"Not seriously, other than my pride," Chad admitted. "Bruised and scratched mostly. I keep in shape and have taken worse falls than that, only with a barrier of clothing."

"I take it that means you want me to find out who took your clothes and caused you to fall?" I asked, wondering how in the hell I would spin this for someone who didn't believe in the paranormal and wasn't sure of this world.

"Yeah," Chad replied softly. "Do you see why I couldn't take this to the department? Ivan said you wouldn't bat an eye at the weird shit."

I *was* the weird shit. I couldn't tell Chad that,

though. "Okay, you are right. The department would have laughed you out of the precinct." I pulled out a contract and slid it across the desk. "Weird shit doesn't faze me, have no fear. I'm not going to climb the rock to investigate. If I remember right, there's a trail that leads up near there."

Chad nodded. "There is. It doesn't go to the cave. I can always meet you up there and rappel you down."

I considered that option, and it intrigued me. "I'd be up there with my partner, Danny. Does the offer include him too?"

"Of course," Chad answered quickly.

"Naked?" I asked hopefully.

Chad burst out laughing. "Isn't Danny your boyfriend?"

I nodded. "Danny can be naked too. I mean, really, it would even the score since you saw my chair throw me across my desk and smash my boobs up into my face, and you stared at my ass."

"I don't think that's even since your boobs were clothed, as was your ass," Chad pointed out. "Which, I am going to take the risk and say is as cute as mine is."

"Sweet talker," I grinned. "Fine, clothed it is. You should market naked rappelling; you'd probably get a lot of takers."

"Maybe," Chad agreed. "But I can't say I want to be below a dude and watching his junk dangle above me. Or, even worse, get the client that is so scared they pee."

Chapter Three

I can't lie. I kept picturing Chad naked. For sure, it was wrong, but it was enticing, not to mention funny in a twisted way. I was on my way to Danny's for dinner and to discuss the new case. My errant thoughts would only benefit him since I was working myself up. I mean, I'd reap the benefits too. Where was I going with this?

I switched gears and thought about the phone call with my parents and would have to get on Gage's case for spilling my secrets. Not that Danny was a secret, was he? Nah, I was open about seeing him. Maybe not as free as Danny was, but I was trying.

Damn, all thoughts led back to Danny, and I wasn't sure what that translated to in the mess that I call a brain. I didn't want to invest the time trying to figure it out either. Not when I had a new case to work on, one that featured a good-looking man who got freaky in nature and rappelled naked, even if it wasn't by choice.

Focus! The easy answer was the widow's ghost, though it didn't feel right in this instance. Spirits couldn't make clothes disappear. They could hide them, move them, ruin them, but they couldn't make them outright disappear like that. A mage could, or someone that could move between realms.

Mages didn't typically hide out in caves, which

would mean one would have been following Chad. That didn't feel right either since Chad was non-magical and lived and worked in Branstone. Several residents of Glimmering Rock traveled to Branstone, so it wasn't unrealistic to think one encountered Chad along the way. Maybe Chad gave them a parking ticket or arrested them.

I was thankful it wasn't another cheating spouse case. They paid the bills, but man, those were brainless. Those cases' only creative thing was finding somewhere to pee while staking the cheater out to get the incriminating photos.

I thumped my fist on the steering wheel in frustration. I wasn't getting anywhere with these thoughts, and my mind was all jumbled up, probably from smelling the cleaner I used on the floor today. That was going to be my excuse, and nothing would change my mind about it.

I pulled up into Danny's driveway and parked. Staying the night was out of the equation since I didn't have a change of clothes, which was fine with me. I had a case that needed my attention and my thoughts. Of course, that didn't mean I wouldn't take advantage of the sexy warlock at the first opportunity that presented itself.

I didn't bother knocking and let myself in. "Danny!" I called out.

"Kitchen," came the answer.

I followed my nose that was smelling the roasted garlic wafting on the air. My stomach rumbled in response to the scent of dinner. "What did you make? It smells divine."

Danny turned to face me, wearing an apron and a grin. "I made dinner," he laughed at my unamused expression. "Roasted chicken, garlic mashed potatoes, and salad."

"Wow, you went all out," I commented and sidled up to the counter to snatch a piece of lettuce.

"I hear Ivan spanked you today," Danny fired back.

"I'm so happy you aren't the jealous type," I winked in return. "Technically, the door spanked me. Ivan was just the cause of it."

"Technically, you are a flirt, don't cop-out. I'm okay with it since that's how you got me," Danny grinned and winked. "That doesn't mean I don't get jealous."

Awkward. "I called Ivan my favorite non-mistake," I blurted out honestly.

Danny laughed. "I know. He ratted himself out already. He brought you a new case?"

Ah, the offered escape. I took it. "Ivan did. We might have to go rappelling naked."

That got him to pause and raise his eyebrows. "I imagine the chafing would be bad." Danny poured me a glass of wine and handed it to me. "Explain."

I took a large swallow and then filled him in on the things Chad told me and how we would need to go check out that cave. "Chad offered to meet us up there and guide us on rappelling down, so we didn't have to hike back out. I asked if we could do it naked."

Danny chuckled and shook his head before turning back to the counter. "Let's go with the clothing. How was the rest of your day?"

"Oh, I called and talked to my parents too," I remembered. "I wanted to ask about the magic thing to see if it has happened anywhere else in my family."

Danny started carrying dishes over to the table, and when I didn't answer immediately, he turned to ask, "Did it?"

"I think so. Neither parent was too clear on it. From the sounds of it, one on each side had a grandparent that blossomed late," I repeated. "One of them was quite powerful. I remember hearing stories about the feats they would pull off and how they were revered by so many."

"That sounds like a good thing, Risa," Danny told me, circling his arm around my waist from behind. "Did you tell Jameson? Oh, and by the way, Gage asked me if he could hire me to do some digital digging."

I mulled that thought over before taking a sip of wine and stepping away from Danny. What would Gage want to dig up, and on who? "No, I haven't spoken to either of them today. Did you accept the work from Gage?"

I wondered why he wouldn't have asked me for help; I'm his mother. I began to pace a small kitchen section while Danny walked around me, setting the table. He hadn't answered me yet, and I started to think he accepted the work.

"I didn't let him hire me, relax, Risa. I showed him some tips on how he could do the digging on his own without crossing any lines. I offered to help him if he ran into roadblocks or if things didn't make sense or he found nothing. I didn't ask who he was looking into either, before you ask," Danny's calm voice irritated me for some odd reason.

"Why?" I bluntly asked.

"Why did he ask me and not you?" Danny clarified as he walked past me again.

"Yes, that." I stomped my foot angrily, knowing it was childish, and not caring.

"You are too close to the situation to be impartial," Danny replied slowly. "Don't take that to mean that I know what is going on. I am assuming that is the reason. Gage is sensitive, and he would know that his asking you for that type of help would worry you."

I hated that he made sense. Even worse, my thoughts were irrational enough for me not to have come to the same conclusion myself. Instead of responding, I dropped into my chair at the table.

"Tell me more about Chad," Danny tried to distract

my mind as he sat down across from me.

"He's fun to flirt with," I announced automatically and then realized what I'd said. "Shit. Sorry." I was an absolute ass.

Danny only laughed. "I gathered that he caught your attention by the suggestion of us naked rappelling with him as our guide."

"I didn't act on it," I offered up feebly and filled my plate with food.

"I know," Danny replied gently. "Other than going up to see for yourself, do you have other thoughts about what could be going on?"

I shrugged. "I'll talk to Mick and see if he has heard of anything in that area. I know wolves roam through there since it's remote."

The last time I'd seen Mick, he was in the middle of getting his rocks off, and since that man was panty-melting hot, you know I looked. I felt heat spreading across my face from the memory. From the moment I'd met Mick, the local pack leader and member of the town council, sexual tension snapped between us. His attitude kept me away, but I'd be lying if I said I didn't want to sample the goods. Yep, for sure, I was an ass.

"Not a bad idea," Danny agreed. He ate his food for a few minutes before clearing his throat. "I know we are in a relationship, and I am aware that it's been a while since you were in one. I don't expect you to change who you are because we are together. I love that you are fun and flirty, wild, and free. I'm not going to lie and say I haven't looked at other females, but I can tell you that it's all it was. I looked, appreciated the beauty, and still find them lacking because they aren't you. All I ask is that you don't touch or let them touch you."

Several emotions lit my blood, and jealousy was the first. "Who did you look at?" The part where he said he'd found them lacking seemed to slip through the cracks of my mind.

"Whoa," Danny cried in alarm. "Your hair is turning green. We got drowned in a pool of bird shit on my clean truck the last time that happened. I wasn't interested in them, Risa."

Breathe, I reminded myself. I was a hypocrite. "Sorry. I'm in control. I won't touch anyone," I lamely promised and shoved more food in my mouth before I inserted my foot. I'd already admitted I did the same thing to Chad, and Danny wasn't flying off the handle, turning green.

Danny sighed but let it go. "If there's a portal up there, do you think if we had safety rope tied to each other that we would be able to pull the other back through?"

"Theoretically, I suppose," I drawled, wondering. "I'm not sure it's a portal, though, or Chad or anyone else wandering around up there would have stumbled through it and disappeared. Or we would have heard tales about it. I'm more leaning towards a hidden door that leads out of the cave or to another area where someone could hide and wait it out."

"Want me to do more research on Widow's Waterfall?" Danny offered. "Maybe the old widow is up there making mischief."

"Possibly," I tentatively agreed. "Seems a lot more prankster like though than a scorned woman. A woman rumored to have killed her cheating husband and threw him over the waterfall would more likely cause harm than steal clothes while people got busy with the slap and tickle."

"I'd say a smack on the back of your nuts was harmful," Danny mused.

"Some are into that," I reminded him with a wink.

Danny's mouth fell open. "Don't tell me more, and

please don't slap my nuts."

With a laugh, the tension fell away, and we finished our dinner and helped ourselves to each other for dessert—no complaints from me with that menu choice.

Chapter Four

I parked in the front of Blue Balls, the pack club that bordered Branstone and Glimmering Rock. Mick's motorcycle was parked in its usual spot, so I knew he was here. I didn't know if he had company in his office, and my promise to Danny hung right in the front of my mind.

Mick and I weren't interested in each other beyond wanting to fuck. It was something I'd never taken off the table with him and teased him with when I wanted information. I also knew that Mick would push the issue but never force it, which gave me a bit of confidence when dealing with the massive wolf shifter.

I put my usual swagger into my step as I walked into the pool hall, immediately noticing my one-time mistake, Chuck, in his customary place. Ignoring his sneer, I sauntered up to the town medium and seer, Crowley, and gave him a little hug.

"Hey, Crowley. Are you winning?" I asked after he patted my back.

"No, unfortunately. This little lady," he pointed at the six-foot-tall woman he was playing with, "is kicking my old carcass like a deflated soccer ball."

I snickered at the little lady comment because she looked like an Amazon. "Well, good luck with that. Have you heard any unusual stories about the cave up by

Widow's Waterfall?" I took a chance with the question.

"Nothing other than it's haunted," Crowley confirmed. "I see that there's something different about you," Crowley squinted as he gave me a once-over. "Whatever it is, it screams not to mess with you. Good on you, girlie."

Interesting. I pecked Crowley on the cheek and made my way to the back room, where I guessed Mick was since I didn't see him out shooting pool with any of the guys. I did notice a bunch of blue uniforms in the non-magical side gathered around a table, though I didn't see Chad among them.

As I approached Mick's office, I slowed my step and knocked on the door this time instead of barging in. At the barked command to enter, I opened the door in my typical fashion, plastered a smarmy grin on my face, and stepped through.

Mick was alone, and the office had the smell of stale sex, greasy food, and beer. Mick was standing in front of a file cabinet, wearing a skin-tight white tank top, jeans that hugged his tight ass, and his standard black boots. All in all, it was a sexy sight that made juices flow.

"What do you want, Risa?" Mick growled out in a tired-sounding voice.

"Looking for information," I answered, surprised. "You okay?"

"Do you care?" Mick turned and leaned a shoulder against the file cabinet, his biceps popping.

I scowled in return, irritated that he thought I didn't. "Yeah, asshole, I do," I admitted, surprising both of us.

"Word on the street is you committed yourself to that poor sap of a warlock," Mick verbally jabbed at me. "Why would you care what happens to me?"

"Because I'm an asshole, but an asshole with feelings," I snapped back. "Fine, don't tell me. I came to ask about the cave up near Widow's Waterfall."

Mick cocked an eyebrow at me. His gaze raked over me with that steamy look in his eyes that didn't help my flowing juice situation. "What specifically?" he finally asked with his eyes resting on my chest.

"They don't speak," I retorted, refusing to give in to the urge to cross my arms over my boobs.

"Are you cold, Risa?" Mick asked huskily. "I've got some ways to warm you up."

Damn the man. I wasn't going to be the woman who cheated on Danny. "Don't get too close, Mick; you might get burned. Have any of your pack reported strange things from that area? Or seen anything out of the ordinary?"

"I'm guessing you are looking for an answer other than people rappelling naked," Mick moved to sit in his desk chair.

I couldn't help but feel slightly jealous that his chair accepted him and didn't fling him around like a rag doll. I also didn't comment on the naked rappelling. "Anything supernatural or paranormal," I clarified.

"Not that I've heard," Mick relented. "Should I warn the pack? Is something dangerous up there?"

"I don't know," I answered, shrugging. "If there is, I'll share the information, so no one gets hurt."

"I'd appreciate that," Mick's voice went back to tired. "I had a female wolf go missing yesterday, though not in that area."

I hadn't heard that. "Where was the female last seen?"

"Other end of town, eastern border area. The girl's parents notified me she hadn't come back from a date, and they have no idea who the date was with, only that she was going to meet him out there," Mick told me with a frown.

"I'll keep a lookout," I offered. "Do you have a picture?"

Mick shoved a photo across his desk of a stunning teenager with raven black hair and piercing green eyes. "I appreciate the help. She's not responding to any commands I issue, but I don't think she's dead."

That *was* concerning. "I'll let Danny know too. He can work some computer magic to see if he can pick up on any chat. What's her name?" I made a mental note to ask Ax, my sasquatch friend, to keep an eye out for anything since he was in that area.

"Maggie," Mick's eyes took on a hard edge. "I don't think it's a shifter, Risa."

Well damn. "Okay. As a safety precaution, can you let any of your pack know that I'll be in the Widow's Waterfall area and for them to be careful? I don't think it's dangerous, but I've thought that before. A non-magical cop will be there as well."

Mick nodded his confirmation, and I knew he was letting his pack know not to be visible. "Thanks for the heads up. If anyone learns of anything weird, I'll be in touch."

That was my cue to leave. I stood up and made my way out of the office. "I'll utilize some of my contacts about Maggie."

"Thanks. Your ass looks great in those jeans," Mick fired off at me before I was out of eyesight. "And don't think I didn't notice the power rolling off of you."

I let out a peal of laughter as I walked back into the pool hall in disbelief that I'd gotten off that easy with the alpha. "Later, Crowley," I called out as I made my way to the front door, where Chuck was still sitting, eyeing me hungrily.

I gave a sassy flip of my hair and, too late, realized that my magic was reacting to the look on Chuck's face when I saw the ends of my hair a hot pink color. I assumed that was some sort of contemptuous feeling as Chuck evoked that emotion in me.

With my hand motion's downward swing, a torrent of what I assumed was the equivalent of napalm shot from my palm, dousing the douchebag. Chuck's girl-like squeal and shout of pain brought Mick barreling out of the hallway, and he tackled me right out of the front door.

I tucked into a ball and rolled with it as we thumped the ground and landed in the parking lot. I heard someone crashing through the door after us, yet my concentration was on the man whose head had landed between my legs. I can't say that it isn't a position I've fantasized about finding him in, but not in these circumstances.

"Tell me you didn't openly attack a member of my pack in my club," Mick growled, pushing to his elbows but not moving from his spot between my legs.

"No, it wasn't intentional," I shifted, not wanting to draw his attention to my crotch. "You know how you said you noticed the power? I've been calling it magical puberty. It seems like my magic is a late bloomer, and I don't entirely have control of it. It happens when my emotions go haywire," I rushed out, admitting more than I wanted to.

Mick's eyes hadn't left mine, yet they were deepening in color, signaling he was close to a shift. "Is that why your hair is changing color before my eyes?" Mick leaned forward and sniffed my neck. "I know what you are feeling right now," he drawled.

I felt my face begin to flame and backed up, no longer caring if he knew my legs were open and he was in a vital position. "It wasn't intentional, I swear," I repeated, getting to my feet once I was clear of Mick.

Mick stood with grace and a predatory smile. "You beguile me, woman."

"I'm not using magic on you," I protested. Damn, I confused myself sometimes.

"I know you aren't," Mick moved closer to me.

"Chuck probably deserved whatever you did to him. Though, I will say you should probably stay away from the club for a bit. His healing will kick in, but he's going to want revenge, and seeing you will cause him to try and break the command I have in place that keeps him from going after you. I don't want to lose my enforcer; he does have some use."

I nodded mutely. Scooting away from Mick, I beelined for my Jeep and got in, locking the door behind me, not that it would keep the alpha out. He moved like he was stalking prey and stood with his face inches from my window.

"You smell delicious," Mick growled. "Go before I stop you."

I wasn't about to press my luck, especially since I was nearly as turned on as I could get. I almost asked if Danny learned that dominant predatory thing from Mick, but I knew that wouldn't get me anywhere except a situation I wouldn't be able to explain away to Danny easily.

I peeled off out of the parking lot and grabbed my phone to call Ax, asking him to keep an eye out for Maggie or signs that she had been in his area. Ax promised to do so and told me that his army would watch too.

Once I could see that the lusty red hue my hair had turned started to fade, I headed to my office. I cursed myself the whole way for using magic in front of non-magical people, police officers to boot. I could safely say that my morning went sideways.

I needed to focus on Chad now and hope to green hells flames that he doesn't hear about me shooting napalm at the club's bouncer from his co-workers.

Chapter Five

After calling a few more contacts to spread the word about Maggie, I hesitated before calling Jameson. I needed to know more about the potion he thinks would help control my magic, yet I didn't want to alarm him or admit that I needed help. Pride was ugly sometimes.

"Hey, baby," I said when Jameson answered the call.

"Hi, Mom," Jameson replied cheerfully.

"I wanted to let you know that I talked with grandma and grandpa, and they both said there were cases of magic blooming later in life in the family," I told him cagily. "It sounds like Ax's theory is correct. I guess that means that there is also a possibility that the potion you were mentioning could be of some use."

"Did something happen?" Jameson cut right to the chase.

I gave him the rundown on the napalm, told him about Maggie, and asked him to work on the potion. When it comes right down to it, I was a threat to magical people by not being able to control my magic around the non-magical.

Then I called Chad. "Hi, Chad, it's Risa. What's your work schedule like this week? I want to get a time set that we can head out to Widow's Waterfall and take a look around, a time that works for you," I told him with a friendly tone.

Honestly, I could go out there without him, and Danny could probably magic us down safely. I'd take that option if Chad's schedule was too booked up. My main reason for having Chad there was to downplay what he called the woo-woo stuff, especially after my blunder with Chuck.

"I can meet you and your partner out at the mouth of the cave tomorrow afternoon," Chad suggested. "I'm off work at two and can be up there by four. That gives us plenty of daylight to get safely down and back to the parking lot."

"I like it," I agreed happily. That gave Danny and me a reasonable window of time to explore what possibilities existed in that cave with magic before Chad got there. "Clothed," I added unnecessarily.

Chad laughed. "Trust me; I didn't want to rappel naked again." There was a pause, then Chad continued. "If I may make a suggestion, take a kayak up and float down the river to where you need to descend to the cliff. It's a beautiful ride."

That could be fun. "Thanks, I'll consider it. Danny might have a kayak."

"Or a canoe, or a raft. A bit cold for an innertube," Chad mused. "Regardless, I'll see you tomorrow around four."

There wasn't much I could do with the case without seeing the cave and searching that area. Danny was doing a computer search on the grounds around the cave to see if anything popped up. That left me with a free afternoon.

At lunch with Wylene last week, she had suggested a day of pampering; hair, nails, waxing. It wasn't something I ordinarily did, and I had to admit that it sounded decadent. I was leery of the waxing part; I'd never done that before. I was brave; I could do it.

My mind made up; I headed out the door and off to

find a salon willing to take a last-minute appointment. Mind you, I could have called Wylene and asked for a recommendation, and I probably should have. Instead, I drove around looking for a place that didn't have an overly packed parking lot.

I finally found one in a not so bad part of town and parked. Buttercup Sparkle-Tips Day Spa, the sign read. I snickered and shook my head. I had a little extra money, and a trim, manicure, massage, and wax sounded good. Mostly.

The place looked newly opened, with everything appearing pristine. I took that as a good sign and pulled the door open with a feeling of anticipation. A striking-looking man leaned against a wall behind the counter, filing his nails. His skin had a blue tint to it, and his eyes were a shade of copper that reminded me of a shiny penny.

He looked up at the door opening and flashed me a brilliantly white smile. "Welcome! I'm Diamante. What can I do for you today?"

A tingle of magic washed over my skin, causing it to pebble up. I shivered and ran my hands over my arms. "Uh, hi. I want a massage, trim, manicure, and wax. Do you have time to work me in?" I felt a little foolish asking that when it was clear that he had time.

"Yes! I'll even offer it all to you for half price!" Diamante gushed and ran forward. "Don't worry about that feeling," he gestured at my goosebumps. "It's the ward to dampen people's magic. I have insurance to cover accidents but thought it was a good safety measure. I've had men that come in for waxing, and they don't do well with it and had their magic go *crazy!*"

I still had my magic and chose not to tell him it hadn't worked. "Perfect. I could use some pampering."

"Oh, this is going to be fun!" Diamante took his place in front of a computer. "We'll have you pay now, so you don't have to dig for your wallet with freshly done nails and ruin them."

With the offer of half off on the table, I wasn't going to argue. I pulled out my wallet and slapped down my card. I recited my name for him, and he chattered on about some beauty things he wanted to do on my gorgeous locks, and I tuned out.

I had some vanity, let's be honest. It wasn't a lot, and I didn't put a lot of work into my appearance. I was a wash-and-go type woman. Sometimes I would put on a little eyeliner and mascara; however, most of the time, I didn't. I thought I looked fine without it for the most part.

Diamante ran the card, and then led me back to a wash station, and I zoned out entirely with the scalp massage. I'm pretty sure I made some orgasm sounds and didn't give one damn. It was divine. He did a trim, some highlights, and while that set, he did my nails. The man didn't stop talking once, and I couldn't tell you a thing he said.

He finished my hair, wrapped it back in a towel, and led me to a private room, where Diamante instructed me to strip for the waxing part, as well as the massage. I was practically comatose by this time, so there wasn't one argument that came from me. I lay face down on the table with the towel over me and waited.

Diamante came in, and the chatter began immediately. The man's hands were a magic all of their own. He started with a back and shoulder rub that left me drooling and numb in the brain. I remember hearing something about sparkling, but I didn't focus on it.

I jolted when the hot wax was smeared on my leg and felt a moment of relief that it wasn't painful. It remained that way even when he ripped the strips off and yanked my hair out. There must be something magical in the wax Diamante was using to help numb it because even when he did the crack of my ass, which shocked me, it was primarily pain-free.

When Diamante instructed me to roll over, and he massaged my face and neck, I think there was a moment when I did fall asleep. Then he started on my legs again and worked his way up. The relaxed haze began to wear off by the time he reached my lady parts. Sure, I knew what a Brazilian meant, I wasn't living underground, but that didn't mean I was prepared for the reality of it.

I ground my teeth together with the strips that were along my bikini line and squeezed my eyes shut to stem the watering that happened. Yet when Diamante moved to more sensitive areas, I could do nothing to dampen the magic that burst from my skin.

A gust of wind came screaming out of my open mouth instead of my voice and literally blew the roof off the building while my body levitated. I might have even peed a little. Diamante let out a high-pitched shriek, jumped back, and stared at the sky instead of his calming blue ceiling with eyes wide and unblinking.

When Diamante's eyes focused back on me, he let out an even higher-pitched sound that I was sure had dogs going nuts for miles. "Your hair! Oh no! The bleach must have been bad. Oh, great green mouse balls, this isn't good."

I was afraid to ask and couldn't find my voice anyway. It had disappeared with the skin from my lady parts. I was never doing this again. "Finish the job!" I squeaked. "Don't worry about my hair."

Diamante was so flustered; I almost felt sorry for him. I felt sorrier for my crotch than the man torturing it. His hands were shaking, and it became virtually awkward for the remaining fifteen minutes it took him to finish.

"Flaming tarts, I need to fix that hair," Diamante fussed after I got dressed. I was walking bow-legged and wondering how I would sit down to drive more than I was concerned with the color of my hair.

"That's a part of my magic," I muttered. "Don't worry about my hair."

"Sit," Diamante shoved me into the chair. "I will dry it and style it. I've never heard of magic changing someone's hair color."

"I defy all logic," I snapped out. I sat utterly still so as not to aggravate sensitive skin in private areas and let Diamante do what he was going to do to my hair. I had to admit, the cut was very flattering, but the odd color of blue was startling. All the previous times that my hair had changed colors, it was only the lower half. This time, it went clear to the roots.

"I'm going to refund your money," Diamante cried mournfully. "I'm so sorry!"

"No, you aren't. You provided a service, and this cut is fabulous. My hair will go back to its normal color when my emotions calm the hell down," I growled. "I should offer to pay for the roof."

"Absolutely not!" Diamante clutched at his chest. "That is why I have extra insurance. You aren't the first to have something happen during a wax. You *are* the first to have their hair change color and give me a heart attack. But it's good, honey."

"Good. We'll call it even," I replied, standing slowly. "I'll recommend you and hope you keep this little event to yourself."

"Of course!" Diamante looked horrified at the thought of speaking of this again.

"Do you have cards?" I asked through gritted teeth as my skin rubbed against my underwear.

Diamante handed me a small stack. "Here. Use this oil tonight; it will help," he grabbed a vial from under the counter. "It's my own recipe."

Chapter Six

The oil did help. As did the remaining bottle of whiskey I found in the freezer and the tacos I ate. It was a pure stroke of luck that none of my sons stopped by to see their mother sitting naked from the waist down and legs spread out while I watched reruns on TV. I don't think they would have recovered from that trauma.

Now it was time to get down to business and help Chad. With the vial of magical soothing oil tucked into the pocket of my very loose shorts with no underwear, I left home slightly feeling disappointed that I didn't think I was up to some extra activity in the wild. Maybe it would change; it was too early to tell. As it stood, things were still on the sensitive side.

I packed a backpack with a few extra clothes to be safe and drove to Danny's. There wasn't much traffic on the road, and I made good time getting there. When I pulled into his driveway, I saw him tying down a two-seater kayak to the top of his truck. It seems Danny had the same idea as Chad.

I grabbed my backpack as I got out of my Jeep and sauntered up to Danny swinging my hips. I couldn't help the cringe that came upon my face as the fabric of my jean shorts rubbed against a particularly sensitive area with the careless move.

"You don't want to kayak?" Danny guessed from my expression. "I thought it would get us there quicker and be fun."

"Oh, no, it's not that," I quickly reassured him. "Sensitive skin issue. Kayaking sounds fun. I've never done it before."

Danny raised one eyebrow and studied me with a slow, roving gaze. "I like your hair. What's with the blue? Is that a bikini top under your shirt? Wait, are your nails painted?"

The questions were rapid-fire as he cataloged the differences in my appearance. "Thank you. The blue is from pain, I believe; yes, it's a bikini top, and my nails are painted. Is that all?"

"Care to strip so I can check the rest of you?" Danny grinned and waggled his eyebrows.

Yeah, that sensitive area was now sensitive for a different reason. "I can't. I'm not wearing any underwear."

Was it mean to laugh when the kayak fell off the truck roof and smacked Danny's shocked expression off his face? Probably, but I laughed anyway. I laughed right up to the moment his hand landed on my bare leg and slid up underneath the loose shorts and found my smooth bare skin. Then my laugh turned to a moan, and Danny's expression changed to that predatory look that set my lady bits on fire.

"You got waxed," Danny breathed out right before his lips crashed into mine. He backed me up against the truck and devoured me with a smoldering kiss.

It took an incredible amount of willpower to break away, and for a moment, I felt like a superhero because I managed the impossible feat. "We have to get going if we want to have time to check things out before Chad makes his appearance," I reminded him breathlessly.

Danny groaned, and my eyes fastened on his swollen lips. He stepped back, adjusted himself, and wordlessly picked the kayak up to refasten it to the roof of the truck. He took my backpack and threw it in the back, and held the door open for me to climb in. "We aren't done with that," his heated voice sent a shiver through me.

"Nope, we sure aren't. I think some birds and fish might get a peep show," I winked. Danny's growl made me wish I didn't have these shorts on anymore.

Once we were on our way to the top of Dragon's Peak, where the trail to Widow's Waterfall was, Danny began to tell me the story of the widow rumored to haunt the place.

"About twenty years after Glimmering Rock became established, one of the prominent families in the area garnered a bunch of attention due to an adultery scandal. You knew that much; most people do. When you dig farther, an interesting story gets painted," Danny glanced at me and hummed horror story music.

"Ah, the dramatic effect. No good story is complete without it," I smarted off. "The widow found out about the affairs, and in a fit of rage, murdered her husband and took his body to the river to sink it. Only it never sank. Instead, it went over the waterfall and bobbed around at the bottom. Fish began to eat at it, and the smell drew in some of the wolves."

"So it goes," Danny agreed. "I don't think that's what happened, though. Alessia and Donal Dagon were both leprechauns. They were known as a power couple in those early years. They had lived in Glimmering Rock almost since its inception."

"Wait, Dagon? Like Dagon's Peak instead of Dragon's Peak?" I blurted out, interrupting Danny.

"That could be what happened. People misheard and started calling it that," Danny shrugged. "Hard to say. I didn't research that. Anyway," he went on, "together, Alessia and Donal ran a successful custom clothing shop. Alessia was a talented designer who created clothes that suited the individual, and Donal made them. They showed a profit within three months of opening and never had a lull."

"Which means Donal was able to come into close contact with several people a day," I mused.

"Exactly. I imagine that some women who valued clothing and wealth would be all over him," Danny agreed. "I also dug up several articles written during that time that mentioned a lot of women turning up at healers battered. It might be putting it lightly, saying battered, but a couple of those articles mentioned Donal by name. It didn't affect the business negatively, but it did make Alessia aware of the claims, and after those articles, I found records where she received treatment for various injuries."

"The cheating bastard was also an abuser? Glad he's dead," I muttered darkly.

"I found tribunal records, law reports, and other documentation that proved he was indeed abusive. My theory is that someone's husband, father, or brother, took out their anger over their loved one's injuries and murdered Donal. I don't think Alessia was broken up over the death, but she took the fall for it. She didn't get prosecuted as they labeled it self-defense," Danny explained. "She lived a long life, and after she died, reports started popping up about her ghost being seen on Dragon's Peak by the waterfall. True or not, I wasn't able to find out. Nothing else about that area popped up."

"It hardly seems like Alessia would resort to stealing clothes or other pranks of that nature," I thought out loud. "She might have smacked the back of his nuts for being overly friendly with two women in the cave, but it's unlikely. I think whoever took the clothes did the physical things, and I don't think it's a spirit."

"Or if it is, it's not Alessia Dagon," Danny stated. "All accounts I read of her showed her to be a gentlewoman with impeccable style and grace. Even after they accused her of killing Donal."

"Okay, so we are both in agreement that we don't believe what happened to Chad was because of Alessia," I continued. "There are no other accounts of hauntings or anything weird. Mick hadn't heard anything, and he has wolves in the area all the time. I am still leaning towards there being another way in and out of that cave."

"Makes sense. At least with the kayak, we'll get a good view of the surrounding area, and between us, we should be able to feel the existence of magic if it's involved," Danny replied.

We entered the trail parking lot and parked the truck right near the trailhead. I hopped out and stretched while Danny got the kayak down. The area was beautiful, lush green, thickly wooded, and smelled of earth and moss, with pine tint.

"Leave your pack in the truck, I'll grab mine, and it will sit between us on the kayak," Danny instructed me. He tossed a lifejacket at me. "You'll need to wear one of these."

I scoffed, "I know how to swim."

"Even still, you are wearing it. Your magic is unpredictable, and who the hell knows what will happen. I'd rather not see you drown," Danny's tone brokered no argument.

I watched in fascination as he stripped to a layer of clothes he had on under his jeans. His muscles rippled as he stretched once and then heaved the kayak onto his shoulder with the pack slung over the other.

I returned the favor when he turned to make sure I was following. I tugged off my t-shirt and tied it around my waist, slipped the lifejacket on, and left it unzipped over my chest. Did I mention that it was white? It was only fair since he made me drool that I did the same.

"Evil temptress," Danny chuckled. "Come on, trouble."

Chapter Seven

Ihad no reservations that this was going to end badly. Come on, it was me, facing a kayak on a moving body of water and a ghost on the opposite bank watching me with humor etched onto the woman's transparent facial expression.

She'd been following us since the parking lot left our view, swiftly answering my question about this place being haunted. The ghost didn't taunt us or do anything to scare us off as if I got scared—laughable thought. Regardless, the apparition seemed more curious than anything else.

My small consolation was that Chad wasn't here watching the shitshow that was about to happen with me trying to get into an unstable vessel on moving water. It didn't matter that Danny was patiently, so far, holding it in place.

"Risa, daylight is wasting," Danny reminded me that his patience had a limit.

"No shit. That water is like ice, and I know I'm getting dumped. I can calculate those odds," I snapped for the third time.

"If you go in, I'll use my magic to dry you off," Danny repeated. "The only way other than hiking through mosquito-infested woods is to get your cute ass into this kayak."

I huffed out a breath and told myself to cowgirl it up. I think that's what the saying was anyway. With an exasperated exhale, I stretched my leg out as far as it would go, my sandal touching the bottom of the kayak, and pulled it as close to me as I could get it. Goosebumps broke out all across my skin as I braced for the impact of the icy river and pulled myself into the kayak, fully expecting to miss it.

When my ass landed in the seat, not the most gracefully, I threw my arms up in the air and let out a whoop of surprise and glee. "Yes! Score one for the mutt!" I shouted.

Danny chuckled, "I told you."

Before he could put the backpack down, I swiveled to see what he was doing and promptly rolled the kayak, landing my cute dry ass right into the icy river. I felt like a glacier landed on my chest; my lungs expelled all my air so fast, and I shot to the surface, spluttering and shivering.

"What the hell?" I spit out between chattering teeth.

The surprised look on Danny's face almost had me laughing, but I was too cold. This time, he moved and picked me up, plopping me in the damn death trap. "Sit still," he ordered me, then his magic washed over my skin in a drying spell.

"Thanks," I whispered, only slightly chilled now.

I squawked when the kayak rolled again, but Danny immediately stabilized it as he got himself situated and took control of the mini torture boat like it was an extension of his body. I wanted to be jealous; only it turned me on instead.

"You look good wet and in a see-through top. Zip up that lifejacket because if anyone else sees what I'm seeing, I'm going to have to go magical Rambo on their ass,"

Danny grumbled.

I hazarded a look over my shoulder and snickered, noticing Dany zipped his jacket. I also saw the female ghost laughing her old ass off at my expense. I slowly moved and zipped the lifejacket, not wanting to rock the boat.

"You can move. Just move easily, not fast. I'm your counterbalance," Danny instructed me.

"Not chancing it," I answered, glancing at the oar across my lap. "What do I do with this?"

"Paddle," Danny chuckled. "Look at my movements, and paddle on the opposite side of me, that will keep us straight. If we need to turn, I'll do it."

"Paddle," I snorted. "Bend over, and I'll paddle you."

"Try it, and you'll be swimming again," Danny warned.

That shut me up, only for a moment. "Promises, promises," I taunted in a sing-song voice. A very girlish shriek followed it as Danny rocked the kayak. I was pretty confident he wouldn't tip us, though there was a slim margin for doubt that crept in as my heartbeat skyrocketed.

I glanced over my shoulder to see the evil grin gracing Danny's face. Instead of commenting, I watched how he paddled and mimicked his movements, and our path through the water increased its pace. It was a nice feeling and peaceful to boot.

The scenery was unparalleled, even with the female apparition that was trailing after us. Lush green forest trees that provided shade for the creatures of the forest. Shrubs showing off berries I wasn't sure were safe to eat, crystal clear water that gave a clear view of the life that survived under the surface, and colorful rocks that I was positive had magical properties. It wasn't any wonder that Chad had been up here exploring.

We paddled for about an hour before Danny directed us to the bank of the river in a nice calm spot. An idyllic setting for exploration of Danny. "Scram lady," I muttered to the ghost. "Unless you've got a fetish for watching people orgasm. I'm not sure I'm comfortable with you seeing what my man's packing under those trunks, even if you do like watching porn."

"Are you telling me there truly is a ghost up here?" Danny asked as he anchored the kayak, so it didn't float away.

"Yeah," I confirmed. "The woman's been following us the whole time. An older lady, you can tell she used to be a looker, as my dad would say. Not aggressive, though the dead woman laughed it up pretty good when I went in. Oh, hey lady," I turned back to the ghost. "Did you spy on a non-magical human up here with his female companions on their adventures?" I waggled my eyebrows. "Was he packing?"

"Seriously, Risa?" Danny groaned. "Are you that curious about this guy that you are asking a ghost what his dick looks like?"

All I got in response was a smirk on the old gal's face. "No help," I curled my lip at the ghost. "Danny, chill. Chad knows I'm with you, and you already stated that I'm a flirt. I know damn well that if naked women were parading around up here, you'd look."

I only felt a little guilty when Danny backed me up against a tree and pressed all that yumminess into me. "Are you regretting committing to me, Risa?"

Oh shit. Danny asked me serious questions and expected answers, and all I was thinking about was the quickest way to dispose of his clothing. "No," I moaned when he gyrated his hips. "No regrets. Only endless curiosity, get used to it, and stop playing dirty."

"You like me dirty," Danny punctuated his point

with a thrust of hips.

"Stop talking, start performing," I demanded, sliding my hands down the front of his shorts.

Twelve and a half glorious minutes later, I understood the draw of public sex. Forty seconds after that realization, I was dumped unceremoniously into the river by the man who had me screaming his name for a different reason.

"What?" Danny shrugged innocently. "We needed to clean off. I thought it would be gentlemanly of me to carry you."

"Ass!" I splashed him, knocked his feet out from underneath him, and proceeded to push him down and hold him there as punishment. Of course, it backfired and turned into an all-out war between us as we tussled in the river. I noticed the sun glinting off my skin like I was covered in diamonds and snickered, only now getting the name of the salon and tying it to Diamante.

"I surrender," Danny held his hands up, laughing. "You are fierce. Come on, let me feed you before we get back in. The waterfall should only be about another mile from here." Danny reached out and tugged me up on the beach. "You do look good wet," he winked and smacked me on the ass.

"That doesn't mean you don't have to dry me off," I prompted with a scowl.

We ate, and I managed to get back into the kayak without going for another swim. I think the ghost was disappointed by that. Once underway, Danny pointed out some fish, a few sprites, and we both saw some strange shadow in the water that neither of us could identify.

"Fish are creepy looking," I decided as I watched one swim under us before we hit the white water we were approaching. "But they taste good." The thought gave me a flashback to the surf and turn the alien creatures were trying to create, and I shuddered.

There wasn't much time for Danny to ask what I thought before something thunked the kayak and had us both shouting in surprise. It took a few seconds for me to recognize that the apparition was frantically waving her hands at us. It was far too late for me to react by the time I figured out she was trying to warn us.

The next thump rolled the kayak, dumping both Danny and me into the river at the worst spot possible, right into the rapids. Danny, the kayak, and the backpack went in the opposite direction of where I did. The icy water sucked me down and tumbled me into some large rocks before letting me bob to the surface to greedily suck in some oxygen.

That's when the panic set in because I heard the thundering of the waterfall and immediately knew my ass was going over. It didn't matter how much I tried to angle myself towards the bank or how many grabs I made for low-hanging branches. All my efforts were fruitless, and thousands of thoughts spun through my head as the unzipped lifejacket began to slide off my body as the river tossed me around.

The hand that wrapped around my calf with a bruising force had me sucking in gulps of water as it pulled me under; this was it. I knew how I was going to die.

Chapter Eight

My heart was about to beat right out of my chest. I had no idea what grabbed me, I was moments away from plunging over a giant waterfall, and I was taking a beating from the rocks I was bouncing off of while I choked on river water—not the best way to have some fun.

Drowning would be an awful way to die, I decided, right as I felt gravity and air encompass my body. Yep, death was imminent. An ear-piercing scream erupted from my lips; my limbs frantically windmilled as they searched for purpose as I began to plummet. The lifejacket slipped from my body, and my fingers grasped it as if it were a parachute.

I distantly heard my name being yelled during my rapid descent, and to my amazement, snow started to fall when I suddenly found myself yanked directly to the waterfall. Expecting to crash headfirst into the rock cliff behind it, I was more than stunned to find myself passing right through it and dropping with a painful jolt onto a cave floor.

My head slammed into the ground, and I blacked out. I don't know for how long. I came to awareness in a dark cavern filled with a thunderous roar and immediately thought that I was in the cave that Chad had his issues. I knew that couldn't be right since I could see the waterfall curtain over the entrance to this one and assumed that was the echoing sound that was making my head pound.

I realized that this was a hidden cave that Chad didn't know about; I slowly pushed myself to a sitting position and took a careful look around the darkened space. I didn't land here by accident or luck; someone had pulled me in here during my freefall to death. It was an act performed by a physical force, not a spiritual one, that ruled out the ghost lady who followed Danny and me earlier.

That also gave credence to Chad's story. Someone else was up here, and they were playing games with the non-magical, probably gullible magical beings fell victim to whoever this was as well. It angered me and piqued my curiosity all at the same time.

I fought back a wave of dizziness as I got to my feet and cataloged each protestation my body made as I moved. Nothing felt broken, granting me a moment of relief, which was immediately followed by an understanding that the next couple of days would be painful ones.

"Hello?" I tentatively called out.

I steadied myself against the cave wall and felt around. I could admit walking back into the dark void gave me a bit of trepidation. That sounded better than saying I was scared. I fancied myself relatively fearless, though I was in a cave and no one knew where I was. Hell, Danny probably thought I was dead. Chad saw me disappear into a waterfall some number of feet above his head.

"I know someone is in here," I tried again, controlling the shake to my voice. "Thank you for saving me."

I shrieked and plastered my back to the cave's wall as the woman materialized in front of me, her form barely visible in the dark space. The ghostly face was contrite, though I saw the spark of humor at my fright. The same glint I saw when she had the laughing attack at my expense on the river bank.

"Funny," I growled. "You know I can't hear you, right?" The ghost nodded and beckoned me to follow her misty form.

As we went deeper into the cave, the manifestation became the only light there was, and I wondered how the ghost was doing that. I had to believe that it took an unbelievable amount of energy to maintain.

"You're Alessia, aren't you?" I asked the apparition. The woman turned slightly and nodded at me. "Did you steal Chad's clothes?" I knew she didn't; the question was only to confirm my thoughts. At the shake of her head, I fell silent, feeling vindicated for being on the right track.

I wondered how far back this cave went when it dawned on me that the light that I saw wasn't emitting from the ghost anymore. There was actual light in this cave, and it wasn't sunlight. The hue was a greenish color and came with the slight smell of something burnt.

My curiosity reached an all-time high as thoughts of crossing another portal floated through my mind. I knew I hadn't since I could clearly see and feel the cave wall, though the sound of the waterfall had long since disappeared the father back we'd traveled.

I could ask the ghost until I was out of breath what was happening and would be in the same position I was already in since I couldn't communicate with the spirit. I had to wait to see what was up ahead, and I found that I was far more interested in the answer than I was worried about the fear of what I would walk into in front of me. I wasn't brilliant all the time.

"Would I have died if I fell to the bottom?" I blurted out, having no clue where the question even came from. The somber nod of the ghost shut me up again, and I followed, biting my tongue, so I didn't ask anything else I didn't want the answer to rolling in my head.

Like that kept more questions from bubbling out. "Am I going to die from whatever or whoever is back here?" The ghost shook her head no, and I breathed out a sigh of relief. "You didn't kill your husband, did you?" I received another shake of the head in response. "Is this mountain named after you, and people just changed it over time?" Another negative response.

Five more minutes of trudging through a darkly lit green light cave, and I stopped in my tracks. We were in an enormous room filled with what had to be magical gems embedded in the walls, which was what was emitting light. That was jaw-dropping enough without the furniture arranged in a living situation.

Danny and I were right. There was someone else here, which meant there was another way to the cave Chad and his booty call clients had been inside. Now, I needed to find that tunnel that led me there and hope like hell Chad and Danny were both there.

"Hello?" I called out again and felt a brush of magic float over my skin. Familiar, but unfamiliar at the same time.

I wandered a little deeper into the room and saw it laid out like a studio apartment. How the furniture got down here was puzzling enough. I shook my head and let my eyes rove over everything and saw a pile of clothes. Cargo shorts, boxer briefs, bras, graphic tees, socks, you name it, I saw it. I began to head towards it when the air shimmered in front of me, halting my movement.

Two imps appeared, and my eyebrows shot up to my hairline. "Now it makes more sense," I mumbled.

Chapter Nine

The larger of the two imps took an aggressive step towards me and squared up as if we were about to battle. My magic responded before I could think about a plan of action, and a gust of air pushed out of me, shoving the imp back to stand beside the other one.

My peripheral vision caught movement, and I angled my head to see the ghost waving her arms frantically at me in a stop motion. "You know them?" I asked her and waited for the confirmation nod.

Imps were known pranksters and mischief-makers that sometimes bordered on the meaner side of things, given they were a sort of demon. I wasn't going to assume they were either good or bad; I was only prepared to defend myself if need be.

"One of you saved me?" I turned back to the pair and studied them.

Both were short, curved horns, darker-hued skin, with dark umber-colored eyes. If I wasn't mistaken, one was female and the other male. Ironically, it was the female that had been aggressive. Both imps were wearing human clothing, all stolen, was my guess.

"I did," a deep male voice responded. "I'm Brindle. This female here," Brindle pointed to the other imp, "is my mate, Chaz."

I nodded a hello. "Thank you for not letting me die. How do you know Alessia?"

"We worked for her. Alessia hired us as house stewards when they moved into town, and her husband summoned us. We worked for her faithfully and loyally until she died," Bridle replied proudly.

"If Donal summoned you, why didn't you work for him?" I asked, slightly confused.

"We're lesser than he wanted to get," Chaz spat out. There was no love lost there.

Brindle put a calming hand on Chaz. "The marks on your leg," Brindle changed the subject. "Did something grab you?"

I glanced down, suddenly remembering the hand that had clamped down on my leg and pulled me underwater. My calf was marred with a big handprint that wrapped all the way around and was bruising. Another sharp pain struck my head, and I blinked slowly, trying to piece it all together. "Yes. I got pulled under right before I went over the waterfall."

"You're just pissing everyone off today, aren't you?" Chaz snarled at me.

"What the fuck is your problem?" I snapped, ready to choke the imp out.

"Did you disrespect the river or its creatures in any way?" Brindle ignored the outburst between his mate at me.

"Not that I'm aware of," I answered him but continued to glare at Chaz. "We floated on a kayak and played in the water." I tried to remember if either of us had peed in the water and didn't think we had. We'd both gone in the forest.

"No comments about the creatures?" Brindle pushed.

"We watched some; that was it. What are you

getting at?” I finally looked back at Brindle.

“Dagon is touchy about those he considers his,” Brindle explained like I knew what he was talking about with this. “Did you do any fishing and kill a fish?”

“What? No,” I frowned. “Who the hell is Dagon? Isn’t that Alessia’s last name?” *Focus, Risa,* I reminded myself. “How do I get out of here? And are you the two who stole clothes from a man and two women who were, uh, using the other cave? Did you physically touch a sensitive part of his body?”

Alessia started to gesture again, Chaz’s attitude quadrupled in size, and Brindle appeared to be trying to calm them both. I halfway expected to see a white rabbit wearing a pocket watch come hopping around the corner with a hookah-smoking centipede on his shoulder at this point.

Brindle took a deep breath in and exhaled slowly. “You aren’t a prisoner. Please don’t worry about that. Chaz is having a moment of jealousy since you are attractive, that’s all. Yes, we took clothes from the man who was yelling your name at the bottom of the cliff. Unfortunately, Chaz did do some harmful things to the young man while he was in a delicate situation. Again, it was her jealousy and short temper taking over. Dagon will take a bit more explaining, though the short of it is, Dagon is known as a fish god, and he has taken up residence in the river recently. He’s a bit temperamental.”

My jaw snapped shut at the sound of a piercing wolf howl, and I glanced around. “That sounds close.”

“There are air vents,” Brindle pointed to a small fissure I hadn’t noticed. “Sound carries.”

“How long have I been down here?” I asked with a frown.

“You were out for a little over half an hour,” Brindle answered quietly. “I’m sorry. I didn’t mean for you to hit your head."

"I'll take that over death," I quipped. "How do you get from here to that cave? And why did you take Chad's clothes? How did you get furniture down here, and if you worked for Alessia, what are you doing in here?" I asked, rapid-fire. "Is Dagon dangerous?"

"You ask a lot of questions," Chaz growled at me.

"Cool your jets, imp," I replied with an edge to my voice. "I don't want your man. Mine is out there right now, probably looking for me. Keep up with this attitude, and my magic will react. My guess is the outcome won't be so good for you."

Brindle physically pushed Chas back farther into the room with some harsh whispers and looked back at me. "Dagon has never harmed anyone unprovoked before that I've seen. I don't know what prompted him to pull you under."

"Wait," I said suddenly, a memory sparking in my smarting head. "Before our kayak rolled, I had said that fish looked creepy but tasted good. Could that be considered a threat?"

Brindle chuckled a dark sound that would have given me chills if I didn't know who or what he was. "It could have. As I said, he can be temperamental. Uh, we had magical help to get furniture down here, and we stole the clothes because a non-magical person was getting too close to our hideout here. Harmless pranks that typically scare people away. Chaz shouldn't have touched him or cut the line, and I'm sorry that happened. We disappeared from civilization because we made a lot of people uncomfortable without the buffer of Alessia to protect us."

"Protect you from what?" I pushed for answers, sensing there was more to this story than just hiding away from assholes. "If whatever secret you are hiding doesn't cause harm to anyone, there is no reason for me to spread it around. I'm a private investigator, and the job that brought me up here was to find out what happened to Chad."

"Stay put," Brindle ordered Chaz. He gestured for me to follow him. "This is the side tunnel that leads to that cave."

"Okay, great," I responded enthusiastically. "What do those gems do?"

"I don't know, but they are great at providing light in that cavern," Brindle gave me a creepy sharp-pointed toothy grin. "We are hiding out because when Alessia was alive, I'm sure you've heard the rumors about her killing her husband. She didn't do it. Chaz did."

Whoa. I stopped in my tracks and stared at the imp. Half of me wanted to go back and snatch the bitchy demon and haul her ass to the Glittering Rock police; the other half wanted to applaud her. From what Danny had uncovered, it didn't sound like Donal was a good guy.

"Care to explain?" I asked with raised eyebrows.

"Donal beat Alessia, he broke his marital vows, gambled their money, and brought shame to their house. Chaz was especially close with Alessia and took the issues personally. One night a disgruntled husband came to the house to confront Donal, only he wasn't there. The man figured that he could instead take it out on Alessia by compromising her morals. Donal arrived before that happened, but instead of getting angry and defending Alessia, he told the man to take her, that she was frigid," Brindle spilled his guts.

I again wanted to applaud Chaz; only her attitude kept me from doing so. "Chaz took the matter into her own hands," I guessed.

Brindle nodded. "She used magic to knock the jilted husband out, then killed Donal. I was not home at the time and didn't know what was happening. I was guarding the shop that night, as there had been some problems with vandalism. When I got home, I saw the mess, and Alessia was comforting Chaz. Donal's death was no great loss, and we all knew that. Alessia wanted to make sure that nothing happened to Chaz because of it, so we took the body, weighted it down, and hauled it up to the river. None of us thought about the currents or that he would go over the waterfall."

I could understand that they were going on pure adrenaline and reacting to the murder instead of plotting out how to make the body disappear. It also told me that it wasn't something premeditated and thought out.

Brindle motioned for me to keep walking, and he resumed his story. "Alessia was more than happy to bear the burden of guilt over the murder, and she wore the evidence of Donal's abuse all over her body. She didn't argue when they declared her guilty of self-defense and accepted that they thought she killed Donal to protect Chaz. After Alessia died, the townsfolk were rude to us due to the nature of our beings, and we began to be shunned. A couple of the farmers ran us out of town, and we headed this way and found the cave purely by accident. We got clothing from scaring people out of the other cave and bribed some fae to help us get furniture in the one with gems so we could live on our own."

Brindle shrugged and continued walking as I thought it all over. There was injustice in there, that was for sure, and I could forgive and understand the murder of Donal. "You need to stop Chaz from physically assaulting people. That crosses a line. Chad isn't aware of the supernatural world, and we need to keep it that way. I can't explain away the scratches on his back or the smack on his nuts, not to mention the cut rope. If she knocks that shit off, I won't report you. However, if it continues, I'll be forced to let the council know you are up here and what's happening."

A few more feet and we passed what looks like a squirrel's nest that had a few bits of fabric mixed in with the branches, and a thought came to me on how to pass this off with Chad.

"I'll talk to her again. It may be that we have to go back to the underworld if she can't control herself. Donal traumatized her, and I'm not trying to make excuses for her behavior. I agree to your terms and ask for a bit of advice, possibly? Can you think of a way we can get some food without having to steal it all the time? Or beg Dagon for a fish? He hates that," Brindle pleaded.

I knew I could ask Wylene to drop food off in the cave. "Give me a list of food that you need, and I'll arrange a weekly drop-off on the condition that Chaz behaves. Pranks are fine if they are harmless. I'm not asking you not to be an imp, only that you don't cross a line to assault or causing someone harm in any way. The clothing theft is somewhat funny since they had to rappel naked, but the physical assault was not. Are we clear?"

Brindle stopped and faced me. "Absolutely. Thank you for understanding. I'm going to take my leave of you now. Ten feet ahead is an illusion spell that looks like a rock wall if you are facing this way. I can hear voices in the cave, and I don't want to be seen. Keep going that way, and there is one turn to the right. The entrance is an optical illusion that isn't magical. It blends with the rock naturally. You'd never see it unless you ran your hands over every inch of that cave and felt the gap."

Before I could agree, Brindle disappeared. I moved in the direction he had told me to go, and I heard Danny's voice, angry and scared as he talked to someone. "Danny!" I yelled, ecstatic to pick up his voice.

"Risa! Keep talking, babe. Where are you?" Danny shouted.

I risked moving backward, grabbed the squirrel nest and dragged it in front of the illusion I could now feel. I'd move it back after I explained away the missing clothes. "Danny!" I called out again. "I'm in a tunnel."

That was the moment that the exhaustion hit me again. My head swam, my knees shook, and all the beatings the rocks had delivered took their toll. I sagged and dropped five feet from the squirrel's nest. Shivering now that I was alone in the dark, I stayed put. I knew Danny would find me.

Chapter Ten

Holy shit, woman," Danny barked about ten minutes later, dropping to his knees in front of me. "I swear on all the gods I am going to put a leash on you and strap you to me."

An insane light hit me in the eyes, making me cringe and groan. "Oh my, you're hurt," Chad whispered.

Danny scooped me into his arms. "Lead us back out," he ordered Chad. "I can't wait to hear this," Danny whispered in my ear. "Your hair is silver, orange, and light blue, and your skin is just as colorful."

I rested my head against his chest, taking comfort in the warmth. "We need to go back down that tunnel and create some more illusions at a later date in case Chad decides to explore some more."

"I thought I lost you," Danny kissed my head, choking up. "I'd agree to anything right now."

"Good. Then don't argue with anything I say," I half-joked.

We made it back to Chad's sexual den to find a confused-looking blonde woman staring at us with an incredulous expression. "Chad?"

Granted, I didn't know Chad that well, and my impression was he was a pretty easy-going, friendly guy. When his face turned stony, I was shocked, and when he spoke with that tone, I moved past shocked to astounded.

"Becky? What the actual fuck are you doing here?" Chad dropped his gear at his feet and crossed his arms over his chest.

"You won't return my calls, so I followed you," Becky whined.

Danny set me on my feet and held me to him, which I was thankful for since I wasn't all that steady yet. A deity had tried to drown me; river rocks beat the hell out of me. I went over a waterfall and would have died if imps hadn't saved me and blacked out in a cavern. It had been an eventful day, yet the woman throwing herself at Chad had me floored.

"Why would I call you? I have no interest in you. Maybe if you hadn't slept your way through the force and given half of them chlamydia, I might have been. Instead, I can safely say I want nothing to do with you. Following me is crossing a major line. I'm a cop; you know I can arrest you, right?" Chad snapped with a tone colder than ice.

"We could have fun with cuffs. Want to know my safe word?" Becky held her wrists out in front of her and tried to play coy. I couldn't stop watching the travesty. Danny slid his hand over my mouth before I could say anything.

"No means no. I like my dick disease-free. Unless you want a criminal record, I suggest you leave," Chad replied in a tone that turned me on. Guess it did Becky, too, because she didn't leave.

"I need you to help me. I can't go back down by myself; it's snowing out there," Becky whined and stepped closer to Chad.

What? Still? I opened my mouth to bite Danny's hand to get him to move, and before I could chomp down, his warm breath tickled my ear.

"Your magic is interesting, babe. When you went

over that waterfall, your magic went apeshit, and the skies opened up with a blizzard," Danny whispered. "Strangest thing I've ever seen, and I have no idea how this is explainable."

"Cut the shit, Becky," Chad moved away from her. "Going down is easier than coming up. I'm on a case, and I am prepared to bring charges against you for harassment unless you leave."

"Can I show you how I go down?" Becky practically purred.

I snorted behind Danny's hand. Even Danny laughed at the pathetic attempt. Chad glanced back at us with a helpless expression on his face. I took matters into my own hands. I pulled Danny's hand away and stepped forward.

"Genital warts don't go away, and no one wants that," I informed Becky. "I'm a little insulted by your behavior. Here you are standing there in a shirt boldly declaring yourself a feminist, yet you are throwing yourself at a man that clearly doesn't want anything to do with you, and you won't take the hint. Have some pride, walk away. You are insulting all females by wheedling and begging."

Another wolf howl split the air making Danny curse and Chad wary. Becky, on the other hand, looked like she wanted to claw my eyes out. I did the only thing I could think of doing in the situation to drive the point home, and I hoped like hell Danny understood.

I walked up to Chad and slid my arm around his waist, pressing my boobs against him. "Go on, go," I purred. "I've got more than enough up there to keep him occupied while you fall a little flat."

Danny grunted, but my ploy worked, and Chad didn't move away from me. We stayed like that until Becky disappeared. After a few minutes, Danny walked to the mouth of the cave and looked down to make sure she was really going and then came back in and removed my arm from around Chad.

"She's gone," Danny spit out sourly.

I shrugged, somewhat painfully. "Sometimes catty and bitchy is the only thing that works. Okay, Chad. I know what happened to your clothes and possibly how you got scratches on your back. Where you guys found me was a squirrel's nest. Scraps of fabric were woven in with the branches and moss. It was a fairly large nest, and I'm guessing there was a little family there, and the mom was trying to keep the babies warm. There were remnants of clothes along that tunnel, so it could be that some other animal got to it too. An animal can also explain the cut line. Racoon claws are super sharp."

Chad was quiet but thoughtful. "Wouldn't I have noticed a squirrel on my back?"

"Dude," Danny cut in. "How hot were the girls you were with up here? There are times with Risa I wouldn't notice an elephant's trunk up my ass."

A sheepish look crossed his face. "Point taken. I wouldn't have noticed a marching band at one point during that experience. A squirrel is small enough that I wouldn't have seen it running out after my nuts got smacked. Guess I'm glad no claws punctured anything."

Yeah, the explanation was far-fetched. I knew it, and so did Danny. It was plausible but unlikely. However, it was far better than telling him a bitchy imp got mad he was screwing two women and flicked his nuts and clawed him because she could. I'd be discussing the elephant's trunk with Danny later in private.

"That tunnel leads to somewhere?" Chad asked, moving back towards where we came out, already past the clothing issue. "Man, I never even saw an opening back here. Look at how well this blends!" Chad exclaimed, shining his light over the wall.

Thinking quick, "The tunnel leads to a cave behind

the waterfall, but the tunnel isn't really a tunnel all the way through. There are some pretty tight squeezes unless you are an animal. I was following the flow of air I felt, hoping to find a way out."

"Damn, when you went over that waterfall and screamed, I almost had a heart attack. Your skin was sparkling like diamonds, like that vampire movie, and I started to believe in that stuff for a few seconds. That might be the only time I say it's a good thing your lifejacket came off and got snagged on that branch," Chad shook his head in amazement. "I saw you hit the waterfall and ran to the bottom to see if I could see your body anywhere. It took me a moment to understand you must have landed on something behind it."

Danny had tensed up again. "Not an experience I'd like to relive."

Chad heaved out a sigh, "Totally get it, man. Now that I know what happened to my clothes, I can say I'm glad I don't believe rumors about a widowed ghost haunting this place. It's just a cave—a home for some animals and a great place to have some fun and intense sexual release. Come on, let's get you both strapped up and get down out of here. Mountains sure have some weird weather patterns. I don't want to get stuck up here."

Non-magical people and those who didn't believe in the existence of magic were sure easy to convince that the magical things happening to them were something quickly explained away, no matter how odd. It was my experience that told me they didn't like their views challenged by something they didn't understand, or didn't want to understand because it scared them. I was happy that this was a case where Chad was quick to believe the offered scenario and didn't push me to expand any further. That wasn't because he was narrow minded, just uncomfortable with his view being altered. Especially on the sparkly skin, odd-colored hair, or the hand that reached out from the waterfall to grab me that he missed mentioning.

"You must be cold," Chad remarked as he fastened the harness around me.

That was all it took for Danny to grunt, and he stripped out of his shirt and yanked it down over my head. "You don't have to look, even if they are pointing right at your face."

I snickered. "Let's get this party started. Chad, show me how to go down," I grinned at Danny's expression.

The blatant phrasing wasn't lost on either man, and Chad laughed in good humor and launched into his directions on how to rappel down the cliff. "I'll go first, watch how it's done."

He disappeared over the side as Danny stood next to me. "Yeah, watch how it's done, Danny."

"You've never complained about me going down before; I think I've got it," he scowled at me. "Sparkle-tits."

"Lighten up," I winked. "We're all alive, and I've got a story for you. The bonus sparkles are from my massage, by the way."

When Chad hit bottom, he yelled up for me to begin my descent. I gave Danny a peck on the lips and rappelled for the first time in my life. I have to admit, watching Danny's ass as he came down was fun too.

While we were packing up the harnesses, a gigantic wolf, it had to be Mick, made a sudden appearance, making Chad about shit himself in fear as he fell flat on his ass, shouting. Just as quickly, the wolf bit my ass and disappeared into the woods with an irritated huff. That was going to be a little harder to explain.

Chapter Eleven

I called Mick to help track you," Danny told me once we got dropped off at his truck. "Risa, we were trying to figure out if you drowned and were stuck at the bottom of the waterfall, or if you really had gone through the falls into some opening behind it. I wasn't going to leave any stone unturned."

We'd told Chad it was a Great Dane mixed with Mastiff that belonged to someone that lived near the area. It was all I could think of spur of the moment. Chad looked skeptical at that, and I didn't blame him one little bit. Mick was huge.

"He didn't have to bite my ass," I grumbled. To ward off any lingering unhappiness with everything that had transpired, I jumped into the story of Brindle and Chaz, leaving nothing out. By the time I got to where I had heard his voice, Danny had calmed down.

"We obviously need to learn more about Dagon, and we need to figure out a way to air the mistreatment of magical races without giving away Brindle and Chaz. You're right. We need to set up another illusion in that cave as well. Chad isn't the only curious one, and I can see him going back just to explore that tunnel we found you in. Chad stumbling across the imps wouldn't be good for anyone."

I laughed at the visual. "No, probably not. I'm going to have Wylene drop off food weekly and maybe some more clothes. I'll probably inform Mick that imps are living quietly down there too, just so his wolves don't eat them or start a problem."

Danny drove in silence for a while. When he finally spoke, there was something in his tone I was scared to label. "I'm not going to take a cop-out on this, but when you openly flirted, I wanted to unleash hell on Chad and let Becky give him genital warts."

I chuckled. "Poor Becky. Cop-out? Pun intended?"

"Obviously," Danny huffed. "Do you need a healer?"

"Nah. I won't turn down a massage, though," I winked and made my tone husky. "We still have the matter of an elephant trunk to discuss. I think there's a story there that you haven't told me."

Danny groaned with a smile. "I knew that was going to come up. There was no elephant sex and that's all I'm saying about that."

Book 5
Feeling Blue

Chapter One

Risa? Risa Sanders?" an unknown female voice called out to me.

I spun around in surprise because I hadn't thought anyone who knew me would be here in an experimental lab. "Do I know you?" I barked out, harsher than I thought or intended.

"No, not yet. I'm Jonielle, and it's nice to meet you," the blue-tinted female held her hand out to me.

I shook it and took in her appearance. Jonielle was taller than me, had thick wavy blue hair, soft green eyes, and a smile that lit her entire face. A pleasant package, even though I had no clue as to how she knew me.

"You know who I am?" I asked, fighting the urge to wipe my hand on my pants. It was not because I thought she had germs but because we were in a lab full of them.

"Risa Sanders, supernatural, paranormal investigator, owner and operator of I S.P.I. and badass female," Jonielle replied with a grin. "You are kind of famous."

I snorted. I wasn't famous in a good way if I was even famous at all. I had a brash mouth, a take-no-shit attitude, could hold my own in a brawl, and more recently, wore my emotions in my hair color. "Not quite, but thank you for the praise, I think."

"Would it be possible to set up a time for us to talk?

I want to hire you. Fortuitous that I met you here of all places since I'm likely to forget to call you until after you are closed for the day," Jonielle told me with a crooked smile. "I get sidetracked easily."

"You and me both, sister," I agreed readily. "I was taking a week off, but what the hell? If you can meet me tomorrow, I'll make it a point to go into the office."

"Really?" Jonielle's smile lit the room like it was a rainbow. "Is eleven too early?"

"Not at all," I reassured the woman. "Do you know where it is?"

"I sure do! Thank you! I'll see you tomorrow then," Jonielle promised and then walked off.

I blinked at the sudden departure as she walked into a closed door. Literally. Jonielle threw a sheepish look over her shoulder at me and pulled the door open, and disappeared behind it. I wondered if we were related after witnessing that smooth move.

"Mom, back here," Jameson, my youngest son, called out.

I turned back and saw him waving me towards him holding open the no admittance door I spotted earlier. "Is this where the secret stuff happens?" I blurted out nervously.

"Yep," Jameson answered wickedly. "Who knows, maybe you'll grow a third breast or male anatomy."

"Are you telling me to fuck myself?" I pushed past him, relying on my sarcastic attitude to beat the fear back.

Jameson belted out a full belly laugh. "No, Mom. Though that would be a creative way to say it."

I practically swallowed my tongue as I saw a sign on the door we were headed to that proudly declared, "Mom's who are being used as guinea pigs." Instead, I rolled my eyes and shot a scowl at my son, who was snickering.

"Relax. I wanted you to laugh," Jameson patted me on the back. "Your hair gives you away. It's an interesting shade of piss yellow. Trust me, Mom. If I weren't confident that this could help, I wouldn't have you here."

A couple of months ago, I had a case involving one of the town's council members and a sasquatch and his dachshund army. A harpy named Mercy was after Ax, the sasquatch, to obtain his land, which held a plant, not from this realm.

Jameson had been able to uncover that the plant was part of a recipe his brother Gavin had asked him to help create. This recipe would allow the person using it to take over someone else's powers. With a bit of research, Jameson uncovered the possibility of this plant being able to help me control my unpredictable powers that were blossoming.

With one of his friends' help, it had taken Jameson almost an entire month to perfect what he thought the potion should be, and he was now ready for me to try it. To say I was skeptical would be an understatement. Not that I didn't trust my son, I didn't trust my magic to behave, potion or not.

Jameson led me to a chair and had me sit down. I spied his friend behind a magical wall waving to us both with a goofy look on his face. I feebly waggled my fingers back and shot Jameson a warning look.

"What's with Dr. Pecker?" I asked my son.

Jameson let out a heavy sigh. "Mom, you know good, and well, his name is Dr. Decker. He's halfway in love with you, so cut him a break."

"Sorry, Jameson." I wasn't sorry. "Did you by any chance see the blue lady out there?"

"Yeah, I saw her. She comes in once a week, and I don't know anything else about her," Jameson recited. "It's unethical to give you any information about her even if

I did know it, and that means you don't get to ask Dr. Decker either."

That's not what it meant. It meant I couldn't ask where Jameson could hear me. "Her name is Jonielle. I have an appointment with her tomorrow at my office."

Jameson raised his eyebrows at me but didn't comment on it. "Okay, I'm going to go retrieve the potion. I want you to drink it; then we will leave you in here and observe you for about fifteen minutes to let it sink in. Then we'll have you start to call on your magic and see if you can get it to respond as it should."

"If you think this is so safe, why are you guys hiding behind that wall?" I fired back.

"For the simple reason of your magic is so strong and wild. I don't want you to feel guilty if either of us gets caught in the crossfire of a spell or casting gone haywire," Jameson retorted hotly. "You know this. We've had this conversation, and that was one of the arguments you tried to use against me not to do this."

I huffed in indignation. It was the only response I had. "Jonielle is pretty, isn't she? Interesting shade of blue skin."

My question made Jameson pause and give me a crazy look. "I don't know where you are going with that. Yes, she is, and that isn't going to change anything that will happen in here. Stop trying to distract me."

My son was too much like me for any of my ploys to work. "Fine. Go get the damn potion and let's get this over with."

Jameson had told me how they kept the ingredients, recipe, and the mixed portions of the potions under heavy lock and key. Ax was the only person with access to the Squatchgold, and since we learned that Mercy knew of it and had been willing to kill for it, Jameson wanted it carefully guarded. As far as I knew, only he and

Dr. Pecker knew what was going on.

I wasn't sure I wanted to know what excuse they told people for why I was here or what was going on in here. I didn't know a lot about this lab other than it was used for experimental treatments for problems other races experienced that regular healers couldn't help.

That again made me wonder why Jonielle was here and what brought her here every week. Did she have some sort of rare disease, and was it communicable? I blinked slowly to stem those thoughts. I doubted that was the case since she was in the open lobby area and wore no protective gear.

A couple of minutes later, Jameson walked out with a martini glass of all things with a fluorescent purple liquid in it. "A martini glass?" I spluttered in astonishment.

"Well, I didn't want you to feel like a guinea pig," Jameson replied wryly. "At least this way, your brain thinks it's going to have a nice relaxing drink."

"Coming from the son who put a sign on the door saying the room was for guinea pig mothers," I shot back at him. "This better taste good."

"Dr. Decker said it should taste like berries," Jameson told me with a dubious sound to his voice.

I sighed and snatched the glass from him before I could chicken out and downed the concoction in a single gulp like I was desperate for a purple martini that had zero alcohol to dull the effects of the fear cascading down my spine. I'd had years to hone the gulping skill, and it didn't fail me now.

Jameson stared at me like I'd grown a second head before he took the empty glass from me and retreated behind the wall. I closed my eyes, tipped my head back, and waited for the third boob to grow. There was a tingly feeling spreading through my body as if I had consumed alcohol, and it carried that sense of calm with it.

We did know that Squatchgold had properties that calmed sasquatch. My genealogy was mixed, but I was confident that I had no sasquatch in my heritage. I could use a little of Wylene's confidence right now. She was a siren that came to me not too long ago needing help and became a good friend.

Suck it up, Risa, I told myself. I don't know why my magic scared me so much or that the thought of being able to control it was an issue. That was the goal, having the ability to call on my magic and have it respond in the way I need it to with a modicum of control instead of the wild spurts that came out of nowhere.

"Mom, are you okay?" Jameson's worried voice filled the room.

"Should I not be?" I called back in response.

"Your wings are out," my son answered with a slightly curious tone to the worry.

I opened my eyes and tried to twist around to see my back. I'm sure it was comical, and after about thirty seconds of making a fool of myself looking like a dog chasing its tail, I stopped. Turning inward to see if anything felt off, I did a slow check of my body. My hair was no longer yellow; I took that as a good sign.

"I feel fine," I said to the empty room. Silence was my only answer from the observers.

It made me pause and look at my limbs again before taking in the rest of the room. It didn't register to my senses that the atmosphere in the room changed. Not until the snow began to fall, and I suddenly realized that my feet were not on the ground any longer.

"Did you try to use your magic?" my son finally found his voice.

"No, does the shock on my face not give that away?" I shouted.

"Focus, Ms. Sanders," Dr. Decker the pecker said

into the microphone. "Try to neutralize the magic in the air."

"You can do it, Mom," Jameson added encouragingly.

Right. I wasn't even thinking of the weather, and I somehow made it snow and began to fly. I thought about a calm day at the beach, the lovely and warm sun heating my skin. I got warm all right. Flames licked at my skin, and sand covered the floor.

"I don't think this is going how you think it should!" I yelled, panicking a little. I could feel the heat of the flames though my skin wasn't getting torched, thankfully. Unfortunately, it did trigger the sprinkler system in the room, and water drenched me.

"Oh, dear," Dr. Decker's voice filled the room again. "Try to relax, Ms. Sanders. We are going to have to go with the emergency plan."

Gas began to fill the room, and before long, I was taking a nap on the wet sandy floor and dreaming of fiery, snowy beaches.

Chapter 2

I felt incredibly well-rested, and ten-thirty the following day found me in my office waiting for the mysterious blue-tinted Jonielle. I studied my office space with a critical eye and thought that I needed to add more comfortable chairs.

The old plastic ones were getting rickety and worn, and I didn't want to get sued if one broke and someone fell and got hurt. I made a mental note to call Gavin, my oldest son, and have him keep an eye out at the market for some better cheap options.

This week, Danny was out of town for a family emergency, which I was almost happy about, sadly. Not that his family was in a state of emergency, but that I had some space from him and the sudden relationship I found myself in. I needed to adjust, and I haven't had a lot of time to do that.

Taking on Jonielle's case should help distract me from that; plus, I didn't have Danny standing over my shoulder checking on me every three minutes, wondering how the potion was working. I mean, thinking of the expression on his face had he seen yesterday's debacle was enough to make me break out laughing.

Shaking thoughts of Danny out of my head, I rounded my desk and caught myself before sitting in my evil chair. I definitely needed to get some more chairs for my office simply to avoid that bastard. I kicked at the base of it with my boot for revenge, not that it did a damn thing other than making me feel slightly better.

At two minutes after eleven, a tentative knock on my office door and a blue head popped into view. "Hello? Can I come in?" Jonielle asked politely.

I fought the impulse to answer sarcastically and replied, "Of course." I gestured her in and then moved to lock the door behind her. "To keep out unwanted visitors since I'm supposed to be on vacation," I explained at her confused look.

"I'm sorry for interrupting that," Jonielle apologized. "I feel bad."

I waved the apology off and rounded my desk. "Oh, don't. It's good for me. It keeps me out of trouble. Kind of."

The look of relief on Jonielle's face distracted me from carefully sitting in the malicious chair. I swear that the damn thing groaned out the words as I sat, "Try a diet fat ass." That was right before the back of the chair gave away, tossing my round, not fat, ass over my head and my toes smacked into the window behind me. I was dangling upside down, and it was like I could hear whatever malevolent shitty entity that chair was, laughing at me.

"Oh, dear," Jonielle murmured. "That chair is alive and not very friendly. Are you okay?"

I used the arms of the chair to pull myself upright and found Jonielle standing and peering over the edge of my desk down at me with a concerned look on her face. "I'm fine." I'd say that even if I had blood pouring out of a wound on my body. "My chair is really possessed?"

Jonielle shrugged. "I don't know about possessed, but it's certainly alive and doesn't give off a friendly energy vibe. Usually, that's me that type of stuff happens to."

Intrigued, I once again sat down without thinking,

and the chair spun me like it was having an exorcist moment and flung me into the wall. More than irritated now, I kicked the object into the corner and sat on my desk.

"Well, that was interesting," Jonielle quipped.

"Any ideas on what it is?" I asked hopefully.

"No. I can only see the energy and that it's living. It's a vicious thing; I'd say," Jonielle hazarded a look over at the innocuous-looking chair. "Anyway, are you hurt?"

"Only my pride," I admitted. "It's only recently it started doing that, too."

"Well, now, that *is* interesting. Are you a witch? Maybe the chair is your familiar?" Jonielle guessed.

"I might have some witch in me, but I'm not a full-blooded witch. I'm more of a hodgepodge of races," I told the unique woman. "I'm sorry, but I feel like we've known each other for a long while," I blurted out, wondering where that had stemmed from in my messy head. Ironically, it was true.

"Anything is possible," Jonielle replied wistfully. "I miss my family; it would be nice to find out we were related. Actually, that's what brings me here."

"The hope that we are related?" I echoed back stupidly.

Jonielle laughed, a joyous sound. "No, me missing my family. I was hoping you could help me find a way home. I'm slowly dying here with no real food source, and if that nasty man gets a hold of me, I don't know what will happen."

Whoa. "Wait. What nasty man? Where is your home? What is your real food source?" I asked the questions rapid-fire, trying to keep up. "Are you hiding out from someone? Where are you staying? Are you in danger?"

Jonielle blinked a couple of times as she processed my litany of questions. "I think I might be in danger, yes."

"That only answers one of my questions," I pointed

out bluntly. "What man do you think poses you a risk?" I decided to try the questions one at a time.

"He's new in town, rich, good-looking, and has this sense of ickiness. I think that's how I'd put it. He's icky. I believe his name is Wiley," Jonielle informed me with a blank face.

"Icky is a good word for him," I agreed quietly, intent on learning more. "Tell me about what is going on."

"You know him?" Jonielle lost all semblance of joviality and fixed her green eyes on me with laser-precision focus.

"I've had a few run-ins with him," I admitted. "He also tried to hire me, and I told him I wouldn't be able to find his balls."

Jonielle burst into laughter again. "Okay, I feel better now. There was a span of a few seconds where I thought you were going to say he was your friend."

I scoffed loudly. "Hardly. The man is slimy. Start talking, chicky. I'd love to take him down."

Jonielle chortled. "Me too. Okay, the realm I come from is called Grapefines, and about fifty years ago, Wiley landed there, only his name was different then. It created a big stir among us because we don't normally get visitors, and it was popular opinion that someone dumped him there, hoping we'd do away with him. Achan was his name there, and he possessed the magic to make some of our people disappear. Well, it was either magic or an artifact he kept on his person; we never did figure that out."

"Achan," I grumbled. "Hold on a second." I reached for my phone and quickly dialed Danny. "Hey, while you are out, and yes, I know you are occupied, can you set your computer to do a deep seek on Wiley aka Achan? As well as doorways to Grapefines?" I quickly asked my absent boyfriend.

"Shoot me a text with that spelling, and I'll make it

happen," Danny promised. "Stay out of trouble, Risa. You are supposed to be on vacation."

"I'm helping a friend," I retorted defensively.

"Right," Danny scoffed. "I miss you. I'll email you whatever I'm able to dig up on him. Remember, he comes across as dangerous, so please be careful."

I half-heartedly agreed and hung up. "Danny is the best at finding things that people want to keep hidden. Whatever he finds will help us defeat the prick. Okay, back to your story. You are a Grapefinian? I've never heard of that place."

A slow smile spread across Jonielle's face. "Oh, I can guarantee that you have. Here in this realm, we are known as purple people eaters," she smiled as she dropped that bomb. Then watching my face, she busts out laughing.

I wasn't sure what expression I had on my face, whether it was disbelief, humor, surprise, or a mix of all of them, but it was funny to her. "I thought they were made up," I finally murmured.

"Most people do," Jonielle chuckled delightedly. "Wrongfully, people often think we are monsters who eat people. On Grapefines, we eat moradas. The best way to describe what that is would be to say they are purple people. Only there, they are raised and grown like what humans do with cattle. Moradas are mean and spiteful, and while they look like a purple version of humans, they are more like animals. They taste more like chicken than they do your beef cattle, though."

I was pretty sure my jaw had come unhinged at this point, and I snapped it closed. "You eat purple people that taste like chicken. Okay." It was less strange than centipede creatures trying to create surf and turf out of cow and lobster DNA.

"We do. The thing is, I'm dying here. I have no food source, and that is why my skin is this color. I used to be a beautiful purple tone like the rest of my people, but without the proper nutrition, I lack the nutrients that keep me thriving. I need to get home," Jonielle pleaded with me. "That's why I've been going to that lab. There is a lady doctor there who's been trying to help me with experimental potions that will replenish what I am losing."

"How did you end up here?" I asked, leaning forward on my desk.

"Achan," Jonielle answered simply. "I still don't know how he did it, but he was abducting my people and sending them places. I wrongly thought I would find others here since so many disappeared, but I'm the only one to my knowledge. He's been tracking me for a long time, and when I arrived here in this town, I thought I'd be safe for a while, and then I spotted him. From what I have been able to gather intelligence-wise," Jonielle's eyes sparkled with a sense of humor, "he's selling various races. I haven't been able to figure out for what purposes, but it can't be good."

"How did you find that out?" I barked out angrily. Wiley was toast; I'd make sure of it.

A sad look crossed Jonielle's face. "It was in Australia. I fell in love with the people's accents and found a small magical town where I could reside without being seen. Sometimes glamour spells don't work on me, and my skin color is a dead giveaway that I'm not like others. I still had a purple tint while I was there, and I made a friend with another who was on the run, too. It was the closest I had come to having a family outside of Grapefines. His name was Booker. Word spread that he was being sought for a supposed crime he'd committed, only he hadn't done anything illegal. A few of the locals started to investigate because Booker was such a good and kind soul, and they found a history of Achan seeking and selling unusual races."

Fury lit my bloodstream. "You are staying with me

until I can find you a way home," I declared with my fist thumping down on my desk. Magic leaked out of me, and Jonielle stared in astonishment as my hair went from blonde to crimson.

"Wow," Jonielle breathed out in admiration. "I wished my hair changed colors like that."

I sighed and did my best to control my warring emotions. "Come on, let's go. If Wiley crosses me to get to you, finding his balls will be the least of his problems."

Chapter 3

While Jonielle took a bath, a luxury she said calmed her; I made several phone calls. First, I left a message for my oldest son Gavin to find me an unalive office chair. Then I reached out to my middle son Gage, the chef, to see if in any of his cooking adventures he'd run across purple meat called morada and if he could get some.

Then I called Ivan. Oh, Ivan. The man still inspired wet dreams and fantasies in my mind. I pictured him singing to me with that deep voice of his while he pulled my hair and rode me hard. I shook my head to clear the forming dirty thoughts and focused on the ringing phone.

"Well, well, if it isn't the gorgeous investigator," Ivan's sexy as sin voice floated across the line. "When can I do you? I mean, what can I do for you?"

I flushed with heat, then laughed to cover the tone I was sure was present in my voice. "Hey, Ivan. I was calling about that portal we discovered in your field. It was permanently closed, right?"

I heard the hesitation like it was a drawn-out five-minute silence instead of a few seconds. "Not completely," Ivan answered slowly, drawing the words out. "I think some of the magical folk can use it, but only a select few know that. I thought you were one of them."

Damn those witches. "No, I didn't know that. Okay,

tell me this, has anyone been out there since the cows came back?"

"Not that I have seen," Ivan spoke freely. "I put that fence around the portal and had a warlock you have intimate knowledge of put a spell on it."

"You could have just said Danny," I giggled, knowing he was flirting with me. "I may need to access that portal. If I do, are you going to rat me out?"

"Is it dangerous?" Ivan's tone changed from sexy to cautious.

"No," I hedged, not knowing the answer to that. "It's information gathering. I'll probably need to bring a witch with me, as well as a new friend."

"Hmm, what's in this for me?" Ivan teased.

"An introduction to my new friend," I answered quickly, my tone huskier than I intended. "She's hot."

"I'm listening," Ivan replied, his voice velvety smooth and orgasmic sounding. "I'll keep your secret as long as there is no danger involved," Ivan capitulated.

"Okay, we'll see you later then," I quickly agreed before he could change his mind. "If you were shirtless, it would be some good motivation to return."

Ivan's rich laugh had me squirming in my seat. "If you were shirtless, I'd agree to anything."

"Good to know," I practically purred. Ivan groaned in response then hung up before I could do damage to my new relationship with Danny. Probably just as well, Ivan was a serious temptation for me to remain single.

My phone chose then to ring and jar me out of my sinuous thoughts. I answered automatically without checking to see who it was.

"Greetings, Risa," Ax's voice penetrated the lust fog in my mind.

"Oh, hey, Ax. What's going on?" I blinked a few times, trying to clear my head.

"I caught a scent that might be the missing girl; only I can't be sure. Can you have the wolf come out?" Ax asked me.

Last week, Mick, the leader of the wolf pack and member of the town council, had asked me to help him find one of his missing wolves. He suspected she wasn't taken voluntarily and had been unable to find her.

"Were you able to follow the scent?" I jumped to attention at the news.

"For a short distance, then it disappears," Ax sounded unsure. "It's the strangest thing."

"Tell me where to have Mick meet you," I demanded, then gentled my tone. "Sorry, I didn't mean it to come out that way."

"No worries, I understand." Ax gave me the exact location and told me he'd watch for Mick to show up.

I dialed Mick and briefly flashed on the memory of him naked. He was another that was a temptation, though I'd been able to resist him so far probably because I knew that one would end in disaster. Not that it wouldn't be a hell of a ride, because that man might be the hottest man I've ever seen.

"Risa," Mick answered with that smug tone in his voice as if he knew what I'd been thinking.

"Mick, Ax called me and said he thinks he caught the scent of Maggie, but he can't be sure. He wondered if you could meet him out in the woods," I dove right into the reason I called to stem any of the other dangerous territories that swirled around us.

"Where?" Mick's tone immediately changed to all business. I gave him the location and hung up. Mick was a man who confused me. There was chemistry between us; there was zero doubt about that. I also felt that if we connected in the way we both wanted to, one of us would have to leave town. The attraction between us was that potent around each other. Jealousy would cause one of us to do something disastrous.

"Mom!" Gage's voice made me jump. "What the hell?"

I spun around, "Do you know how to knock?"

"I was knocking! You are, like, so lost in whatever thoughts are in your head that you didn't even notice me calling your name three times," Gage admonished me. "What the hell kind of message was that you left me? Purple meat? Are you high? Did that potion mess with your head? Where is Jameson?"

Jonielle chose that moment to walk out into the living room looking all sexy with her wet blue skin and a giant towel wrapped around her. It worked on distracting my son from reading me the riot act, but that wasn't a union I wanted to have happen. I'd rather sacrifice Ivan.

"Hello," Jonielle gave a brilliant smile to Gage. "Your energy is beautiful. Risa," Jonielle turned to me, "do you have some clean clothes I can borrow?"

Gage had a dopey look on his face as he took in her blue beauty. I ushered Jonielle out of the living room to my bedroom and flung open the closet. "Help yourself to whatever."

I ran back out to see Gage still staring after her and snapped my fingers in front of his face. "Who is that?" he focused on me.

"Jonielle. I'm helping her out, and I met her yesterday. She'll be staying here until I can find a way for her to get back home. Off-limits, and you are in a relationship with Zhor already," I reminded him none too gently.

"Zhor isn't meant to last," Gage replied distractedly. "Jonielle is mesmerizing."

"Be that as it may, she's destined to get back to her realm," I declared in my best motherly tone.

"What realm is that, and is she why you are looking for the elusive purple meat?" Gage finally turned back to me.

"Grapefines," I leveled a look at him that told him to cool his jets. "Yes, Jonielle is the reason I was asking about purple meat. She's dying without it. Wiley is hunting her, and that's why she's going to stay here until I can get her home."

"I've never heard of that realm," Gage let out a little smitten sigh. "It sounds delightful. What is she?"

My sigh wasn't smitten; it was irritated. "Purple people eater," I told him with a small smile as his face morphed into shock.

"I'm going to guess Wiley is the reason your hair is red," Gage finally found his tongue. "What happened with the potion?"

"I made it snow, flew, tried to set myself on fire, covered the floor with sand, and made the sprinklers come on," I summed up the experience as briefly as possible.

Gage's face wore the stunned expression once more as he stood there and blinked at me. "Yeah, um, okay. That explains why Jameson hasn't returned my calls. It means he's buried himself inside that lab trying to do something to fix the potion."

"Maybe my magic isn't tamable. I wasn't even trying to perform magic," I told Gage with an agitated tone.

"Bullshit," Gage spat, his own irritation rising. "You haven't trained extensively with it, so, of course, it's going to take a bit to learn. You just need someone to help you focus and direct the magic, Mom."

"Don't you need to be at work?" I crossed my arms and glared at my son and his logic. He snickered lightly, kissed me on the cheek, and left.

Chapter 4

My Jeep wasn't exactly inconspicuous, and I'm sure that word would get back to Danny that I was at Ivan's. It didn't worry me too much, but the thought was present as Jonielle, and I pulled into his driveway. I didn't contact the witches who helped with the portal yet. It would be just me and Jonielle crossing into that realm this time.

I wanted to see if I could find Cujo again and see if he knew anything about Grapefines and how to get there or purple meat. If it weren't possible for someone to create a portal from the realm we were on, maybe it would be possible from that realm. That was my hope, at least.

We'd had a bit of a delay when a tire suddenly went flat on our way there, and Jonielle only shrugged, saying things like this happened all the time. Luckily my leprechaun luck kicked in, and a passerby stopped to help us.

Now, as I climbed out of the Jeep, my mouth went utterly dry. A shirtless Ivan stepped out of the barn I'd parked in front of to minimize our walk. Jonielle stumbled out of the Jeep, just as affected by the sight as I was.

"Who is that?" she stage whispered to me.

"The mistake I should have made," I whispered back through a tongue that felt covered in cotton.

"Oh, I'll make it for you," Jonielle offered.

I wanted to shove her into a closet and run away with Ivan. I bit the inside of my cheek and forced a smile. "Have at it, but I want details. Explicit details." Not a chance in hell I was introducing her to Mick. Where that thought came from, I don't know. I had no claim on either of these men.

Ivan motioned for me to take my shirt off, and damn it, I almost did. Only the pressing thought of Danny that surfaced in my mind kept my clothes on. I briefly wondered if he'd put a spell on me, so that happens.

"It was worth a shot," Ivan smirked at me. "Who's your friend?"

Jonielle came around the front of the Jeep with a swing to her hips that made her stride go off balance, and she tripped over her own feet. I bit back a laugh and then tried to smother the jealously that surfaced when Ivan lunged to catch her.

"Hi there, I'm Jonielle," the blue woman told him breathlessly.

I couldn't help but question if the fall had been on purpose, given the look on Ivan's face. He was as enraptured as Gage had been. I rolled my eyes at the expression on Jonielle's face after she heard Ivan speak.

"Would you sing me to sleep?" Jonielle gushed, and I snorted, almost laughing until I saw the look on Ivan's face. Damn it; my hair was turning green now.

"Come on," I snapped, not happy with the rising jealousy. I had Danny, and he was nothing to scoff at; I shouldn't be feeling this way.

Jonielle scurried after me. "It's been a long time for me," she hissed in my ear. "That man is delicious."

"No shit," I glared at her. "Let's get our info before you dance on Ivan's pole."

Jonielle giggled. "Deal." She trotted after me and tossed a look over her shoulder to make sure Ivan was behind us. "He's coming with us?"

"Not through the portal, but chances are he'll stick around outside of it until we are safely back through. He's a gentleman like that," I admitted reluctantly.

Jonielle stumbled again, and this time I did laugh. "I should stop trying to be sexy," Jonielle muttered as she stood back up, brushing the grass off her clothes.

"You don't need to try. You already are sexy," I scolded Jonielle gently. "Be you; he's already interested."

"I think he's interested in you, too," Jonielle commented offhandedly.

"He is, but he knows I'm not exactly available, too, and he's just torturing me," I smirked. "Torture him back."

"Oh," she groaned, "with pleasure. I want to lick the man."

I bent over at the waist and slapped my knees with laughter. "Girl, I had the same reaction, then I heard his voice and almost had to go change my pants."

"I can hear you," Ivan called out, sounding embarrassed.

"Good, serves you right for looking like that," I shouted back. "Okay, obviously, you've been through a portal before. This one goes to a world I saved Ivan's cows from this year. There's a three-headed talking dog there that I am looking for; I can't pronounce his name, so I called him Cujo. He seems to be knowledgeable about things, and I'm hoping he'll have answers for us on if we can portal you home from that realm."

"A Cerberus?" Jonielle paused and gave me an incredulous look.

"I guess. That's the closest I could come up with though Cujo walks on two legs as well as four. Cujo's sense of humor is lacking," I added as an afterthought. "You seem to have an opening and welcoming effect on people; let's hope that continues, so he doesn't want to kill us. Oh, and if my magic goes wonky, try to avoid standing in the line of fire. That place had a strange reaction with my powers."

"Noted," Jonielle stated thoughtfully. She studied the fence as we walked up to it. "That fence has a major repellent on it," she told me.

Not paying attention to where she was walking, she stepped into a low spot on the ground and took another tumble, her foot slipping in a still steaming and warm cow pie. Jonielle's body crashed into mine. I heard Ivan shout, and there wasn't a thing he could have done to stop the domino effect of the collision.

I landed flat on my back with a splat in another cow pie pile. Jonielle landed on top of me with her forehead between my boobs. It looks like I was the one getting motorboated this time, only the impact wasn't pleasant, and her skull bouncing off my sternum hurt like a bitch.

Ivan ran up to us, looking worried. He pulled Jonielle up off me and checked her over while I tried to unglue myself from the pile of shit I'd landed in involuntarily. I ignored the amused look on Ivan's face as I stood, silently grateful that my head hadn't been what got covered in cow dung.

"Irony," Ivan mused as I tugged off my foul-smelling shirt. "Karma decided since I delivered on my shirtlessness that you had to pay up as well."

"I don't think shirtlessness is a word," I grumbled, happy that I put my sports bra on before we'd left.

"I'm so sorry, Risa," Jonielle told me contritely. "Did I hurt you?"

"You've got a hard head," I told her, rubbing my sternum. "I'll be fine. I think my shirt is a lost cause, though. Ivan, you better have a clean shirt for me to put on when I come back out of this portal."

Ivan chuckled, "Yes, ma'am. Meanwhile, I'll enjoy

the view and the rainbow-colored hair.”

“Oh yeah,” Jonielle breathed out. “It’s like purple, pink, yellow, and orange.”

I rolled my eyes and briskly rubbed my now bare arms. “Whatever. Is there something I need to get through this?” I asked Ivan, pointing to the portal. I figured it had been keyed for entry in case of emergency and that Ivan had the key. At least that was my thought process after he told me it hadn’t been completely closed.

Ivan nodded and reached into his pocket, pulling out a piece of crystal. Jonielle edged away from it with a frown, picking up on the energy signature imbued in the stone. He held it out to me and dropped it in my open palm.

I think before my magic awakened, I wouldn’t have felt the thrumming energy resonating with me; now, it felt like it was vibrating, and I was fascinated for a moment. I could feel the portal communicating with the crystal.

Ivan grew serious and gave me a pointed stare. “I mean it, Risa. Come back unharmed. A pissed-off Danny isn’t fun to deal with under any circumstances. Much less if you are hurt. Give me a contact number for someone in case something goes sideways.”

I pursed my lips in defiance and then relented and gave him Mick’s number and Wylene’s. I figured if something went south while I was in the portal, either of those two was badass enough to handle whatever came of it.

Chapter 5

aybe we should have brought your chair with us," Jonielle whispered after we stepped through the portal. "We could have sacrificed it to whatever the energy is in this place."

I hmphed in agreement. "Sacrificing that chair is a good idea no matter where we are."

This world looked much the same as it had the last time I was here. Dark and eerie with vegetation that looked like it was watching us. It probably was. I halfway expected the centipede-looking scientists to be hovered around the portal, trying to find a way to get more cows.

"What do we do now?" Jonielle asked, clutching my arm.

"Relax, don't cut my circulation off," I tugged on my arm. "Cujo!" I called out, keeping the shrill tone from my voice that spoke of my fear.

"No need to shout, humanoid," the demonic-looking dog stepped out of the shadows. "The crackling of the portal gave away your presence."

Jonielle let out a small shriek and tried to hide behind me. "That *could* be Cujo!" she blurted out as her nails gouged out skin from my arm.

Cujo ran his six eyes over me, making me feel decidedly naked even if my sports bra covered my nipples. "This is a pleasing form, as is the one hiding behind you."

"Yes, well, it's a spoken-for form, so no touching," I quipped, ready to admit my relationship status freely in this case. "Though the one behind me is available," I threw out as an option, mostly joking.

Jonielle pinched me to show her unhappiness, which made me laugh a little. "Not available," Jonielle squeaked in fear. "You can understand him?"

"Chill, yes I can," I hissed over my shoulder at her. "Cujo, I need help. Have you heard of a realm called Grapefines? Or a race called Moradas?"

Cujo shifted and began to circle me, and I distinctly remembered that he was a guard and ordered to kill things that didn't belong here in this place. He raked his eyes over us, and I hoped he wasn't hungry.

"I've heard of Grapefines, yes," Cujo finally admitted after his third time around our bodies. "What is in it for me for sharing this information?"

I sighed in relief. "You need to learn how to bargain better. You should have asked that before telling me you know of it," I smirked at the creature.

Cujo stepped right up to me and stared down at me with teeth showing. Was that a smile? I was afraid to ask. "I admitted I know of it, but I have shared nothing valuable with you. Now, what is in this for me?"

"The pleasure of knowing you helped someone?" I offered weakly. I didn't bring anything to bribe him with since I didn't think he would require that.

"Not enough. I found myself in a perilous situation after you left here last time. It's my sheer physique and strength that keeps these people from harming me," Cujo inched closer. Our bodies were almost touching, and my stubbornness kept me rooted in place, refusing to back down from the threat.

"I'm sorry," I apologized. "I never meant to put you in a bad position. I'm not sure what I can offer you."

Jonielle let out a snort, "I can tell you what to offer him."

"Can it, blue woman, or you are going to get a cow pie facial," I warned her.

Cujo reached out and fingered my hair, "This is different. So is this creature with you. She is not the same as you."

"Thanks for pointing out the obvious," I huffed. "Did the blue skin give it away? What do you require to share information? It's a matter of life and death."

"Yes," Cujo agreed, "it is. On many levels. Mine, yours, and hers." Cujo took a step to the left and glanced down his noses at Jonielle. "You wish to live, yes?"

Jonielle stammered out a yes and moved to the right. "Enough with the intimidation tactics," I interrupted. "Speak your terms so negotiations can begin."

Cujo eyed me with the same intensity he had the first time we'd met. I knew he didn't want to kill me, not yet, anyway. Though he mainly remained a mystery to me, and his motivations weren't precisely clear. Despite my proclamation, I wasn't going to offer Jonielle up as a bargaining chip.

"I want to leave here with you," Cujo finally told me.

Holy hell. I hadn't expected that, and I was entirely sure that Glimmering Rock was not prepared for Cujo. "You want to go to earth?"

"I desire to be somewhere other than here. If that is where we go, then so be it," Cujo declared.

"Uh, well, they don't take too kindly to random killing there," I hedged carefully.

"Do you think me so primitive that killing is all I am capable of?" Cujo growled menacingly. "I didn't kill you."

"That's because you found me pleasing," I reminded him, again fighting off the urge to step back away from the dog.

"You asked my terms, and I stated them," Cujo stood his ground. "That is the price for my help."

"Wait, he wants to go back with us?" Jonielle asked me, stunned.

"Seems that way," I answered without looking away from Cujo.

"You mistake me, humanoid. I want to leave here. Returning with you is an option, but I did not state that was the only place I wished to go," Cujo clarified his answer.

"Well, that's the only place I am going, so excuse me for misunderstanding," I fired off at the imposing figure.

"He can come with me," Jonielle offered quietly. "If I can get back home to Grapefines, he can join me. I love dogs."

There was a subtle shift in Cujo's expression as he carefully took in Jonielle again. "She is more pleasing than you, humanoid."

Speechless for a moment, I stared at the two of them aghast. "Look, dog, I have a name, and it's Risa. Second, what the fuck is happening right now? Jonielle, you are cowering behind me terrified and are offering him to come home with you?" I totally ignored the stab of jealousy at the 'more pleasing than' me comment.

"There's something sexy about him," Jonielle answered with an awestruck tone. "Besides, think about it, three tongues."

My jaw dropped. Of all the things this woman could have said, that was not what I expected. I was well and truly speechless now and slightly turned on.

"I've been told I have skill in using them," Cujo growled to Jonielle. Too bad that she couldn't understand him, and no way was I repeating that. "Do we have a deal, humanoid Risa?"

"Uh, Jonielle, he is willing to accept your offer," I

recited automatically. "Are you sure?"

"Can he understand me?" Jonielle locked her eyes on the towering three-headed dog.

"Yeah, he can," I assured her, fascinated, despite my misgivings about the whole thing.

"There is a man after me, and I am positive he wants to do me harm. Can you help protect my family and me if you come home with me?" Jonielle moved out from behind me. "I promise that I can take care of you," her voice dropped to a husky tone that I easily understood.

Cujo dropped to a knee, bringing him just below her height. "I can smell your arousal. I accept and look forward to it."

Flabbergasted, I stared between the two of them while Jonielle stared at me expectantly, waiting for a translation of what Cujo said. "I don't know how this is going to work," I muttered. "He said that he could smell your arousal, and he accepts."

Jonielle's blue skin took on a reddish hue for a moment as she leaned forward and kissed each of the three heads. Given the possessive growl emitting from each of them, Cujo was pleased. "I will disembowel anything that tries to harm you," Cujo promised her.

"Uh, yeah," I shook my head. "Okay, you get what you want. Now, dish information. If I bring someone here with magic that can create portals, will Jonielle be able to get to her home realm from here? She is currently trapped on my realm, unable to access her home from there."

"The simple answer is yes, but it will require the assistance of the magic inside you," Cujo responded. "You must leave now; someone is coming, and it is not safe for you here."

Needing no further encouragement than that, I grabbed Jonielle's hand and forcibly yanked her through the portal back to the patiently waiting Ivan.

Chapter 6

After explaining everything to Ivan and Jonielle both, which was a weird experience in itself, I left for home. Jonielle stayed behind to warm up for the experience of three tongues at once, and since Ivan didn't seem the least bit bothered by that, I left her there after he promised to bring her back to my place, so he wasn't in danger.

I didn't consider myself a prejudiced person in the slightest. However, I found myself balking at that pairing with Cujo, and I shouldn't have. It was no different than Ax and his girlfriend, or me and Danny, for that matter. My entire family history was filled with couplings like that. Maybe it was just that he was Cujo, threatening, and not very friendly. Whatever, it was Jonielle's choice.

I made the necessary calls to the witches who had done the portal work on Ivan's property and secured their agreement to help with a portal to Grapefines and, in return, owe them a favor at a later date. I could live with that arrangement. We set up the date for tomorrow, figuring time was of the essence, given Jonielle had been starving for fifty years.

After Ivan dropped her back off, looking extremely satisfied, I might add, I grilled her for details and ended up going to bed horny and unfulfilled. Every dream I had was a dirty one, and each featured three men, I'm guessing because Jonielle threw the idea of three tongues out there.

Ivan, Mick, and Danny spent the night starring in dirty fantasies. There was something wrong with my brain, but man, what a dream trio.

After I stuffed my face while Jonielle sucked down a pot of coffee, we set out for Ivan's. Once we hit a long stretch of backroad that had forest on one side of it, my Jeep suddenly careened off the road due to magic. I knew that because of the slimy feel of it washing over my skin like an oil spill.

Our heads bounced off the roll bars as my Jeep turned over and settled in a ditch upside down. I unbuckled my seatbelt and dropped down on my shoulders as I tucked my head. "Unbuckle and run," I whispered harshly to Jonielle. "Into the forest."

I quickly sent my location and an urgent text to Mick's phone and followed Jonielle, unwilling to leave her alone. I desperately needed to bring Wiley down, but to do that, I needed proof of what he was doing. Getting Jonielle safely home was a bigger priority at the moment, and I focused my energy on making that happen.

We charged up the hillside in front of us and ran into the thicker part of the forest. I yanked on Jonielle to have her head in the direction of Ivan's, and we kept running. The one thing I'd noticed since drinking Jameson's potion was my magic wasn't reacting wildly anymore, but it was also still sort of elusive.

"Someone is behind us," Jonielle panted. "I can feel their energy."

I hoped it was Mick or one of his pack that was in the area. Our relationship was tenuous at best, but he wouldn't let me get killed; I was pretty sure of that. "Keep going," I reached out and pushed her. "If it's friendly, it will make itself known."

As we dodged rocks, fallen trees, holes in the ground, I sensed Jonielle was losing steam fast. We needed to get out of this forest and onto the road. Preferably in a car speeding away from danger. My skin began to prickle as my magic welled up underneath it. Right as we came to a screeching halt because an eight-foot-high rock blocked our path, a concussive force ripped out of me and shot backward.

Trees felled with the blast, and not wanting to waste time, I bent over and heaved Jonielle into the air and hoped she grabbed the rock to pull herself over it. Seeing she grasped what I was up to, I prepared to jump and follow.

My heart was thundering painfully in my chest, and the expenditure of energy that using my magic caused made me slower than expected, but I made it. Dropping to the other side of the boulder, I found we were at an impasse. A howl pierced the air, and I let go of a sigh of relief.

"That's either Mick or one of his pack," I told Jonielle on a gasp of air.

"There isn't anywhere for us to go but down," Jonielle pointed out, resigned. "Oh, your head is bleeding, and your hair is pink and red."

I wasn't sure if that was from blood or my mood-colored hair doing its thing, and we didn't have time for me to figure it out. "Down it is. Use the trees to slow your descent," I instructed Jonielle.

"Shit," she muttered. "This isn't going to go well for either of us."

Probably not, but I wasn't sure of our chances with meeting Wiley face to face with my magic on the fritz again. "Hurry, we don't have a lot of time to spare. I don't know how long that blast will hold him back."

Jonielle gave me a fleeting look of worry but dropped down to her ass and slid over the side of the cliff. She was clutching the small tree next to her for support.

There was less for me to hold, but I held on to a shrub, hoping for the best.

It held for two seconds before agreeing with my chair that I should be on a diet and ripped right out of the ground. I plummeted and landed with a tree in my crotch. It was every bit as painful as I imagined it would be for a man. Air whooshed out of my lungs on an excruciating exhale, only to have it turn to a shriek when Jonielle landed on the same branch, and we continued our descent.

If we weren't in peril, this would have been a hilarious comedy of errors. Right up to the moment that we plunged into a thicket of thorny bushes like we were the size of the boulder we had scaled over. It sucked ass. The only positive was I doubted Wiley would follow us into sticker bushes.

Carefully, and I use that word loosely, we made our way out and stared at each other, covered in blood, wood pieces, thorns, grass, and various bugs. We looked like a bear, or a porcupine had mauled us.

I quickly got my bearings and kept us moving in the direction of Ivan's farm, not slowing down once. We eventually came to a small creek that we needed to cross. Parts of it were deep, but it mostly flowed fast and shin-deep over rock.

I took the first step and crossed over a stream of water, and turned to hold my arm out to Jonielle to help her cross. No sooner than I did that than she stepped out on her own and promptly slid, falling right to her ass in the middle of the stream. It looked like she was happily sitting down to take a bath in the flowing water.

Insane laughter bubbled out of me. I couldn't help it. We were running for our lives, been in an accident, ran through the woods, scaled a boulder, fell down a cliff into sticker bushes, and now this. It was too much. I was deliriously happy that Danny wasn't here to witness this debacle.

A slight chuffing sound had me looking up to see a giant wolf. Mick. Great, there was a witness to this humiliation after all. "I think Wiley is after us," I sobered and told the wolf. "I need to get Jonielle to Ivan's and into the portal."

The air around Mick shimmered, and with a cracking sound, he shifted into the magnificent male specimen that he was, and to my delight, utterly naked. Jonielle, still sitting in the water, gaped at him while I unabashedly stared at his dick.

"Risa, I swear, you are determined to give me blue balls," Mick shook his head at me. "One of my pack is half a mile that way with a vehicle," Mick pointed. "Get to him, and he'll get you to Ivan's. I'll head off whoever is after you. I can hear someone thrashing about not too far away."

I hefted Jonielle out of the water and wasted no time in getting the hell out of there. I kept Jonielle slightly ahead of me so I could catch her if she fell again. Our pace was a tad slower than before, most likely because she was waterlogged, but we made it to the road and found the vehicle.

Fifteen minutes later, we were at Ivan's and racing towards the portal where they were waiting for us to arrive. Ivan's eyes widened at our appearances, and he reached in his pocket and tossed me the crystal. "I want an explanation for how you look," he warned as I leaped over the fence.

"Later," I promised. Carolyn and Willem, the witches I'd called, hurried after me. Out of the corner of my eye, I saw Mick's massive form loping across the field towards Ivan.

"Damn, he's hot," Jonielle said on an exhale, spying the wolf.

"If he's here, that means he's here to protect the

portal. Get in," I shoved Jonielle towards the portal. "Hurry, the witches need a few minutes to call up a portal, and they are going to need your help."

I was calling for Cujo the moment we plunged through into his realm. Carolyn and Willem immediately began their work, pulling Jonielle over to the side with them, my magic assisting however it worked. I frantically looked around for Cujo and finally saw him stalking in our direction.

"Risa," Jonielle called to me a few minutes later.

I turned back to her. "What?"

"Thank you for your help. I'd probably be dead right now if it weren't for you," Jonielle held her arms out for a hug.

I had to admit; this woman had a draw to her I couldn't resist. She was so open and friendly that I found myself falling into her embrace. "Be careful and stay safe," I whispered in her ear. "If you ever come back here, I want details on Cujo because now I'm curious."

Jonielle laughed, "Deal."

A few minutes later, a portal opened. "Humanoid Risa, don't waste time here. They will come looking to see who performed this magic, and they will try to take you as a prisoner," Cujo warned me. "They remember you."

Carolyn handed Jonielle a crystal, and then my new blue sister friend and her three-headed dog/man disappeared into the void.

Chapter 7

I was met with a wet tongue licking blood off my abdomen as I pulled my bloody shirt off. "Mick, knock it off," I swatted at him. "We have a problem with Wiley. Oh, and did you catch the scent of Maggie?"

Shimmering air surrounded him, and I was staring at his naked junk again. Not exactly a hardship for me. Carolyn stammered out an apology and rushed out of the area like a blushing virgin.

"I did but lost it," Mick responded with a grin at the witch's retreating forms. "We definitely have a problem with Wiley, and the issue is going to be obtaining proof. By the way, I like you with no shirt on."

Ivan belted out a laugh. "Me too, man, though I can do without the vision of your junk. Risa, are you okay?"

"I'm good," I assured him. "I need to rest, and the scratches will heal. No permanent damage."

"I've got the taste of you on my tongue, woman," Mick growled low in his throat. "Fucking addicting. I'll be seeing you soon; we've got work to do."

Shivers raced up my spine and I reached for the shirt that was on the ground and pulled it over my head. "Looking forward to it, wolf," I replied huskily.

About the Author

Michelle Lee is a Pacific Northwest native with a mind open to possibilities. Growing up, people often saw her with her face buried in a book and not much has changed. She's living her life dream of writing books that set her imagination free and explore the possibilities and mysteries she sees in the land all around her.

Find novel-length works by Michelle and additional *I S.P.I.* installments at:

www.BlueForgePress.com